CW00351930

Without Motive

by

Cyrus Ferguson

**Grosvenor House
Publishing Limited**

All rights reserved
Copyright © Cyrus Ferguson, 2009

Cyrus Ferguson is hereby identified as author of this
work in accordance with Section 77 of the Copyright, Designs
and Patents Act 1988

The book cover picture is copyright to Inmagine Corp LLC

This book is published by
Grosvenor House Publishing Ltd
28-30 High Street, Guildford, Surrey, GU1 3HY.
www.grosvenorhousepublishing.co.uk

This book is sold subject to the conditions that it shall not, by way of
trade or otherwise, be lent, resold, hired out or otherwise circulated
without the author's or publisher's prior consent in any form of binding or
cover other than that in which it is published and
without a similar condition including this condition being imposed
on the subsequent purchaser.

A CIP record for this book
is available from the British Library

ISBN 978-1-906645-62-5

Dedication

*To the memory of my mother Winifred Ferguson
whose constant encouragement first brought
me to writing. Also to the memory of my late
brothers Des and Paul (Late of California)
whose friendly and intellectual company is
sadly missed. Thanks for everything. Cyrus*

Acknowledgments

Special thanks to Gillian Williams, an already over-worked author whose helpful and friendly advice over a long period proved invaluable. To my friends in the Heswall writing group, particularly Andrew who helped and cajoled me along the way, I am most grateful. A special thanks also to my colleagues at Edge Hill, Ormskirk, for constructive criticism advice and encouragement. To my good friend Trevor Williams and his wife Jackie for giving up many hours of their precious time to guide me through the minefield of error avoidance, and continuity. To my family and friends who patiently accepted my endless promises to have this novel completed by the end of next week.

Cyrus Ferguson January 2009

Prologue

Even through the thickest walls of Gloucester prison the noise was deafening. John Stretton barely glimpsed the curiously majestic lines of Concorde as it passed overhead, bent on creating its own niche in aviation history. He looked towards the tiny window allowing him a narrow view of the blue sky beyond. Maybe he should have felt a sense of pride, the old bulldog spirit. But deep down inside he was conscious only of a numbness that was threatening to drag him under at any moment. It would be easy to give in, surrender to the system, and get the earliest possible parole date.

Stretton wondered if he would ever again be allowed the peaceful enjoyment of life's most simple pleasures; walking to the corner shop for a daily newspaper, or standing at the bar of his local pub, and ordering a pint; even feeling the power of a woman's scent. Thoughts of better times lay somewhere in the dark recesses of his mind, buried in a black hole of despair, locked in a seemingly unending nightmare from which there could be no release, only death. What if the appeal failed? What chance of success? Thoughts hammered away at a tired brain. A life sentence meant there could never be a tomorrow, only today. A future only ever one day at a time for the rest of his life. When even the most basic things in life are out of reach, they soon become compulsively desirable.

It had taken just ten months for Stretton to lose his marriage, his wife and his freedom. It seemed unbelievable that less than a year ago they were happy together, melting excitedly into the crowd, walking the Kings Road in Chelsea, hoping to catch a glimpse of the 'Rolling Stones' hanging around the Chelsea Drug Store made famous by them. Nobody could ever have guessed that 1968 was about to become a watershed in both of their lives.

His thoughts suddenly distracted, Stretton looked down. Walking slowly, soundlessly towards him the black steel backed cockroach showed no sign of fear, no desire to escape. It stopped for a moment in the space between his shoes. Instinctively he raised a foot to crush the life now crawling beneath, only to turn away at the last second, allowing the creature to proceed unmolested. A piercing whistle burst into his nightmare, bringing it to a temporary end.

'Level Two Stand-by.' The order was crystal clear and understood. The call was for Category 'A' prisoners to gather in a place where only murderers mingle; the most notorious block in any prison. Already he was marked down as a high-risk prisoner, a 'lifer,' a killer. Stretton stared at the floor. The cockroach was nowhere to be seen in a room with nowhere to hide. His mind went back to the day when the police knocked on his door and broke the news of Ella's death.

He'd found himself having to explain how things began to go wrong between them. How Ella had wrongly accused him of having an affair. She'd had him followed. Suspicion soon became obsession. She'd refused to sleep with him, convinced there was another woman. Nothing he'd said made any difference. Only he knew the truth. A once strong relationship soon lay in ruins.

When Ella was brutally murdered, the police listened, took several statements, then arrested him. There was no evidence of sexual assault or robbery. Only one person stood to gain from her death, her husband. What began as a nightmare gradually unfolded into stark reality, then total misery. A passionate plea of innocence fell on the deaf ears of an unsympathetic jury. The absence of any other motive had strengthened the circumstantial evidence against him. No-one, it seemed, disliked Ella enough to want to murder her. No-one maybe, except him.

He fought to overcome emotions threatening to expose him as a weak and vulnerable character. In exactly one minute from now, on the second whistle, he would be meeting the other tenants of level two as they queued in orderly fashion to slop out, wash, and queue again for a meagre breakfast. One tiny scoop of margarine to cover two thick slices of bread with bitter marmalade. One small ladle of sugar free watery porridge and a green tin mug of insipid lukewarm tea. Stretton had never been much of a breakfast person.

Already he had been warned that any sign of weakness in the early days of incarceration would be exploited without mercy by the hardened prison element. The cell door swung open allowing his entry into a world of harsh metallic noise, and loud voices. This was the beginning of the first day of a life sentence. Looking neither to his left or right, Stretton stepped out on to the landing of his new world.

'Stretton 877018. Sir.'

CHAPTER 1

It was a ritual, a frustratingly bad habit, a sign of insecurity. One final check before pulling the zip across the top of the black canvas holdall. A Minolta XG series 35 mm camera, top of the range, sat alongside a telephoto lens, a pair of binoculars, spare film, and a notebook; essential tools for an enthusiastic bird watcher. The early spring was mild, almost warm for the time of year. It was an ideal opportunity to snap the young fledglings as they struggled to make that first stuttering flight.

'What time will you be back?' Joy had given up trying to sound interested. It was a loveless, sometimes violent marriage.

Pascoe barely glanced in her direction. 'No idea. Why?' His voice was sharp, brutish.

'Just asking.' She continued towards the kitchen, her back towards him. Fingers ran nervously through lank hair, no longer highlighted, or waved. There was little point these days. She would only have to explain how she managed to save the money and be told how better it might have been spent. She wasn't allowed to question him.

'Might call in at The Lion when I've finished.'

Joy knew what that meant. She could be dragged out of bed, sometimes at midnight, losing a handful of hair in the process. Other times it was his foul breath, filthy hands and earthy smell as he forced unwanted attentions on her. Joy frequently wondered how she had mistaken sullen nature for shyness. In those days she was convinced that love and mothering would bring out the best in him. But it never worked out like that. Pascoe was jealous of her quiet ways, taking every opportunity to belittle her, and undermine her self confidence. If that didn't work there was always another way. When the mood came on him, she could expect anything from fists to a leather buckled belt.

Recently, she'd heard Pascoe mention a peregrine falcon, reputed to have been seen around the Martin Mere wildlife sanctuary, for the first time since the end World War Two, almost twenty four years ago. He seemed unusually keen, almost anxious, to catch sight of it. A small bird but a busy hunter with a voracious appetite, capable of speeds as high as 115 mph, was never going to be easy to catch on film. His apparent concern for the wildlife was fairly recent. Rabbit snaring and pheasant poaching used to keep him well occupied but his bird watching activities seemed to be more intense, more focused, leaving less to chance. This new challenge was keeping him away from the house more often than she would have expected. Hearing the front door slam, she reached for the kettle. Communication between them was over, to be resumed when he decided it was necessary.

Pulling away from the small terraced house, Pascoe set off towards the town centre, following the contour of a long sloping hill winding its way past the Ormskirk parish church. He passed the same spot almost daily without paying the slightest attention to its unique design. The tower and spire, standing together at one end of the church, had attracted the curiosity of visitors for hundreds of years. He had no interest in either religion or architecture. Dropping down the hill he turned right at the traffic lights towards Preston, following the road through Burscough towards the junction for the Martin Mere wildlife sanctuary.

Pascoe ignored the sign on the bridge and a sign in bright colours that pointed towards Southport. Continuing along the main road for a mile or two, he eventually made a sharp left turn into a single-track lane. After a few hundred yards, the car came to an abrupt stop close to an overgrown footpath. He climbed out of the car and glanced around as if checking the light. The sun over his left shoulder was ideal for his photography.

Lifting the canvas bag off the back seat he locked the car and began to walk along the path. On the right hand side a small group of terraced cottages came into sight. He'd known about them for years. They were old farm cottages, built by the landowners to house the families of farm workers. In recent times they were being sold to the new country folk who wanted to live out of town, had cars and didn't mind commuting.

Pascoe knew exactly where to go. A small opening in dense hawthorn allowed him both access and camouflage. Jerking the zip on the holdall he pulled out the groundsheet, carefully spreading it over an area the size of his body. Lying flat as he dragged the holdall to his side, Pascoe immediately began to stare towards the cottages, binoculars tightly gripped. It had been a bonus when he'd spotted her in town, window-dressing a boutique. Standing so close to her in a public place made the whole thing more exciting. What would she do if she knew what had been going on these past weeks? That the man pausing to gaze into her shop window had been mentally using her body as a tool for his own gratification? Pascoe's thoughts were interrupted by the sighting of his quarry, a dark diffuse figure moving behind frosted panes of glass. As usual she was preparing her bath. Next would come the undressing routine, then the bathing, before returning to the bedroom to dress. She was an unhurried creature of habit that seemed to have little need for privacy. The cottage boasted views uninterrupted to the horizon and the woman obviously didn't feel the need to draw curtains. He sucked in air between clenched teeth as the door opened and she entered the bedroom.

Sitting on the edge of the bed, she removed a polo-neck sweater, folding it neatly before putting it to one side. The slight pause allowed him time to focus on her breasts. The stark contrast between the white brassiere and her tanned skin sent a surge of excitement through him. Now she was stretching her hands backwards and slightly upwards as nimble fingers sought the clasp nestling between slender shoulder blades. Pascoe imagined he could hear a faint click as the straps parted, then breathed sharply as her bra slipped away, exposing a semi-naked body. His hand moved downwards as if to check a reflex action. There was a sudden movement to his right. A frightened rabbit darted away from a nearby bush, disturbed by his heavy breathing and movement.

The woman now stood before a wardrobe mirror gently pressing her breasts. She did the same thing almost every time he watched. The hand gripping the binoculars tensed as the other fumbled awkwardly between the groundsheet and his leg. His voice growled in angry frustration.

'Dirty filthy bitch!'

4

After a few seconds, but what seemed an age, she moved a hand downwards. Turning slightly, reaching to the side of a plain light grey skirt, she pushed the zip fastener to the end of its track before releasing the button on the waistband. The top of the skirt peeled away exposing snow white briefs neatly embroidered with some sort of motif. Her fingers released their grip on the waistband allowing the skirt to drop to the floor. Sitting down again, she folded the skirt neatly before laying it across the end of the bed. Next she carefully removed a pair of dark coloured stockings, rolling them down her legs slowly and methodically. Finally she was able to remove her briefs before rising to her feet and standing once more, now completely naked.

Still facing the mirror she turned slowly, exposing every aspect of her nudity. Suddenly she stopped and stared at the floor as if looking for something. Whatever it was caused her to bend downwards. The heavy breathing now reached a peak as the watcher began to jerk convulsively backwards and forwards. Now she was reaching for the phone, making herself comfortable on the edge of the bed again and smiling. It made him feel angry. It was as if she was mocking him personally.

'Dirty filthy bitch ! I know what I'm going to do with you.' Quickly putting aside the binoculars Pascoe used his free hand to grasp the camera. A probing forefinger set the telephoto lens to the precise range. There followed a continuous click-clicking of the shutter as he followed her every move. It was souvenir time. The breast shots were always easy. It was the more intimate ones which often proved difficult. Now she was standing again, full frontal, just as he liked it and reaching to put the phone back on to its cradle. If only she would move closer to the window he might get the extra shot.

At last she was walking again, still naked, into the bathroom and out of sight for the moment. Pascoe rolled over attempting to dry some of the wetness which he had brought upon himself during his vigil. It wasn't long before she was back again, preparing to dress. This time she was wrapped in a bath towel. Bending over the dressing table, she carefully selected a body spray before allowing the towel to drop away.

The telephoto lens continued to follow her movements, interrupted only by the rapid clicking of the camera shutter.

Now sitting comfortably on the edge of the bed, she bent forward pulling on a clean pair of plain white briefs, followed by tights. Her fingers now moved quickly through the straps on her bra. Slightly hanging breasts rose sharply as she pulled the clasp together.

A red warning light flashed. The film was fully exposed. 'Bastard!' Pascoe almost screamed the word aloud. Having to rewind the used film before loading a fresh roll wasted valuable time and took his attention away from the subject. Fumbling fingers only made things worse. Finally he gave up, deciding to watch her through the binoculars. The peepshow ended. An hour had passed since his arrival and the sun had disappeared. Pascoe wondered where the woman might be going and with whom. The thought that some other male might get even closer to her angered him. 'She'll never let you take the pictures I've got.' Sliding backwards out of the gap in the hawthorn he sat upright, carefully packing the equipment back into the bag. Slinging it over his shoulder, Pascoe climbed to his feet and walked back to his car.

Not a bird in sight but a very successful evening with a naked woman and a rabbit.

The key turned in the front door lock. Joy had been in bed for an hour trying to sleep but had found it impossible. No use pretending. It would make no difference to him. The luminous dial on the bedside clock showed eleven fifteen. Footsteps on the stairs confirmed his intentions as the supper she had left in the kitchen remained untouched. A heavy feeling instinctively rose through her stomach reaching high into her chest. A foot kicked open the bedroom door.

Pascoe climbed into bed without bothering to wash. No words were exchanged. A huge hand curled around her shoulders pulling hard as he drew her towards him, still lying on her back. It was what he called his 'entitlement.' His breath was vile as ever, as she felt the pain of uninvited penetration. There could be no love-making, no foreplay. Without love there could only be lust or rape. She couldn't tell the difference anymore. Joy breathed a sigh of relief when he withdrew and pushed her away muttering something that sounded like 'Fucking useless bitch.' Five minutes later he was snoring loudly.

Slipping quietly out of bed Joy headed into the bathroom. Soaking a facecloth, she rubbed vigorously, obsessively, in a vain attempt to cleanse herself and disguise the smell of his body, stale sweat and alcohol. Alone in the darkness tears ran freely. Joy wondered whether she might ever be freed from this awful marriage. It was almost twenty minutes before she was able to return to her bed. Sleep never came easy; the dawn not soon enough.

The next morning Pascoe left early for work, unshaven and wearing the same grubby clothes. Not that it mattered much in his line of work, cutting trenches for pipe layers, though most men would at least make some effort. It was his way of waving two fingers at the world and God help anyone who might try to stop him. There was little point inquiring about the peregrine falcon. Any success and she would have known about it. Pascoe was a braggart.

It was Joy's day for shopping at the market. She knew where to find the bargains and how far she could spread the pittance he handed out each week. Before starting the food shopping, she liked to walk around the stalls, enjoying the colourful displays and merging into the street scene. It was busy and noisy and every once in a while she would nod to an acquaintance. People had come from far and wide for hundreds of years to this quaint market town. Joy knew many of the stallholders by sight, being an occasional customer when funds permitted. She stopped to admire figurines of a West Highland terrier and a Border collie, her favourite dogs, marked at two shillings and sixpence each, and thought long and hard before walking away. Maybe one next week and another the week after. The stall lady would put something on one side for her if she really wanted it. Wandering between the close-packed stalls she cast envious eyes at the people giving themselves little treats. Skirts, sweaters and shoes seemed to be on sale everywhere. What must it be like not to have to count every penny? Why should she have to risk a beating for some minor infringement of his rules? Those were the times when Pascoe would say that she needed to be taught a lesson.

Turning the corner of Market Street she now headed towards the next line of stalls, stopping to pass the time of day with one of the farm ladies. The stall next to it was offering poster size pictures of the Bay City Rollers, The Beatles, The Who, The Bachelors, Matt Monroe and many others, all in a blaze of colour. At the back was a range photographs of footballers. Even Joy recognised George Best.

Suddenly her heart missed a beat. Pascoe was just a few yards ahead, walking in the same direction. Shoulders hunched, head slightly bowed and looking neither left nor right, he seemed to be heading towards The Lion. Panic forced her to double back so they wouldn't meet. From a safe distance she watched and waited. Surely he wasn't looking for her, spying on her? Pascoe said that if ever she tried to leave him he would mark her so that no other man would ever want her, and she believed him. It wasn't as if she wanted another man.

Walking slowly along the backs of the stalls Joy was able to keep him in view. At the junction by the clock tower, on the corner of Market Street, he stopped and seemed to be staring at something across the road. She watched, curiosity mixed with apprehension. There were just a couple of bric-a-brac stalls in front of him with an alley between. Behind them stood a ladies boutique. Pascoe leaned against the wall of the Bank remaining still for almost ten minutes before moving off towards The Lion.

'Twenty five per cent off everything today love.' The man smiled at her.

She knew him vaguely. 'No thanks, I'm only vegetable shopping today.'

Joy scurried away, embarrassed, without a second glance at his bargains, hesitating outside the boutique for a moment, not knowing which way to turn for the best.

A well groomed woman wearing a princess line light grey skirt with a white polo neck jumper was putting the final touches to a display. She smiled through the window and pointed to a sign 'Up to 50% off all marked prices,' it said. Of course. She remembered, it was the beginning of the Easter sales; an invitation to spend money she didn't have. But how could she explain that to the woman in the window? Joy smiled, nodded her acknowledgment and moved away.

Why was Pascoe hanging about such an unusual spot? The question was puzzling. Obviously he wasn't looking into a ladies' boutique, not unless he had designs on being another Lady Chatterley's Lover! The thought was laughable. Pascoe must have been waiting outside the bank for a reason but she probably would never find out and she would never dare to ask. If he suspected she was spying on him, he would probably kill her. The thought stayed in the back of her mind all the way home. Maybe he was holding back from going to the pub too early if he was short of money. It was the only explanation that made any sense.

The Lion was always packed on market days but if the boutique woman called in for a glass of wine, he'd know instinctively. Pascoe knew exactly where she'd look for a seat in the lounge and positioned himself so he could keep watch from the bar area. He knew her favourite drink, her times of arrival and departure. In or out, she was an unsuspecting creature of habit.

He ordered a pint of bitter, carefully counting the coppers given in change from his three silver shillings. He turned his mind to the coming weekend. There was plenty of developing and printing waiting to be done. By letting

Joy go to chapel on the occasional Sunday he gained the free use of the kitchen for a couple of hours. The last thing he needed was a pair of prying eyes in his darkroom.

He thought about the Irish woman he had been watching recently. She was always home between licensing hours and very careless in her bedroom habits. 'Fucking near caught me once', under his breath. He was pretty sure she called the police but didn't hang about to find out. On another occasion a fox bolted from its lair and caused a rumpus which nearly got him trapped. She was a heavy boozer, an alcoholic, not that it mattered. She only drew the curtains when she remembered. Better still, it was a bungalow which made for easier viewing from the high ground to the rear.

There was always the young cashier from the Spar shop. She was another possibility and much more interesting. Pascoe had enjoyed intimate sessions that she never knew were being shared with a stranger. He gained a great deal of pleasure from watching the things she did to herself in the privacy of her bedroom. The photos might have been better. He liked to see a face as well as a full figure lying stretched out. On the days following each session he made it his business to call into the shop to get as close to her as he could. Somehow it added to the excitement of his perverted actions and, in some evil way, prolonged his self gratification.

Grudgingly, Pascoe reached into his pocket, then carefully counted out the correct money for another pint of bitter. Standing at the end of the bar, facing into the lounge, he watched and waited. She might call in, even at the last minute. His thoughts were suddenly distracted by a buzz of excitement around the bar, Pascoe looked towards the barman.

'What's goin' on lad? What's it all about?'

The barman glanced sideways towards him.

'The space ship, one that went to the moon a couple of days ago is in trouble.' He turned up the volume on a radio behind the counter. Apollo 13 was in difficulties. The voice of the astronaut, echoing from space was crystal clear. It was the mission commander in charge of Apollo 13, James Lovell.

'Houston we've had a problem here.'

An eerie silence descended across the pub as ears strained to hear what was being said as hearts and minds concentrated on the words of the astronaut. Suddenly she was there, sitting in the window seat in her usual place. She listened with the others, her eyes glistening at the news. She must have walked in at the precise moment he looked away. Not so much as a glance in his direction. Somehow he hadn't noticed her arrival and neither was he listening to the radio. Pascoe had other things on his mind.

Chapter 2

The dark nights and mornings of winter were now quickly receding. April, heralding sunshine and warmer days, made the fishing all the more pleasurable. So far, today had been kind to Deakin. Too kind, almost. Time and opportunity is as crucial to a fisherman, as it is to a criminal. He reeled in his line to avoid contact with an approaching barge. The owner acknowledged his gesture of goodwill. Deakin nodded. The sun, edging towards the horizon, was directly in to his eyes, preventing him from having a clear view of the skipper.

Deakin watched as the narrowboat came, almost lazily, to rest alongside its mooring points. It was heading from Burscough, north towards Wigan. His best guess was that it would be joining the main Liverpool to Leeds section at the Bridgewater canal junction. The hand-painted ornaments lining the roof, the polished brasswork, gleaming windows and neat curtains told him plenty about the owner. This was no hire boat. It was lovingly maintained to the highest standard. He recalled with some amusement that surgeons, accountants and, above all, bank robbers, are also notoriously meticulous.

Chief Detective Inspector Deakin had been involved in a love affair with fishing for many years. The canal allowed him all the solitude he could wish for. It gave him time to think. To work things out in his mind. He also had a great affection for the well ordered wildlife, at last beginning to show signs of movement after a long winter in hibernation. There was a flurry of nest building and egg-laying in a world where only the strongest survived.

The sun, finally touching the horizon signalled the end of a peaceful day. Carefully, methodically, Deakin began to pack away the rod sections into their canvas carrier. The reel with its fancy locking winder, keep net and folding stool, all slotted into the large wooden box. He stretched and exercised his cramped legs before setting off along the towpath. It was almost time to collect Laura.

The skipper had finished securing the boat to its moorings and seemed to be tinkering with something on the deck. He glanced up casually as Deakin drew alongside. He was a big man, with a face that looked younger than his greying temples suggested. The two nodded to each other. There was something vaguely familiar about him. Deakin struggled to put a name to the face but for the moment it was escaping him. It annoyed him when things like this happened. In his line of business it wasn't just important but often vital.

Turning off the towpath he walked over a small hummock, following a shortcut back to his car. Once home he stored the fishing tackle carefully in its own special place in the garage. Laura really couldn't stand the smell which seemed to hang about the place even though he always returned his catch to the water. Deakin lay back in the bath and relaxed, resolving not to fall asleep. Who the hell was that boatman? Where had he seen him before? Stupid, maybe, but annoying thoughts. At least they stopped him from falling asleep in the bath. Slacks and a warm sweater made him look smart but casual. Nobody would expect to see him in a suit on his day off. Stepping out into the chill evening air, he hardly noticed the drop in temperature. A short drive across town brought him to the doorstep of his mother in law's home.

'Hello sweetness.' Deakin kissed his wife gently on the lips.

They always kissed on the lips. It had real meaning. Her eyes flashed their pleasure. She rewarded him with a gentle squeeze of the hand, as she led him down the brightly lit hall into a comfortably familiar lounge. Laura had somehow managed almost to maintain the slim figure of earlier days. Maybe the food rationing during the war years and after, had something to do with it. She still had the desirable figure of a much younger woman.

'Hello Mum.'

Deakin gave Sally a bear-like hug before releasing her to return to the kitchen. He settled into the winged armchair and winked broadly at Laura. Any moment now the old lady would re-appear as if by magic, carrying a well laden tray displaying a variety of his favourite snacks, a meat pie, custard creams and maybe even a chocolate éclair and a mug of steaming coffee. It was her turn to do the spoiling and she enjoyed every minute of it.

Laura caught his attention and pointed towards the floor.

'Don't forget to notice Mums new shoes,' she whispered.

He glanced at the shoe box lying at the side of his chair. Sally came back, carrying the tray exactly as predicted. Laura looked on, amused at the way he allowed the old lady to fuss around him.

'Just a little snack darling.'

The treats Dad used to get when he was alive were now being lavished on his well loved son-in-law, and appreciated. Leaning back into the armchair he had a contented look about him.

'You remind me so much of Dad when I see you in that chair. What are you day dreaming about?' Laura wanted to know.

'If I told you, you'd think I was going soft in the head.' He looked a bit sheepish. 'I was just thinking how your dad used to sit in this chair and remembering the night when I plucked up the courage to ask him if we could get married. How he called your Mum in from the kitchen to see whether or not she approved.' He grinned like a schoolboy with a guilty secret.

Laura's expression never altered. 'No regrets, I hope?'

'I was a bag of nerves. A young beat bobby with no experience and no money, and working three shifts, but I was determined to have you, in the nicest possible way of course.'

Her eyes twinkled. 'Dad knew all that but he must have thought you had prospects, as well as the desire to take over his second most treasured possession.'

Sally walked back into the room. 'Couldn't help hearing you two twittering like love birds.'

'It's your daughter trying to tell me how lucky I was to get your permission to marry her.'

'I'm strictly neutral. I love you both.'

'Bought anything nice today Mum?' Deakin changed the subject.

'Just a pair of shoes.'

She picked up the box and reached inside. The red label stuck to the leather sole said, 'Sale'.

He pretended to examine them 'They're lovely. Let me treat you.' He knew exactly what she was about to say.

'Course not. Don't be silly.' Sally's face lit up at the offer.

He handed over the empty tray which she took from him before disappearing back into the kitchen. Deakin reached out and left a five pound note on the sideboard just as Laura knew he would.

Climbing out of the armchair he walked through to the kitchen checking the locks on the back door, the windows, and finally, the double locks on the door leading into the garage. Satisfied that everything was in order, he came back into the lounge giving Sally a pat on the shoulder and a goodnight peck.

'Give you a ring tomorrow Mum. Bye for now.' Laura waved from the car as it pulled away, heading for home.

'Mum needs to be careful at the moment. There's a peeper roaming loose in this area. Didn't want to mention it in front of her. Might make her nervous.' Deakin spoke without turning his head.

Laura looked out into the darkness. 'I thought you were being extra vigilant tonight. I'll give her a ring later, make sure she's alright.'

The black Ford Classic swept through the open gates coming to a standstill on the driveway. A glimmer of light showed through the lounge curtain giving the impression that someone was already home. It was a good neighbourhood with mostly new privately owned houses but that was no reason to relax their vigilance.

With five minutes to spare before the news started on ITV there was no need to rush. Thursdays it was followed by his favourite programme, University Challenge. Switching on the imitation coal fire, he waited for the flames to dance over the black ceramic bricks before taking up his usual seat opposite the television. Laura went upstairs to put her bargains into the wardrobe before settling down with some unfinished knitting. The phone rang.

'Bloody hell. I knew today was too damned good to be true.' Deakin picked up the receiver, expecting the worst and listened intently for a few seconds, before interrupting the caller. 'Yes Mum, I did check the curtains and no-one can see through them. No Mum, you're no trouble at all, so stop worrying about it.' He hesitated for a moment. 'I'll tell Laura. Goodnight.' Replacing the receiver, he sighed. 'Oh God, never underestimate the elderly.'

'She knew all the time about the peeper. Said she didn't want us worrying about her and she's not one of the Bluebell Girls anyway.'

He turned his attention back to the news. Out of the corner of his eye he saw Laura exchange her knitting for a crossword puzzle, then pick up a pencil. He already knew that she would put it down again shortly to make a cup of tea. Laura could always put a crossword down without losing her train of thought. It was one of those womanly traits, being able to do two or three things as the same time.

Shortly before midnight he followed her into the bedroom. Clothes being neatly folded ready for the morning was a harmless habit, carried on from his years in the military. Everything done, he climbed into bed, switching off the bedside light. Crooking one arm around Laura's shoulders, he pulled her gently towards him. She snuggled up close, basking in the warmth and safety of his powerful body. Reaching forward to kiss him goodnight, she felt the same twinges of excitement which first swept over her all those years ago. Lovemaking was important, as well as exciting, but they had learned a long time ago about patience and compatibility. Their desire for each other had never abated but was well under control and always mutually pleasurable.

It was still dark when the telephone rang again. Automatically he reached out dragging the receiver to his ear. Laura, raising herself on to one elbow, switched on the bedside light. At this unearthly hour it had to be business.

'Deakin.'

'Jones, chief. Sorry to disturb you.'

'That's alright sergeant. What's the problem?'

'Suspicious death. I thought you ought to know about it. Nightman answered a triple nine. There's a body in an unadopted road between Higher Lane and a group of terraced cottages.' Jones paused for a moment. 'Fatal head wound. Real messy. Doesn't look like a hit and run to me.'

Deakin frowned. 'Where are you now?'

'Higher Lane, chief.'

There was no need for a note pad. 'I'll be along shortly. While you're waiting, call the Home Office Pathologist. It's probably Julian Hayes. Tell him it's urgent. Tell the traffic men to look out for him and I'll see him there. Make sure the road is blocked off. I don't suppose there'll be any traffic problems but you'd best mention it to the traffic office as well. Secure the scene and have the team ready to start at first light. Thanks.' He replaced the receiver.

Laura had already slipped into her dressing gown and disappeared downstairs. When he came down, she was sitting by the kitchen table, a cup of hot sweet tea ready and waiting for him. Being married to Deakin was a full time job even without children. Within ten minutes he was ready to leave. Relieving him of a half empty cup as they walked to the front door, she could sense the urgency in his stride.

He stopped briefly to kiss her. 'Sorry about this sweetheart. I'll call you as soon as I can. For breakfast I hope.'

'Take care and keep yourself wrapped up; it's chilly out.'

She watched as the sleek lines of the car moved slowly out of the drive, turning left into the road before picking up speed and disappearing from view. Deakin knew nothing of the nerves which played havoc with her stomach every time he answered an emergency call. It had been like that for more years than she could remember. Her husband had a box full of commendations for bravery. Any one of them could have been his obituary. Locking the front door, Laura went back into the kitchen to make herself a drink, no longer interested in sleep.

The grey light of dawn had yet to force its way through but already Higher Lane was a hive of activity. There was no mistaking sergeant Jones. Younger and slimmer than Deakin, he was light on his feet, moving quickly between the small groups of men that made up their team. At the moment he was busy briefing the search team. Speed was of the essence.

'Morning chief, we're over there.' He pointed to a ditch a short distance away. Deakin stepped forward, following him for a few yards before catching the scene in the beam of his torch. A crumpled heap came into view. At first sight it could have been a piece of old carpet discarded by some lazy home decorator. He quickened his pace, before stopping and staring downwards. 'Jesus

Christ!' Slender fingers reached out ahead of the body as if pleading for mercy. He reached down gently touching them. They were stiff and freezing. Rigor mortis had set in. The style of coat she was wearing suggested a person of mature years but not elderly. It was hard to tell from the blood soaked hair what colour it should have been. Jones came across, obviously still moved by the scene which had greeted him on his arrival.

It wasn't possible to study her features, or see what other wounds might have been inflicted. She could not be moved or contaminated in any way until the forensic team had visited the site. The photographer had also to complete his unenviable task. Those were the rules of murder investigation. Even in death there has to be some order.

'Don't touch anything until the doc has examined her.' Deakin barked the order.

Already he could feel the anger welling up inside him. The thought of how and why a woman came to die in this remote spot was worrying. Did she die here or was she brought to this spot and her body dumped? Deakin glanced at his watch,

'Any sign of the pathologist yet?'

Chapter 3

Jonathan Hayes closed the door gently behind him, leaving his wife to the warmth of their bed and the remainder of a peaceful night. Outside in the cold and darkness he hesitated, struggling with the zip fastener on his suede jacket. Throwing the Gladstone bag on the passenger seat, he drove away quickly. The journey across town was brief at this hour. The orange glow from the overhead lighting on the dual carriageway and the rising mist of early spring gave the road a spectral appearance, reinforced by the absence of traffic.

Turning into Higher Lane, headlights on full beam, he began to look out for the side road somewhere ahead. He knew the area generally but not the actual spot where the incident had occurred. A minute later, a blue flashing light came into view. It seemed to be tucked away behind a hedge. Two police vehicles had sealed off the entrance to the side road, forcing him to slow down before coming to a complete standstill. He reached for the black leather bag before stepping out of the car and paused just long enough to close the zip up to his collar as protection against the biting cold. A uniformed officer came towards him.

'Morning sir. Can I help you?'

'Hayes, Home Office Pathologist.'

'Chief inspector Deakin is expecting you sir. I'll let him know you're here.'

He pointed towards a wide circle of corded rope with small red triangular flags hanging from it at intervals. It was a scene with which Hayes was all too familiar. Two uniformed officers stood at the perimeter ensuring no-one entered the hallowed circle without the Chief's permission.

'Through there sir.' One of them pointed the way.' Nothing touched. Just as we found her.'

The officer left the doctor to get on with his unenviable task. Deakin was easily identifiable even though his back was half turned away. He walked directly towards the group.

'Good morning gentlemen. What have we here?'

'Good morning. Sorry to have to drag you out at this unearthly hour.' Deakin offered a welcoming hand that was firmly grasped.

'Youngish female, discovered an hour or so ago. She didn't die by accident. This is exactly as our lads found her.'

Hayes reached into his bag, producing a pair of surgical gloves and a large chromium handled torch. Pulling tightly on the gloves, he managed to stretch them over both hands before kneeling down to begin his examination.

'Female, face down, arms ahead as if to soften the fall and in an advanced state of rigor mortis.' The new style Sanyo pocket electronic memo recorder with its tiny recording tapes, was proving to be invaluable. Hands free he could talk for fifteen minutes at a time before turning the tape over. All he had to do was toss it into the secretary's basket at the Pathology office and she could play it back and type the report directly from her transcribing machine. 'Clothing appears to be undisturbed.'

He looked down the beam of his torch towards the heels. 'No scuff marks.'

At least she hadn't been dragged to the spot where she now lay. But it was still possible that the body been carried or even tossed into its last resting place. Putting the machine aside for a moment, he reached into his bag and pulled out a thermometer. Taking temperature readings from two parts of the body, he estimated death to have occurred approximately eight hours earlier, no more than nine. Rigor Mortis was not yet ready to reverse itself. It could take anything from twelve hours to three or four days, depending on the circumstances. Glancing again at the watch he double checked the time.

'Time of death, probably nine o'clock last night, give or take thirty minutes, bearing in mind the time of year, the external temperature and exposed position.' He thought for a second before making the next note.

'Not possible to measure the lowest blood levels because of the position of the body.'

There would be other factors to consider later such as partly digested food or the presence of drugs in the bloodstream; maybe fluid in the lungs. Occasionally a broken watch would provide an accurate time of death though not to be relied upon without supporting evidence. More like corroboration. Hayes knew only too well that the precise timing of death was always crucial in a murder enquiry.

The doctor now turned his attention to the wounds. The first blow had been struck with such force that death would almost certainly have been instantaneous. Those which followed had landed on a skull already shattered like an egg shell, serving no purpose other than satisfying the desire of a maniac. Even by torchlight, he was able to note blackened bruising around the neck muscles, indicating some attempt at strangulation, or maybe a means of keeping the victim quiet. Closer examination of the exposed side of the face showed deep indentations made by a thumb being forced underneath the jawbone.

'Sergeant, can you help me for a moment please?'

Jones moved forward alongside the pathologist. 'Hello Doc. What can I do for you?'

Hayes turned his head. 'Can you help me turn this lady over please.'

Jones looked towards his boss. 'Photographer finished chief? The doc wants to turn her over.'

Deakin nodded his agreement while continuing to speak with the officers who were first on the scene. The sergeant leaned forward to take the weight while the pathologist turned the victim on to her back, now able to note that she had died in a semi crouching position. The rigid state of the body gave it a grotesque appearance. It was as if she had been praying and reaching out. Hayes turned his attention back to the machine and began speaking again.

'Female now lying on her back, knees fully contracted towards the chest, arms outstretched ahead. Facial injuries consistent with a forward falling motion. She fell into the ditch, probably from the force of the blow to the skull. Mud in the nasal cavities. No excess bruising on the knees and minimal damage to her tights.'

He shone the torch over the rest of her body, gently moving aside her outer and inner garments with his free hand and carefully putting them back into place.

'Clothing undamaged. No obvious staining or seminal residue. No immediate evidence of rape or intercourse.'

Jones listened intently as the doctor made his recorded notes. 'No sexual assault?' He didn't intend it to sound as if he was questioning the doctor, it was just the way it came out.

'I think not sergeant. But we'll know more later. I can tell you she died here and wasn't dragged or carried, if that's any help, and probably around nine o'clock last night.'

Jones waited to hear anything else which might be of some help at this early stage.

'Whoever did this would have been saturated in blood, and probably have some brain membranes stuck to him as well. It will be on his skin, clothing and even down to his feet, in tiny droplets.' He smiled, 'What we call the watering can effect which results from fractures of the skull and brain damage.'

All too frequently Hayes was called upon to explain to detectives and dinner-jacketed audiences, that when a skull is fractured there are numerous small vessels in the head which rupture while already under pressure from a heart still pumping at anything up to two hundred pounds to the square inch. Blood spurts from the cavity, spraying like water from the nozzle of a watering can. Anyone standing close to the victim would certainly be caught in the fine, but powerful eruption. Probably sergeant Jones already knew about it but it didn't do any harm to remind him.

Hayes leaned back on his heels for a moment. Certainly the unfortunate victim had been given no opportunity to defend herself. The position of her hands indicated some attempt at protecting her face, perhaps just a reflex action. Had she been on her side, it might have been different. She must have been taken by surprise.

'How's it going doc? Anything for me to start with?'

The familiar voice brought the pathologist from his kneeling position to his feet as he found himself facing Deakin.

'Morning chief inspector, someone else asked me that already.'

Deakin was willing to accept whatever help he could get at this stage.

'The basics, you already know. He paused for a second as if gathering his thoughts before proceeding. 'Time of death somewhere between eight thirty and nine thirty last evening, still to be confirmed.'

Then came the words the detective needed to hear.

'Cause of death almost certainly a massive fracture to the rear of the skull. No question of suicide I'm afraid.' He hesitated, picking his words precisely. 'You already knew that that much. There appear to be a number of blows to the head and strangulation marks, but she was already dead in my opinion. Sometimes air escaping from the lungs and stomach gives the impression that life still exists which might account for the throat marks. The face lacerations happened as she fell forwards from the force of the first blow into the bracken, which probably left her in a partial kneeling position. She wasn't punched.'

Deakin listened intently without interruption until the doctor finished, before putting one question which concerned him.

'Any thoughts on the type of weapon used?'

Hayes had already considered the shape and depth of the wound in the skull.

'I might do better later, but my initial guess would be something tubular, maybe a solid steel bar of some sort.

Possibly half to three quarters of an inch in diameter, no larger than that. It would have to be pretty solid.'

Deakin turned to his sergeant. 'Pass that on.' It was an order. He looked back at the pathologist. 'Any indications of sexual assault?'

'Not on first examination. No initial sign of leaking semen, blood or bruising in the vaginal area.' He had, however, noticed something else. 'See the wedding ring on the wrong hand? She may have been married and divorced, unless of course it's a family heirloom.'

Deakin nodded his appreciation of the thought. 'We can't rule out robbery yet, because there's no trace of any personal effects, but it seems an odd place if that was the motive.'

Their discussion was interrupted by the flashing of photo bulbs as the police photographer took his last pictures of the surrounding area. He turned back towards the chief inspector.

'Got all my pictures now, sir. Any specials you need?'

Deakin thought for a second. 'Take a picture of the right hand and mark it carefully. Let me have all the proofs as quick as you can, please.'

Hayes waited until the chief had finished giving out his instructions.

'Any idea who she might be?'

'Not yet, but there were some car keys by the body that belong to a vehicle in the lay-by down the road. That should give us our first lead.'

Casting a final eye over the victim in order to satisfy himself that nothing had been omitted or forgotten at this early stage, the pathologist carefully removed his surgical gloves before checking his watch again.

'See you at the mortuary. I'm off for a bite of break-fast. Say about eleven o'clock?'

What would it take to put you off a meal? Deakin wondered. 'Eleven it is. Bye for now.'

Deakin returned to the business in hand. 'Area secured sergeant?'

'Yes chief. Service road's blocked off, and the main drag is an urban clearway, so we can stop any uninvited guests.' Jones was familiar with the depths to which press reporters and photographers were liable to sink when it came to a human interest story.

'OK, make sure the search team scans right down to the main road. It's likely the car belongs to her, unless of course she borrowed it, but at least we can be reasonably sure of her movements in this area. Tell the lads to keep an eye for an iron or steel bar of some sort, maybe a half inch round and probably not less than about twelve to fifteen inches long.'

Jones was about to confirm the orders when he was interrupted by a tap on the shoulder.

'Excuse me boss. I'm late and I've got deliveries to make.'

It was Tommy Johnson, the milk roundsman who discovered the body while making his early morning deliveries. He had been attracted by the gleam of a patent leather shoe in his headlight and what looked like a bundle of clothes. Tommy would remember the moments that followed for the rest of his days. Closer inspection revealed a body lying hunched in the ditch at the side of the lane. Suddenly he was at the sharp end of a real murder enquiry. 'No, I didn't see anyone in the vicinity. No I didn't notice any cars driving round the area. No I didn't go near the body or touch anything.'

The questions had seemed endless. It was as if he was the prime suspect.

'OK Tommy, you can get off now.' Jones pointed to one of the young constables standing nearby. 'Make sure he has your details. We'll be needing a full statement later. Thanks for your help.'

Without waiting for an answer he moved on to deal with the next query. Tommy needed no second invitation and two minutes later headed back to his milk float, anxious to get away as quickly as possible. There would be plenty to tell the missus when he got home today. 'Bloody hell, I'll be in the papers, maybe even on the bloody tele.'

The sergeant watched the float rattle its way up the road. Wonder what it must be like to be home the same time every day and have regular days off? He watched as it turned a corner, the small red tail lights disappearing from view.

Deakin returned from his tour of the area. The nearest properties were only a couple of hundred yards away, comprising a block of terraced cottages set back from the road on a gentle incline, with typical rural open aspects. Some of the tenants had been roused by the arrival of the police and their blue flashing lights. Others were still in bed. Arrangements had already been made for all of them to be interviewed. It was possible, even likely, that the victim was on her way home to one of the cottages and her car had broken down. It shouldn't take long to find out.

Deakin needed answers, and urgently. He took one last look at the crumpled heap, so recently a human life, no doubt with feelings, hopes and dreams. Who are you? Why are you here? Where are you from? Who hated you so much that you had to die? The answers wouldn't come soon enough as far as he was concerned. His thoughts again interrupted, he turned towards his sergeant. 'Sorry Chief. Can we move the body now and get her off to pathology for the post mortem?'

'Yes, I think so. Tell the lads we'll hold the team meeting later, sometime this afternoon.'

Jones walked away towards the body attendants standing a couple of yards from the scene, waiting quietly and respectfully.

'OK boys. Gently does it.'

Deakin watched as the two men carefully wrapped sheets around the body before lifting it on to a stretcher, then placing it carefully into the private ambulance. The silence, while the body was eased into place, was almost religious, as if the funeral was taking place there and then, on the very spot where she died. It was only a few minutes after seven.

'I'm going home for a shave and clean up. Make sure the scene is protected until the search team have done their bit.'

The sergeant watched Sam Deakin leave before going back to the crime team. The first light of the day had now broken and although still weak, it was enough for the search team to get started on their inch by inch coverage of the immediate area. He never ceased to be amazed at the items unearthed during searches.

Laura was already up and about when Deakin arrived. 'Hello love.' She gave him a peck on the cheek. 'Hungry?'

'Just give me half an hour sweet. I'll have a soak in the bath: might make me feel fresher.'

'I'll run it for you.'

She was already on the move, leaving him in the kitchen with a mug of hot sweet tea, turning things over in his mind. It was too early yet to start worrying about what might or might not be. There was always a chance that some maniac was targeting the patch. It was every detective's nightmare. At this moment in time there was no way of knowing whether they were dealing with the results of a domestic dispute gone wrong, two drunks squabbling, or something much worse.

Laura interrupted his thoughts. 'Bath's ready.' She looked at him sympathetically. 'Bad one is it?' It wasn't a gossip seeking inquiry.

'Young woman lying dead in a ditch. Not by accident.'

He decided to spare Laura the facts. It would be bad enough when the papers got hold of it. Recognising the signs, she decided not to ask further questions, leaving him to get on with his bath.

CHAPTER 4

Food shopping had become a nightmare for Cathy
Wilson ever since Linda went on yet another of her slim-
ming rampages. She was already planning the weekend
menus and it was still only Thursday. Cathy recalled her
own youth and the hardship of food and clothing short-
ages brought about by a world war. Today's generation
had no notion of such things as queuing for hours at a
time, to be rewarded with a few potatoes and a cabbage
or perhaps a handful of carrots and the occasional luxury
of an onion.

Who needs kids? She looked down at a box of pink
grapefruits conveniently stacked close to the cashier. How
long before the next craze overtakes this child of mine?
How much is it going cost to satisfy that little whim?
Cathy smiled to herself. A voice cut across her thoughts.

'Anything else madam?' The cashier asked politely.

'No thank you. Not unless you can send me somewhere exotic where I don't have to cook and clean.'
Cathy's face took on a forced, wistful look.

'Fancy just having to shop for jewellery, make-up and
clothes.'

Another customer joined in; 'Can I come too?'

The cashier smiled, 'Don't go without me girls.'

Straining under the weight the shopping bags,
Cathy was pleased that she had been able to park near

the entrance. Oblivious to a pair of eyes following her movements, she piled everything into the back. With a sigh of relief she took her seat behind the wheel. Fifteen minutes later the grey Austin saloon came gently to rest outside the small semi-detached house. The tiny patch of grass beyond the low brick wall was showing signs of a new season breaking through at last. Cathy pushed open the wooden gate with her foot.

It was hard trying to manage on her own with a teenage daughter who couldn't understand why her father had walked out on them. Sometimes Linda blamed her. Other times it was her father and occasionally both of them, depending on her mood. The truth of the matter probably lay in a fear of waking up one day and finding herself completely alone in the world. After all, if Dad had already deserted her, why not Mum?

Cathy needed to speak with Bill Wilson about the delays in payment of the court order for her and Linda. In recent times he had become erratic and was causing them unnecessary hardship. She couldn't help wondering whether his new wife, Betty, was paid her housekeeping on the fourth Friday of every month, or whether he kept her waiting while he robbed Peter to pay Paul. Bill Wilson had commitments and whether he liked it or not, they would have to be met. You push me too far and I'll have you back before the court. One way or the other you'll pay. Words said under her breath had so far not come to fruition. Bill still flouted the order whenever it suited him. But his time was running out.

Once inside the house Cathy quickly unloaded the shopping into the kitchen cupboards. She had barely finished before Linda appeared as if from nowhere.

'What's to eat? I'm starved.'

Cathy turned to face her. 'Hello Sweet, there's plenty today. I've got some nice celery soup and there's some jacket potatoes to go in the oven. You can have beans or cauliflower cheese with them and a nice side salad. Ready in about half an hour.'

She waited for the accolade, but the fact that Linda was already taking her place at the table, was the only sign of approval. Relieved, Cathy got on with the job. Whatever problems followed the divorce, they had to eat.

Almost on the stroke of seven the pair sat down to their evening meal, two courses, neatly presented and accompanied by crusty cobs. Cathy took the empty plates into the kitchen, allowing Linda to wander back to her room. She believed strongly that children should be allowed their childhood and not be pressed into endless household jobs before their time. She wanted Linda to enjoy her youth. Womanhood would come soon enough, and with it, a whole new way of life. Cathy had almost finished washing the dishes when the phone rang.

'I'll get it.' She glanced towards the kitchen clock, it was almost seven forty five. 'It'll be Grandfather, I expect. Grandma's not well today.'

Cathy had to keep an eye on both of them, particularly her mum who had been coughing far too much lately. Expecting to hear a familiar voice, she spoke cheerfully.

'Hello, 5525.' The welcoming smile quickly faded, turning into a frown. After a few seconds she interrupted. 'If the damned money was paid into the bank at the proper times all this would never have been necessary. It's bad enough having to wash our dirty linen in public, without having to explain myself to a bank manager every month.'

Linda appeared in the doorway as Cathy's frustration showed itself.

'No, I don't like the idea and it shouldn't be necessary either.' Finally she conceded. 'Oh alright then, eight forty five, no later.'

She slammed the phone down in temper. 'Damn him and his blasted tart. Why can't he just pay the damned money into the bank when it's due?' Still muttering to herself she headed upstairs. 'Better still, just get to hell out of my life and leave me in peace.'

'Was that Dad on the phone?'

'Don't start asking questions, I've got to get ready.'

'Where are you going?' Linda persisted.

Cathy was in no mood for a question and answer session. 'I've just got to go out for an hour. You can manage without me for that long surely?' She thought for a moment. 'By the way, if Grandfather rings, tell him I'll be back by nine thirty.'

'Alright but what about the washing?'

'What about it? Can't that wait for an hour, or do you want me to do it now before I go? For God's sake Linda, I've been working all day, then shopping and cooking. Are you completely helpless? Either do it yourself, or leave it in till I get back. Just this once try making a decision. It's not that difficult.' She could feel her anger rising.

Linda didn't give in easily. She tried again. 'Going to see Dad, are you?' It was months since she'd seen Mum in a state like this after one of his calls. Mostly it was about money.

'Now just mind your own business and stop asking questions. Get on with your homework till I come back.' Cathy turned back to the mirror, surprised at the look on her face and feeling slightly embarrassed.

Realising that the argument was getting her nowhere, Linda wandered back into the safety of her room and sat staring at the books laid out on the small desk. There was still plenty of homework to be done.

The clock in the hall showed eight–thirty as Cathy poked her head round the door. Linda gave the impression of being absorbed in her reading, but the frown on her face suggested she might be sulking, not studying.

'I'm off now. See you shortly.' As an afterthought she added, 'We'll have a nice supper when I get back. See you later.'

Linda nodded her approval. The peace offering was accepted. 'Give my love to Dad.'

'Do that yourself. If it wasn't for him, I'd be settling down in front of a warm fire now instead of dragging myself out.'

Cathy slammed the door behind her, leaving her offspring to get on with something better than useless banter. She walked out into the cold night air, pulling the lapels of her coat together as protection against the biting wind. Once in the car she reached for a cloth to wipe the mist from the windows before starting the engine. A minute later it moved away from the kerb heading across town. The smell of petrol fumes aggravated her. *Must get that exhaust fixed, if ever his damned cheque arrives.* She made a mental note.

The road was unlit. Cathy had been there only once before, purely out of curiosity. She was not familiar with any of the landmarks. The last time she came to this damned place it was in daylight, snooping around wearing a headscarf and dark glasses like an amateur detective. It was that awful period of uncertainty when, feeling very low and rejected, she had to know why the grass was apparently so much greener on this side of town. She had to see the love-nest for herself. It turned out to be an old farm cottage even smaller than the nineteen thirties home he'd left behind. Looking back on that afternoon, it would have been comical in different circumstances. Even now she still couldn't fathom why he strayed.

In the darkness everything was completely different. Cathy remembered passing a pub on the right last time and then a parish church before heading out into the countryside for a mile or so. Somewhere nearby was a junction she had to cross before turning into Higher Lane and reaching the lay-by where she hid the car last time.

Frustration and a touch of nerves began to show. Cathy could feel her anger simmering again. *Why the hell did I agree to this? He knows the cost of living and I shouldn't have to beg for every penny. The sooner this is over the better.* Cathy could feel her anger beginning to simmer again. *The sooner this is over the better.*

Following the beam of the headlights she kept a sharp eye for the lay-by which she had used on her last visit, bearing in mind it was opposite the short road leading to the cottages where Bill now lived. She needed to be certain that she had the right place. Within a couple of minutes, but what seemed like an eternity, Cathy spotted the parking place and breathed a sigh of relief. Pulling over and looking across the road towards the cottages, she could make out the tail lights of a parked car. In a remote place like this it couldn't be anyone else except him.

Let's get it over with. She locked the door and walked quickly across the carriageway into the lane, heading straight for the parked vehicle. The fingers on the luminous dial of her wristwatch showed precisely eight forty five as she walked towards the dark figure standing slightly ahead of the car.

Well at least you're on time. I suppose I've got a right to expect that much. Cathy looked at the figure now standing almost alongside her.

'Hello. What a hell of a place to meet on a cold night.' She spoke aloud, surprised at the firmness of her voice. There was a ring of authority about it that had been missing for a while. Maybe the new job was giving her confidence. Cathy waited for her greeting to be returned.

'What the hell has happened to you?'

Bill Wilson's frame seemed to fill the small doorway at the rear of the cottage making him seem bigger than his normal five feet ten inches. Betty stared at her husband as he came into view by the kitchen door. He was white as a sheet. Cuts on his face, nose and left eye were still bleeding. His jacket and trousers were ripped and stained, while both hands and knees still dripped red.

'Have you been in a fight? What have you been up to?'

Bill's face was twisted with pain.

'What happened?' she persisted, noticing for the first time the blood on his shoes.

'Sorry about the mess. I tripped on mother's path in the dark and fell on to some broken glass.' He hesitated for a moment, clearly shaken with the trauma of it all. 'You're home early tonight.' He half turned away. 'Just let me change and clean up. Won't be long.' Limping towards the stairs he left Betty standing in the hall frowning after him.

'Well aren't you going to say 'hello' or something, or is the honeymoon over?' She refused to be ignored.

'Sorry love. Just give me a couple of minutes,' he answered.

Betty didn't give in easily. 'Let me have a look at those cuts. And that hair needs washing.'

She could see more clearly now that both knees were still weeping and grazed. His hands and wrists had blood on them as well. Bill looked as if he had been dragged through a bramble patch.

'Take those trousers off; they're ruined. I'll get some clean ones.' She stood back allowing him the space to carry out the order.

'No, honestly, it'll be fine.' He tried to side step her.

'If there's any dirt or glass in that cut, you'll need a tetanus injection.'

It was pointless trying to argue with her. Bill slipped out of his trousers, exposing fully the cuts on both knees and a trail of blood to the ankle.

'You look like some kid who's just fallen off the back entry wall.' It was like treating a small boy. She regained her composure. 'Soon sort this mess out,' she said. 'How the hell did you manage to fall off the path?'

Betty waited for an explanation as she reached for the jug and a sachet of Vosene hair shampoo. Ten minutes later, plasters covering the worst of the cuts, and now dressed in clean trousers and shirt, Bill sat down to a cup of hot sweet tea.

He was embarrassed. 'Sorry about that sweetheart,' he said. 'Now don't go telling anyone. Promise me?'

Betty felt relieved. He'd looked awful when he first came home. 'I just hope you haven't been on your knees to some other woman.'

'Darling would I lie to you?'

'Well you did to your first wife. Anyway how was your mother?'

'She was out. I was going to stick a note through the door till this lot happened. Anyway, 'I've got a headache, any Aspros handy? Where's the Aspro?'

He gave Betty a peck on the cheek, before taking up his now customary place opposite the fire and the television. The brightly coloured screen looked out of place in the tiny lounge with its low beamed ceiling. He wondered how farm labourers ever managed to bring up large families in such cramped spaces.

'For future reference, they're kept in the medicine chest in the kitchen.'

Betty handed over the bottle. Without waiting for his response, she turned on her heel, busying herself preparing supper. 'Cheese and pickles OK?'

Linda Wilson awakened with a start, not realising she had fallen asleep or for how long. Looking up at the clock on the mantelpiece, she frowned in surprise. *Half past ten Mum. And no supper. What are you up to?* Her thoughts began to race. Since the divorce Mum and Dad couldn't give each other the time of day, so there was really no need for her to be out this long. *Hope you haven't had an accident.* It was her first thought even though she knew that Mum was a good driver. She also knew her to be a creature of habit and not given to wandering off anywhere or keeping late hours except on special occasions.

'I'll give you until eleven o'clock and no longer,' Linda spoke aloud, then laughed nervously at her own joke. Deep down she was worried. It wasn't like Mum to be late. She was a very punctual person. Linda glanced towards the chimney breast where a portrait of

Grandma and Granddad smiled down at her from a space once occupied by Mum and Dad's wedding day photo. Feet now tucked underneath, her slim body pressed into the seat that Dad once liked to call his own. She could still feel his presence. Eleven o'clock soon came and went. Unwrapping her ankles from the armchair, Linda straightened up and walked into the kitchen. She began to fill the kettle. *Mum'll think she's dreaming if she walks in now!*

Chapter 5

It wasn't the most welcoming of places. A sparsely furnished waiting room boasting only two chairs and a
rickety, oval shaped mahogany table. No ashtray, not
even an old magazine. No window to look through. The
faint smell of hospital disinfectant drifted into his nostrils as he walked across the room towards a single door
bearing a black and white sign which simply said 'Ring
and wait.' Deakin had a strong dislike for what he
called the two M's, murder and mortuary. Pausing to
take a deep breath he pressed the bell. Post mortems
and scenes of crime were an essential part of his working life. Having to be present while the pathologist was
still working called for a strong stomach. At least he
wasn't sick anymore.

The high pitched whine of an electric saw echoing
beyond the door stopped abruptly. Too late to prevent
his stomach tightening, he prepared to face the ordeal of
yet another forensic style post mortem. Knowing as he
did, what was happening on the other side of that door
only made things worse. Not bothering to sit, he stood
and waited. *Hope to God I die of natural causes.* Deakin
kept the thought to himself.

'Come in Chief.' Julian Hayes held the door open,
nodding his acknowledgment and allowing the detective
to precede him into the post mortem theatre.

Deakin walked across the room towards a stainless steel table on which lay the half naked body of a female. The trunk was now wrapped in plastic and partly covered with a white sheet. He could see at a glance that she was in the thirty to forty age range. He looked down with neither curiosity nor embarrassment. He didn't see a naked woman, only marks on a body, each one with its own tale to tell.

The bruising on the face, particularly around the eyes, gave impression that the victim had been lacking sleep. Deep black and blue indentations around the neck now showed clearly what the doctor had mentioned earlier. Slowly his eyes moved downward taking in details of every mark. Both knees grazed, hands bruised, but the fingernails remained clean and polished. That, in itself, meant something. There had been no fierce resistance, no scratching of anyone else's skin. Looking closer he could see a clearly defined thumb mark under one side of the jaw bone making it seem as if someone had tried to lift her physically by the neck, using just one hand. Without removing the folded white sheet from her midriff, it wasn't possible to see the inside of her thighs and neither was he able to see the detail of any indentations to the rear of the skull. The doctor stood patiently on the opposite side of the table until Deakin had completed his initial survey before interrupting him.

The pathology examination had now confirmed the time of death as having taken place sometime between eight thirty and nine thirty on the previous evening. Hayes continued to talk his way through the results of his examination, speaking into an overhead microphone.

'Confirming my overnight notes. We have a female, age mid-thirties, fair hair, hazel eyes, slim build, height five feet five inches, weight one hundred and twenty five pounds, just about nine stones. She was fully clothed on her admission to this unit.' Pausing only for breath he continued; 'Generally in good health prior to sudden death; no heart, liver, or kidney problems, no fluid in the lungs, no atrophy or signs of disease. Two dental fillings but no recent extractions. Contents of stomach indicate a meal taken around 7-00pm yesterday partly digested.'

Deakin stood silently absorbing every word. She'd had tea probably two hours before meeting her death. She wasn't going anywhere to eat. Maybe she had already eaten out somewhere. Shouldn't be hard to get to the bottom of that query. All part of the process of elimination.

'Cause of death: haemorrhage, shock and trauma, due to a massive insult to the skull. Evidence of attempted strangulation, but she was already dead when that took place. Not yet identified. Married, possibly recently divorced, judging from the ring mark on her third finger left hand, but no ring worn and no evidence of it being forcibly removed.'

Already dead, Hayes had said, when she was being held by the throat. Deakin found the thought worrying. He found himself wanting it to be a domestic killing but somehow it wasn't working out that way. Maybe she was divorced and had gone out on some sort of blind date. It was difficult to keep an open mind on the subject.

Without taking his eyes from the body Hayes continued. 'There are a number of severe lacerations to the skull clearly indicating a frenzied attack.' He looked across at the detective. 'This was no cuff behind the ear. Someone really wanted her dead.'

Moving the head gently sideways Hayes indicated the full extent of the wounds. Deakin's stomach heaved, but was quickly overridden by anger.

Hayes continued, 'From the angle of impact I would say that the assailant is right handed and about five feet eight or nine inches tall.' He hesitated again.

'Any sign of sexual interference?' Deakin interrupted him with the first of many questions which would need to be answered.

'No,' said the pathologist. 'No bruising, no semen, no obvious attempted, or forced penetration. In fact I would say she hasn't been sexually active for some time. The hymen is almost closed'

'That almost puts paid to the blind date theory. Anything else doc?'

Deakin waited for a response which might just point his enquiries in any one of a number of directions. Wounds can often speak volumes for the dead. They can spell out the word 'frenzied', sometimes even 'professional'. Statistics indicated that the majority of murders in the United Kingdom result from some form of domestic dispute and therefore were unlikely to be repeated by the same person. Deakin was only just beginning his search for the right category.

The doctor was almost at the end of his commentary. 'She wasn't wined or dined. Partially digested food only amounts to a jacket potato and some sort of cheese sauce or similar, about two hours or less before she died. Looks to me as if she might have had her evening meal and went more or less straight out.' He continued, 'There's no evidence that she fought back; no hand bruising, blood or skin under the nails, which might suggest she felt comfortable right up to the point of attack.'

Suddenly he looked rueful, realising he was beginning to cross the line between pathologist and field detective at a time when he should be sticking to the medical facts. 'Blood samples indicate no evidence of drugs or medication such as tranquillisers, sedatives, or aspirin based pills.' He Stopped, as if expecting more questions and allowed the detective time to consider the situation. 'Was that her car in the lay-by?' Without waiting he added 'If it was, she walked in darkness, without a torch, along a lane for about thirty or forty yards before meeting her assailant. She certainly wasn't pulled or dragged to the spot. She would also need to be confident, a woman walking alone in a place like that.' Hayes' voice was mournful. 'All it tells me as a doctor is that she had damned good eyesight and rotten instincts.'

Deakin looked thoughtful. 'Yes, I believe it was her car but we won't have a positive identification for another hour or two.' His mind switched to something else. 'Did someone really hate her that much? Or was it something she represented? If it isn't domestic, or sex orientated and we know it's not robbery, then what the hell is it all about? Vengeance, maybe. But in return for what?

Hayes switched off the microphone. 'No doubt you'll be able to answer that one sooner or later.' He leaned forward and picked up the folded white sheet from the foot of the stainless steel table. Spreading it gently over the length of her body, as if to protect her from further invasion of her privacy, he hesitated long enough to touch her forehead, almost like a father patting his child. It was his final gesture, an attempt to restore some of the dignity so brutally snatched from her only a few short hours ago.

Deakin found himself strangely moved by the actions of the pathologist, the gentleness of a man to whom death was a way of life. They walked together into the doctor's private office, one whose job almost done and the other hardly started.

Deakin sat down and waited for the coffee to arrive. 'Well at least I know what I'm not looking for, a rapist.' He hesitated. 'Thank God for small mercies. And, if it's not domestic, we're searching for a madman.'

Hayes tapped his fingers on top of a file of papers. 'That means more killings. You know as well as I do that, once they start, there's no stopping till they're caught.' He returned the detective's gaze across the desk. 'Let's just hope it does turn out to be a domestic.'

Deakin put down the cup and glanced at his watch. It was time to be on his way. 'Thanks for all your help. We must have lunch sometime soon and get a couple of hours away from all this depressing stuff.' Rising to his feet. 'I'll give you a call when the report comes through.' He hesitated. 'By the way, someone will ring shortly to arrange identification of the body, hopefully before the end of the day.'

Hayes nodded. 'Twenty minutes notice should be plenty. I'll make sure she's ready. The report will be with you tomorrow and if there's anything else, don't hesitate.'

The two men shook hands before going their separate ways. Deakin was part way down the corridor leading to the outside world when he fancied he could hear the whine of an electric saw somewhere behind him. Outside he was met by watery sunshine. Though not warm, at least it was dry. Deakin was busy trying to dismiss the pictures now crowding his thoughts following the pathology ordeal. In his mind's eye he tried to visualise a woman walking away from her car and into a dark unlit lane, straight to a man who was lurking with one intention only.

Maybe her car had broken down. Maybe her assailant had pretended his car had broken down. Maybe she was walking towards the cottages to get help and he stopped alongside her. Too many questions. Not enough answers. Deakin was well aware of the options and possibilities at the outset of an enquiry of this nature. Time would soon resolve most of the questions.

Logically it seemed to bear the hallmark of a domestic argument, unless of course she'd been having an affair, perhaps with a married man. He thought about the pathologist's comments concerning the ring finger and the chance that she might be separated or divorced. But if she was having an affair it could only have been platonic, because no sex was involved. Hardly worth dying for. Climbing into the car, he reached for the radio microphone hanging on its coiled heavy wire.

'Deakin. Is Sergeant Jones back yet?'

The radio room controller recognised his voice. 'Yes Chief, I'll put you through.' Deakin hated radio phones which seemed to crackle with interference almost continuously, particularly if the car engine was running.

'Morning chief.' There was a distinct air of optimism in Jones' voice.

'How's it going?'

Jones was practically purring after getting off to a good start with his own enquiries. 'Pretty good, confirmed the victim's name and address. Might even have a motive.'

Deakin wanted to be moving and cut the conversation short. 'Good. I'm on my way back: be with you shortly.'

He left the hospital grounds taking a diversionary route which brought him to the old Kirkdale cemetery where his parents lay buried. On a sudden impulse he pulled over and went into the florist shop opposite the gates, emerging a few minutes later with a large bunch of flowers. He drove into the cemetery and along the narrow winding pathways, finally coming to a standstill alongside the family grave. Slightly ahead was a monument standing about twelve feet high. It was in brown mottled marble and bore an inscription to the memory of Chief Officer Henry Wilde who lost his life in the Titanic disaster of 1912. Sadly, his wife and children, also listed on the monument, had passed away during the two years preceding his death. Turning towards his parents' grave he read again the inscription which he wrote for them before going off to war.

Pray for the repose of the soul of John Deakin who departed this life on the 10th of October 1935 aged 40 years. A loving husband and father.

Below the first inscription there was another.

Pray also for the repose of the soul of Sarah Deakin beloved wife of the above who passed away on the 10th June 1937 aged 41 years. A much loved wife and mother.

Removing the pepper pot metal vases from their marble seating, he walked to the water point, filling each one carefully, before returning to the graveside and sliding the flower stalks into the holes until each was full. At the foot of the grave, hands clasped, he paid a silent tribute to his loved ones before making his farewells.

'Sorry I haven't been for a while but things are hectic at the moment.' Apologies made, he climbed back into the car and made his way to the station.

Jones knocked and entered, already armed with two mugs of steaming coffee.

'Thanks, grab a chair.'

Deakin reached out for his mug. The detective sergeant sat down. Obviously something was exciting him. His eyes still showed the strain of the late night vigil, though his face was reddened with enthusiasm.

'Name's Catherine Wilson, chief. Divorced about eighteen months ago and living with her teenage daughter.'

Deakin noted the intensity in his voice. He didn't normally sound so excited about his enquiries without good reason.

The sergeant leaned forward, almost confidentially. 'I've spoken to the daughter and her grandparents, this morning while you were with the doc. Linda, the daughter, told me that her mother had an argument with the ex-husband on the phone and then went out to meet him last night.'

Deakin raised his eyebrows. 'What time would that be?'

Jones had a confident look about him. 'She left home about eight thirty.'

He pondered what the doc had said about her dying around nine o'clock. What else did he say? Someone wanted her dead? 'Got an address for him?'

'Yes, very close to where we found the body. Talk about making a mess on your own doorstep. Shall we have him in?'

'Please, and a search warrant for his home.'

Deakin stared into his cup as if it were some sort of crystal ball with the answers to all his problems. 'You know someone wanted her dead. The motive was neither robbery nor rape.' He considered his words. Was this only about hatred? Or perhaps money? The answer might be coming sooner than expected.

'Well Chief, let's find out if Mr 'ex-husband' Wilson can provide some of the answers.' Jones' gut instinct seemed to be working overtime but Deakin wasn't quite finished yet.

'Did the daughter say anything about her dad? Good or bad?'

'She doesn't visit his house because she's not fussed on his second wife, but she is in fairly regular contact and sees him whenever she can.'

Deakin tapped his fingers together. 'Sounds more like the average ex-family man to me. Do we know the grounds for divorce?'

'Undefended, no violence. Overtime, bickering, and unproved adultery, which turned out to be true.' The sergeant pondered for a moment. 'The usual family arguments, then the parting of the ways.'

Deakin interrupted. 'Any arguments over money?'

'Don't know yet chief. I haven't had time to take a full statement but we're due to interview the grandparents shortly. They might know what the situation was like.'

'Go and get him and let's see what he has to say for himself.'

The phone rang. It was Tom Lloyd from the front desk.

'Just thought I'd let you have an update on the Peeping Tom job boss.'

Deakin had almost forgotten about the prowler. 'Whereabouts was he seen?'

'Around 83 Bridge Road, near the canal, past the Blue Anchor pub. No proper description though. The lady making the complaint is a heavy drinker and says he looks just like her ex-husband. No other suspicious sightings anywhere else at the moment.'

'Christ; not another bloody ex-husband. How far is that from the A59 towards Preston?' He already knew the answer but wanted confirmation.

'Less than five minutes by car. Fifteen on the bike.' Lloyd knew every inch of the area.

'So, we've got a prowler on one side of the canal, a killer on the other and a pub somewhere in the middle.' Deakin filed it away in the back of his mind.

'Thanks, keep me in touch if you will, please.'

Putting the receiver back on its cradle he reached for another bundle of statements, only to be disappointed at the lack of helpful information. He already knew that no-one had heard or seen anything of consequence. The killer had struck silently, swiftly and moved on, all in the space of either a few seconds or a minute, depending on whether Catherine Wilson knew him and held some sort of conversation which led to murder, or whether she had never even seen him coming. Linda Wilson appeared to be pointing the finger straight at her father. It was a strange thing for a daughter to do. Unless of course, she was blaming him for the breakdown in the family.

Deakin tried to keep an open mind. The idea of someone walking behind the victim and killing randomly without some sort of motive was too hard to contemplate at this moment, yet it couldn't be discarded. No evidence of a struggle; no last desperate fight for survival, no telltale skin under the fingernails to indicate an injury to anyone else. Catherine Wilson had been caught completely unawares. His thoughts were shattered by the ringing of the phone.

'Sarge' Lloyd, chief. Will you give your good lady a call, as soon as you've got a minute.'

Deakin glanced at his watch. 'Christ, I've done it again.'

CHAPTER 6

Fridays in the new Spar supermarket were becoming pretty hectic. The concept of one-stop shopping was beginning to attract the attention of the public, particularly workers and weekend shoppers. The pace of life seemed to be increasing almost daily. Today was different. The discovery of a woman's body near to the old cottages off Higher Lane had introduced an air of excited curiosity. Nobody seemed to be in their usual rush. Everyone wanted to chat, to find out the woman's name and whether she was a customer.

A year or so ago they would probably have congregated in the greengrocers, the grocery store, even the fishmongers'. Gossip would have travelled fast. The small shopkeepers, usually havens of local news were in danger of being overwhelmed by supermarkets and their impersonal approach to the local community. Cashiers had no time to chat and there was always a queue of people impatient to be getting on with their lives. Today though, nobody seemed in a rush to leave the shop. People kept glancing around as if to discover who was missing from their mini social circle that might have been there on a Friday morning.

Betty Wilson sat on her swivel chair swinging left to right in a robot like motion as each item passed her check point. She could sense the apprehension in some

55

people this morning and real fear in others. The discovery of a body so near to her home was worrying but at least it wasn't a friend or neighbour. The woman must have been a stranger, probably arguing with a man friend. Betty remembered when that stretch of road was called 'Lovers Lane.' It was in the days when few people owned cars and courting couples walked the area, looking for their own bit of privacy. Maybe the woman was one of that sort. She might have learned more if she hadn't been in the bath when the police called. It was left with Bill to deal with them. A hand touched her on the shoulder.

'Betty, you're wanted in the manager's office. I'll take over when you've finished with this customer.'

It was Angela, one of the floating cashiers whose job included relieving staff for their tea and lunch breaks and emergencies.

'Thanks Angie, won't be a minute love.'

Betty finished off the sale, signing the till roll which showed the date and time of her relief. She stood, allowing Angela to move smoothly into the vacated swivel seat. The changeover was done without fuss, yet there was still time for a quick word.

'Hope everything's alright.'

Angela knew that Betty was only a part timer and the firm had a reputation for hiring and firing according to seasonal demand. Betty seemed unconcerned.

'Don't know what he wants, but we'll soon find out. Hope I'm not in trouble.'

Angela settled in to serve the next customer, leaving Betty to make her way towards the manager's office, which overlooked the warehouse area at the back of the main shop.

Betty looked up at the goods which were stacked from floor to roof in the stores, all waiting to be taken into the sales area. *This lot must be worth a bloody fortune and the pittance you pay us!*

Flushed and slightly out of breath, she paused to regain her composure before obeying a sign which read 'Manager. Knock and Wait.'

'Come in.'

'Good morning' Mr. Swift. You want to see me?'

There was another man with Mr Swift, someone she didn't know and for a moment she wondered whether he might be an area manager. One of those characters who seemed to be forever popping in and out in their smart suits, starched white shirts and silk ties. This one seemed to fit the bill, though he did look pretty serious. Dark rings round his eyes suggested a lack of sleep. Perhaps they wanted to lend her to another branch.

'Good morning Betty. Please come in. Take a seat.'

Mr Swift had been very polite with her when she joined the company, but she had a feeling he was a bit too oily. Not quite manly enough for her. It seemed to have become more noticeable recently perhaps because some men were beginning to be more open about their predispositions. She sat down and waited.

'This gentleman is Detective Sergeant Jones from the CID and he would like a few words with you.'

The thought she automatically associated with the police and her work was shoplifters. In this business they practically belonged together. The police were regular, sometimes daily visitors. It wasn't unusual for detectives to visit and warn staff about gangs working in the area. She began to relax.

The man seemed to be almost studying her before he spoke.

'Hello Mrs. Wilson. I wonder if you wouldn't mind helping me with some enquiries.? Is your husband William Arthur Wilson?'

What kind of a damn fool question is that? *Oh God. Something's happened to Bill.* For a moment she froze, her world turning upside down. A single thought flashed into her mind. *He's dead. I just know it.* Her mind raced as she tried to gather herself together to face whatever it was.

'Yes, has something happened to him?' Tears began to well in her eyes as panic set in. 'It must be serious or they wouldn't be sending police here to speak to me.'

Jones' natural instincts told him to have some pity for this unfortunate woman but he had a job to do. 'Nothing to worry about as far as accidents are concerned. Your husband is well as far as I know.' He had now to come to the nasty part. 'You probably know that a lady was found dead last night, not far from where you live and I wonder if you wouldn't mind helping with my enquiries?' He cleared his throat before going on. 'I thought you might feel better chatting here rather than the station.'

Completely confused, Betty looked at the detective with a mixture of curiosity and relief. Detective, CID, of course it made sense now.

'Would you mind telling me what time you got home from work yesterday evening Mrs Wilson?'

Her heart thumped in her chest as she looked first at the manager then back to the detective. Jones sat back and waited. 'No, not at all. I just don't understand why you are asking me, but if it's the same for everyone then I don't mind. I was working till eight o'clock and by the time we cashed up, and tidied up, it would be around twenty past. I would have got home at about a quarter to nine. She was surprised how cool and calm she sounded, now that she knew Bill was alright, and the rush of adrenalin had passed.

'Was anyone at home when you arrived?'

It seemed an odd question but she took it in her stride. 'No, my husband didn't get in till just after nine.' She thought for a second and carried on, 'Bill was round at his mother's and I was preparing supper for both of us. Is it that important?'

Mr Swift intervened. 'Betty, would you rather speak to the sergeant alone?'

'No thanks. I'm alright so long as you don't mind us being in your office.'

Jones tried to smooth the path of his enquiry. 'Mrs. Wilson, we're checking the movements of everyone who was in the area last night; between, say, eight o'clock and ten, and particularly the Higher Lane area.'

'Mr. Jones, 'Betty started indignantly. 'I hope you're not suggesting.' The words stuck in her throat, as a terrifying thought suddenly became locked in her brain. The blood on Bill's trousers, his hands, wrists, knees. The bruises suddenly took on mammoth proportions. She stared wide-eyed at the detective. It took a mountain of courage to ask the question, but she had to do it. Bill had been to his mother's and she was out, or at least he thought so. He came home covered in blood. *Of course, that's why the police think Bill had something to do with this person's death.* Inwardly she breathed a sigh of relief. *This little mess wouldn't take long to clear up and they could get on with searching for the real killer. Bill would never do anything like that, not to anyone.*

Jones watched Betty's face closely, taking her question in his stride. Her sudden change of attitude surprised him but there were things he needed to know and Betty looked as if she might have the answers. 'What don't I think, Mrs Wilson?' They were now eye to eye.

'I just hope you don't think that either me or my husband would get involved in killing someone.' She realised there was something important she didn't know. 'Anyway sergeant. Are you at liberty to tell me who has been killed? Is it anyone we should know?'

'The lady who was murdered was called Catherine Wilson, and I have reason to believe she was your husband's previous wife.'

A terrible blackness engulfed Betty as she slumped to the floor before Jones could get anywhere near her.

Ignoring Bill Wilson for the moment, Deakin turned his attention to the two young CID Officers. Still in the infancy of their CID training, both men were keen to learn the techniques of interviewing suspects, as well as studying the psychology of the criminal mind, something that had never formed part of Deakin's apprenticeship.

'Has Wilson been cautioned?'

'Yes sir; once at the time of arrest and again at the outset of this interview period.'

Taking his place at the interview table, and looking the man straight in the eye, he addressed the suspect for the first time. He could tell a lot from eye contact. A lot more than most would credit.

'William Arthur Wilson, my name is Deakin, chief inspector Deakin and I am making enquiries into a murder which occurred not far from your home yesterday evening around nine o'clock.'

The calm and matter of fact approach was his usual opening, suggesting to the opposition that he was not a man to fool with. He watched carefully for any sign of reaction from the suspect, seeing only fear and lack of comprehension.

'Can you tell me what your movements were last night, say between eight and ten o'clock?'

It was like the opening move in a deadly game of chess. Wilson's eyes flashed defiance. He'd already answered the same question three times.

'I've already told your associates where I was.' He nodded towards the two officers keenly observing the proceedings. 'Haven't I?'

Both men stared back at him without speaking.

'Wilson,' Deakin's voice was clipped, 'I'm asking the questions now and I want answers.' He was in no hurry with the interview, neither was he in the mood for pussy footing around. 'I asked you a question, now think carefully then tell me where you spent yesterday evening between eight o'clock and ten.'

Wilson hesitated. 'I got home from work around seven thirty, had a drink and went to see my mother. She lives in Upholland village, on the estate near Ashurst Beacon. I came back and had supper with my wife. We went off to bed around eleven and that's all.' He looked hopefully towards the detective.

'Your wife and mother will be prepared to make statements to corroborate what you're saying?'

Wilson looked worried.

Deakin pressed on. 'Is that a problem?'

'Well, as a matter of fact, my mother wasn't at home when I called. She was at Bingo, I think. But my wife of course would be happy to make a statement.'

Deakin held his gaze, knowing that sooner or later some reaction would take place which he might then be able to identify. 'Wilson, I need to eliminate people from my enquiries, but in your case it's proving a bit difficult.'

Wilson looked frightened, his hands tightening their grip on the edge of the table. Deakin watched him carefully. No doubt when he had agreed to assist the police with their enquiries down at the station the thought must never have occurred to him that he might be suspected of murder, or that he would be given a grilling. 'Assist', to him probably meant help, not a verbal battering and being told his answers weren't good enough.

'Why? Why are you asking me Inspector?'

Deakin leaned forward looking steely eyed. 'I'll tell you why I'm asking the questions mister Wilson. It is because we have reason to believe that the murdered woman is Catherine Wilson, your former wife.' He watched as the colour drained from Wilson's face. Was he really shocked? Moved by the sudden death of someone he once knew and loved? Or was he a bloody good actor? Deakin had seen it all before, the good, the bad and the evil. He waited and watched.

Wilson gulped loudly, catching his breath. 'What the hell was she doing near my house?' It was all that came to mind.

Deakin never budged. 'I don't know. I was rather hoping you might tell me the answer to that one.'

'How the hell should I know?'

'Maybe, just maybe of course, she was on her way to see you about something?' Deakin was accustomed to cat and mouse games.

'She certainly wasn't coming to see me. I only see her on odd occasions when I call to pick up my daughter from our old home.'

'Wilson, have you had an argument with your former wife recently? About money possibly?'

The question seemed to anger Wilson, especially in view of the fact that he had only just denied seeing or speaking to Catherine. He leaned backwards into the chair reaching for a handkerchief clutching it tightly in his right hand before dabbing at his nose.

'No, I've not had an argument with her or anyone else for that matter!' His head seemed to ache with the strain. Hands moved either side of it rubbing in a circular motion. His face was taking on a slightly haggard appearance, made worse by a dark stubble waiting to be shaved.

'On the telephone maybe?'

'Why would I want to phone her?'

Deakin didn't like questions being answered with questions. He was in no mood for negative answers. He glanced down at his watch. Time was beginning to run out on this interview. The suspect was entitled to a tea break and also to be fed at the proper times. He tried once more. 'I don't know. That's why I'm asking you.'

The question and answer session was interrupted by a knock on the door. One of the officers stepped outside to take a message. Walking back into the room he spoke quietly into Deakin's ear. The detective nodded his acknowledgment, leaving the officer to return to his position by the door.

'Wilson, are you going to continue to deny that you have spoken to your former wife recently?' He hesitated. 'As recently perhaps as yesterday?' His tone had clearly hardened.

Wilson took his hands away from the sides of his head, now exposing the dark rings of stress and exhaustion. He raised himself up to confront the detective once again. 'Mr. Deakin, I've repeatedly said that I haven't spoken to my ex-wife in ages and that's all there is to it.'

Deakin leaned forward. 'By no means is that all there is to it, Wilson. By no means whatsoever.' His voice had a chilling edge. 'Let me see your hands Hold them out, palms upward.'

Wilson lifted his hands from the table, holding them forward.

'Where did you get those scratches? They look new to me.'

A look of relief seemed to spread over Wilson's features. 'Tripped on Mum's path last night, fell into her bushes and landed on a broken milk bottle.'

'What time would that be?'

'Eight thirty....Eight forty five...thereabouts.'

'What time did you say you got home?'

This was the fourth or fifth time the same question had been put to him but it still called for an answer. 'Around nine o'clock, maybe a couple of minutes either side.' He thought for second before going ahead again. 'Actually it was just after nine, because the news had just started on the television. I remember missing the headlines.'

Deakin rose to his feet, collected his file of papers and turned to the nearest detective standing in the background.

'Get him a drink and see if he wants a bite to eat. I'll be back later.'

Wilson started. 'What do you mean? A bite to eat?'

Deakin turned back. 'I have the power to detain you for four hours initially, and then for up to seventy two hours if I have reason to believe you can assist with my enquiries, and I happen to think you can. I'm going to leave you to think things over for a while.' He looked once more at his adversary seeing only a pair of frightened eyes. 'Never know what you might remember once you're on track.'

One P.C. stood aside while the other opened the door. Deakin headed out into the corridor, papers tucked under one arm. Back in his office he picked up the phone.

'Find me Sergeant Jones please, right away.' He replaced the receiver. Two minutes later Lloyd knocked and entered, a document in his hand.

'Search Warrant for the Wilson house Chief.'

'Thanks.'

Deakin took possession of the paper checking it carefully. Signed by a senior magistrate it gave explicit power to enter the home of one William Arthur Wilson for the purpose of retrieving any evidence which might be concealed on the said premises in connection with the death of Catherine Wilson and such power being granted after hearing prima facie evidence from a representative of the Constabulary. The phone rang again. It was Jones returning his call..

'Hello Chief,' you wanted to speak to me?'

Deakin wasted no time. 'Are you still with the surviving Mrs. Wilson?'

'Yes Chief, I had to stall part of the interview because she became unwell. But she's OK now.'

'I've got the search warrant on my desk. You can collect it, take her home and do the search at the same time.'

'On my way Chief.'

Deakin replaced the receiver, picked up the steaming mug and sat back to think through the events so far. A young woman, divorced, good looking, tells her daughter she is going out for an hour after receiving a call from the ex husband. She is later found battered to death near his home but not raped or otherwise sexually assaulted. Ex-husband denies all knowledge but displays recent cuts and bruises. He is five feet ten inches tall and quite powerfully built. Catherine Wilson went knowingly and willingly to meet her killer unless by pure chance she walked into the spider's parlour. There's always a million to one chance that she was in the wrong place at the wrong time. No! What sort of defence could the husband could offer if it became necessary? Granted, everything so far was pretty much circumstantial but the witnesses were genuine. It would be all too easy if some of his blood turned up on the body.

Turning once more to the statement made by Linda Wilson, it was clear that she was in a distressed state but she was the next to last person to see her mother alive, and her evidence would be crucial. He studied the references to the telephone call received by Cathy Wilson, which had prompted her to go out. Linda was very sure it was her father on the phone even though she was surprised that he didn't bother to speak to her. She thought he might have been embarrassed.

'I could tell from the way they were talking and not wanting me to hear.' The statement was positive.

The fact that he didn't speak to her might have been due to the argument. There had been a lot of arguments when his affair first came to light, but more recently things had quietened down and the mother seemed to be getting her life together very well. Grandfather and Grandma still held their former son-in-law in pretty high esteem and refused to believe that he was capable of any sort of violence, certainly not murder.

What was the motive? There had to be a reason. Money? Jealousy? They were often the cause in this type of case. In Wilson's case he had recently acquired a new wife and should have no reason to be jealous of the previous one. However, there had been arguments over money several times. That much was fact. It was a troubling thought, the possibility that someone would kill for a relatively small amount especially one which could be negotiated reasonably peacefully.

'Morning chief.' Jones interrupted his theorising.

'Morning. How's the new Mrs. Wilson?'

'She's OK but very frightened with everything that's going on at the moment. Seems her husband came home covered in blood, went straight upstairs for a bath and told her just to get rid of his bloodstained clothes.'

'I hope she didn't.' He needed an answer.

'Don't know till we get to the house. She put them in the bin but the refuse collection is not due till tomorrow.'

Deakin pointed to the search warrant. 'You'll be needing that.'

'See you later.' Jones picked up the warrant and left as quickly as he had arrived.

Deakin pushed the half empty mug aside, picked up the file of papers and walked back to the interview room. Wilson should have finished his break by now and more questions needed to be answered. Deakin took his place at the table, thanking God that the suspects didn't get fed in the interview room. He hated the smell of stale food, ever present on prison visits.

'Wilson, I don't need to remind you that you are still under caution?'

Deakin guessed that Wilson had only nibbled at the bacon sandwiches. At home he would probably have eaten twice as much. But the hot sweet tea certainly seemed to have revived him and he now looked more in control of himself.

'Now, let's just run through things again.'

'Chief inspector, I've run through your questions five or six times today. No matter what you say, I can't make the answers any different.'

Deakin glared at him, ignoring the comment.

'I'm not happy with those answers. You say you never phoned your ex-wife last night?' He waited, looking for some clue in the face of the man sitting opposite.

'No I did not phone her.' Wilson's eyes never flickered.

He began again, trying to contain his impatience. 'Supposing I were to tell you that I have a witness to the fact that you did make such a call?'

'That's not possible!'

Deakin thought for a moment before making his next move. 'I think I will terminate this interview for the time being and give you the opportunity to consult a solicitor. I believe you may find yourself in serious trouble.'

Wilson paled visibly. 'A solicitor?'

'Yes, I intend to detain you on suspicion of murder and to keep you in custody pending further enquiries.'

'For God's sake, I never killed anyone. I couldn't. I'm just not capable.'

'Wilson, if you intend to consult a solicitor then I will place a phone at your disposal to make that call. Your wife is now aware of your situation.' Deakin was anxious to be as fair as possible in the circumstances and clearly there were problems with this suspect. But the police had every right to hold him.

Wilson looked at him despairingly. Slowly it had sunk in that he was the prime suspect in a murder hunt. 'I'm telling you, I never killed anyone and never had reason to kill anyone.'

Deakin ran things through his mind again. She was Wilson's ex-wife and was found dead near his home. She had been subjected to some sort of violence. Even worse, he'd arrived home covered in blood and with cuts and bruises. Wilson was in the vicinity at all relevant times and without a proper alibi. But certainly with a motive. His own daughter seemed sure of her facts. Deakin tried hard to imagine in what other circumstances the victim might have left her home at such short notice at the same time expressing the intention to return within the hour. Who else could possibly have phoned her? Young Linda was adamant it was her dad.

Wilson stared across the table at his inquisitor, and for the first time, Deakin saw fear in the man's demeanour. 'I think I'd like to see a solicitor.'

'Very well Mr. Wilson, I'll arrange for you to make the call to any solicitor of your choice and if you don't know anyone we will provide you with the Law Society list of approved lawyers.'

Deakin rose to his feet and walked through the door without further comment, leaving Wilson to ponder his fate.

CHAPTER 7

WPC Giles glanced upwards as the reception door swung open. Middle aged certainly, but undoubtedly handsome. She continued writing something into the station day-book for a few moments. He walked the mandatory seven paces from the door to the counter. There was an air of assurance about him, confident but not intrusive.

She raised her head. 'Can I help you sir?'

'Howard Phillips. I'm here to represent my client William Wilson. I understand you're holding him in cells.'

'Solicitor, are you, sir?'

'Yes, that's right.'

He seemed pleasant enough. 'Won't keep you a moment sir. I'll just enter your details in the day book if you don't mind and then we'll see if he's ready. For a visit that is.' Head bent over the day book, she made an official record of the name and reason for the visit before reaching for the phone. 'WPC Giles, front desk sir. A solicitor, Mr. Phillips is here to see Wilson in cells.'

Phillips was impressed. She was young, pretty and efficient. Hardly the type of girl you would expect to see slapping a pair of handcuffs on a Saturday night drunk. He moved to the end of the counter watching her performance with a mixture of amusement and admiration. Dark hair, tied in a bun just above the collar, regulation style, bobbed as she nodded her head then sat poised, ready to drop to shoulder level the minute her shift ended.

'Yes sir.' She replaced the receiver and looked around for him. 'Chief Inspector Deakin will be with you in a few minutes. Would you would like to take a seat?' She pointed towards an uncomfortable looking wooden bench which sported a variety of carvings and graffiti. Phillips walked away from the counter and stood next to it, grateful that it wasn't Friday or worse still Saturday night. From his days as a duty solicitor he knew only too well how crowded the reception area could be at weekends.

A door marked 'Private' at the end of the counter behind the WPC swung open bringing the lawyer face to face with his adversary. There was no need for any introductions. The two men had known each other for around fifteen years.

'Hello Howard, nice to see you again.' Deakin stuck out a hand which was grasped and shaken firmly.

'Nice to see you too Sam. Be nicer still if it was a burglary and not a murder. Win or lose, murder cases always leave a nasty taste. What's it all about?'

'I'll take you through to cells. We can have a word on the way.'

Phillips nodded his appreciation towards the young woman before disappearing through the door. The two men walked together towards the rear of the building. A brightly lit but windowless corridor guarded the approach to cells and interview rooms. There was only one way in or out, apart from a solid steel emergency exit. Deakin now spoke in a quiet but serious tone.

'Woman battered to death last night in a small side road off Higher Lane. It seems she is the ex-wife of your new client.'

Phillips glanced sideways, noticing for the first time the signs of age now beginning catch up with the detective. He wondered whether it was just the profile. Full face, Sam Deakin still looked to be in his mid to late forties. Considering his unrelenting battle against serious crime he was remarkably well preserved.

'Doesn't exactly make him a killer, does it? Wouldn't just bring him in for being an ex-husband, would you? I know you better than that.'

Deakin hardly checked his pace.

'The murder happened close to his new matrimonial home, and to make matters worse he arrived home covered in blood at about the time of the murder.'

Phillips shrugged his shoulders. 'The mystery deepens then?' He decided to stick with his first line of thought. 'Still could be coincidental though.'

'Not necessarily. There are other factors.' Deakin stopped near to a cell door. 'Go and have a word with him and we'll speak again when you're finished.'

'Thanks.' Phillips walked through the door, leaving the detective to go about his business.

Wilson stood to greet his lawyer, holding out a desperate, rather than welcoming hand. Phillips had seen it all a thousand times before. He was a great believer in first impressions and the man before him was no bluffer or heavyweight. He was too nervous and obviously inexperienced in the ways of the police and their suspects. In the tiny concrete and steel room, measuring nine feet by six feet, neon lights and lime green paint were the only indication of modern times. The stainless steel bucket in a corner with its shiny lid was there for emergencies. In this cell there could be no privacy. It was in truth, no more than a cage for humans. A place of misery where they could be housed until some decision was made which would affect their future. The tiny sliding panel in the steel door was all that stood between the two men and total isolation.

Without his tie, trouser belt, or even shoe laces, Wilson was a sorry sight, not being allowed anything with which he could possibly harm himself. After only a few hours his face had already begun to take on a gaunt, bemused appearance. His dejected reddened eyes only added to his air of misery. The two men stood face to face for the first time.

'Phillips.' He spoke while disengaging his hand. 'I'm here to represent you.' The only place to sit was on a biscuit thin mattress spread over a metal framed bed, which was securely screwed to the floor. A thin pillow lay on top of a neatly folded blanket at one end of the bed. Phillips sat down next to his client before removing a large notepad from his briefcase.

'Today, we'll only be dealing with Legal Aid and a short statement, plus the usual boring details; name, age, date of birth, marital status and address. I'll try to answer any questions you may have, but can't make any promises at this early stage.' Trying to make it all sound very matter of fact wasn't as easy as it sounded. The formalities seemed to be taking time which might have been better spent on matters of defence, but until the minor details were out of the way they couldn't begin to make any headway.

'Do you mind if I call you Bill?'

Wilson nodded. 'Call me what you like, so long as you get me out of here. For God's sake just look at me. A few hours ago I was leading a fairly normal sort of life.' He tugged at the soiled collar of his shirt, then pointed downwards as if indicating something the solicitor should already have noted.

'No tie, no belt, not even shoe laces. They've already found me guilty' He pointed towards the door.

The conversation was becoming sidetracked. Wilson was in danger of being distracted from the real issues of his matter.

Phillips picked up on a point not previously mentioned. 'There is something I have to say before we go any further. Neither myself nor any member of my staff will ever ask whether or not you committed the offence with which you may be charged.' He noted the confusion. 'If you were to tell me that you had committed a murder or any other crime, I would become an accessory after the fact and no longer able to defend you, except through a plea of mitigation. That means I would have to submit on your behalf to the court a statement that either you didn't know what you were doing, or didn't know it was wrong, or perhaps even that you were provoked into the act. But we would have to admit that you did commit that act.' It was asking a lot for a man already stressed to the limit to take everything into his brain at the first time of asking, but Phillips had to get on with the preliminaries.

'When it becomes necessary, and I hope it doesn't, I will ask you only how you wish to plead, that is guilty or not guilty. Your case will be based upon whatever response I get at that time. In the meantime, remember that you are not yet charged with any offence, though the police have a right to hold you on suspicion for a limited period and then they must either charge or release you.'

He paused to let the detail sink in.

'As far as the removal of your personal effects is concerned there are many cases on record of people attempting and succeeding in committing suicide while in custody. It's police policy to remove anything with which you could possibly injure yourself.'

Wilson stared through weary, darkening eyes. 'Just for the record, I never killed anyone but I can't say I won't become suicidal if they keep me in this hovel much longer.'

A short statement for the purpose of Legal Aid was soon completed and finally they were able to turn their attention to the question of Wilson's wife.

'She knows where you are and why you're here. I'll arrange for her to visit you, if the police decide to oppose bail.'

Wilson's voice dropped almost to a whisper. 'The police have told me that they can keep me here for up to three days. I just hope she doesn't think it means I've got anything to do with this.'

Ignoring the remark, the solicitor pressed ahead.

'Your former wife was murdered near to your home last night. The police arrest you on suspicion and I'm called in almost immediately to represent you. It seems to me that they must think there are grounds to detain you otherwise we'd be having this conversation in my office.'

Wilson appeared to be hearing every word that was being said to him but didn't seem to be making much sense of it. The shock was certainly playing havoc with his powers of concentration. If he were innocent then it could be ten times worse.

'Are you listening to me? I need some answers and I need them now.'

'Sorry Mr. Phillips, I'm having trouble taking it all in. What was it you wanted to know?'

'Why do you think the police arrested you?'

At last a flicker seemed to show itself in Wilson's eyes. 'They say they've got a witness who heard me arguing with Cathy an hour or so before she died, and that they knew I had an arrangement to meet with her at the time she was killed.'

'Anything else?'

'No. They just keep asking me to repeat where I was last night and the names of any witnesses.'

'What about the bloodstains?'

'I told them the truth. I tripped over and fell on a broken bottle on my mother's path and ended up in her hedge.'

The lawyer put his notes and forms into his brief case, locked it carefully and rose to his feet. 'From now onwards you have nothing to say to anyone unless either myself or a member of my staff is present to advise you.' He looked down at the hunched figure. 'Is that clear?'

Wilson sat, utterly dejected, lost in his thoughts.

'Have I made myself clear Bill?'

At last the answer came. 'Yes.'

Phillips pressed the bell for the cell door to be unlocked. 'I'll be seeing you again very shortly.' He left his client to his own deliberations as the door sung open. A minute later he was outside Deakin's office.

'Come in. Take a seat.' Deakin stood to greet him. 'Tea or coffee?'

The offer was gratefully accepted. Visiting people in cells was a dehydrating, as well as depressing job. 'Tea, please; milk and two sugars. Are you going to oppose bail?' Phillips came straight out with it.

Deakin seemed to consider the matter for a moment. The truth was that he didn't know. 'It depends on the results of our search warrant; we should have a report shortly.'

'You've moved very fast on this one. You seem pretty sure you've got it right.' It was a bit of a fishing expedition.

Deakin nodded. 'We do have a witness who heard him arguing on the phone with the victim, and we can place him very close to the scene at the time of death, and he has injuries which occurred at about the same time. We also know that he made an arrangement to meet the deceased around the time of death.' He sat back, waiting to see how well his points had been received.

'How reliable is the witness?'

'His daughter, a teenager; intelligent, distraught and loves her dad.'

'Can I have a copy of her statement?' The request was made in the knowledge that sooner or later he would be entitled to a copy anyway. Once charges were laid everything would have to come into the open. It might be helpful to know the strength of it now, if bail were to become an issue. Wilson would certainly be banned from going anywhere near his daughter if he did succeed in getting him out. The detective picked up the phone and a minute later a young woman detective entered the room.

'Run off copies of these two statements if you will please.' He turned back to Phillips. 'You might as well have a copy of the wife's statement, because she's not doing him any favours either.' He sat back and waited for some response.

Phillips was now trapped between his duty to the client and the honesty of his adversary. There had been odd occasions when the two men had almost argued a case from beginning to end, something which only could be done between those who shared trust and honesty. On the face of it, things didn't look too good for Mr. Wilson.

'Motive?' he enquired.

'Money,' said Deakin. 'Pure and simple. She was putting the squeeze on him for more and he was already up to his ears in a mortgage and with a new wife to feed. They argued, he lost control of himself, and the rest is history.'

'It's all too easy. Doesn't seem that type to me.'

'Neither did Crippen.'

He might be inclined to agree with the solicitor but had to stick with the facts as he understood them. Soon he would have further evidence which might just swing it one way or the other,

Deakin looked serious. 'You know, people don't just turn up in places and get themselves murdered. It's not as if she was on the main road to somewhere or going home from some dance hall or pub, or perhaps even asking directions.' He stopped as if considering his position further. 'This lady was in a specific place, at a specific time She wasn't casually walking a dog or visiting a sick aunt. Only one person knew she was going to be there. At this moment it looks to me like you've got him for a client.' He stopped again, almost pausing for effect. 'It seems more likely that she was on her way to his home but was stopped before she got there. Who prevented her from getting to that house? Who knew she was on the way there?'

Placing the empty mug on the desk, Phillips prepared to make his exit.

'Thanks again. If you want to do an interview later, I'll send someone over from the office but if you wait until tomorrow, I'll be free from around eleven-thirty.'

Deakin consulted the list on his desk. Tomorrow would suit him better.

'Shall we make an arrangement for twelve o-clock tomorrow for a full interview?'

Phillips walked back to Wilson's cell. 'Don't bother to get up.' He towered above the client as he explained the arrangements.

Wilson was thoroughly dejected. 'Does that mean I can't go home today?'

'Don't worry, I'll make sure your wife visits later today armed with fresh food and clean clothes for you to wear.'

Wilson looked up at him with a despairing expression. 'I've done nothing wrong. Honestly Mr. Phillips. Why am I being kept here?'

The lawyer, about to leave, turned back. 'Because the police believe they have reasonable grounds to suspect that you murdered your former wife. They don't intend to let you hamper their early enquiries, so they arrest you on suspicion and that entitles them to detain you for a short period without charge. I'll see you tomorrow' He wondered how many of his words were hitting the target or whether they were just going over his clients' head. 'Till tomorrow then.' Wilson barely nodded, not seeming to be listening, staring at the floor.

Phillips breathed in the fresh air of freedom as he walked back to his Vauxhall Cavalier. Back in his office, he gave strict instructions not to be disturbed for at least an hour. The witness statements needed to be studied word by word.

Linda Wilson was clearly the key witness, and if her version of things stood up to scrutiny, her father was likely to find himself in serious difficulty. She seemed convinced it was her father who phoned and that her mother had no intention of going out prior to that call. It also seemed obvious that Cathy Wilson had no secret lover tucked away in the background. Her life appeared to be very much an open book.

He weighed up the possibilities. Supposing his client never made that call, then who could have made it? The question troubled him. There had to be an assumption that the killer made the call otherwise Catherine would never have left the house. On Linda's say so, there was the further assumption that her father was the last person to see her alive and yet he was denying all knowledge.

The more he thought about it the more it could go either way. Two further possibilities might help swing the weight of evidence in the right direction. What evidence might the search of the Wilson home produce? Bloodstained clothes and shoes were a foregone conclusion but whose blood? That was the crucial question.

Secondly there was the possibility of tracing the actual phone call which was made to Catherine Wilson's home. It was unlikely it came from the new Wilson home. If it did then Wilson might just have to throw his hands up and start telling the truth. Wouldn't it be more convenient if some random killer suddenly came to light and it transpired that Catherine Wilson was just in the wrong place at the wrong time?

He finished dictating the letter to the Legal Aid Board to secure authority for payment of his fees. Holding the phone in one hand, he ran his finger down the Law List, stopping at one particular name. He pressed the internal number for his secretary.

'Call Mr. Sellars' clerk and see if he can be retained for the Catherine Wilson murder defence should it become necessary. Let me know right away.' It was his way of ensuring the prosecution didn't get either first choice or any psychological advantage that so often comes with a big name. The answer came back quickly. Mr. Sellars would be delighted to assist and his diary was marked accordingly. The team was beginning to come together even before a charge had been laid. 'Now let's see what happens tomorrow, after the search warrant has been executed.' He had an idea. Reaching into his drawer he pulled out a business card. 'Ralph J. Bergman Private Investigator.' Phillips smiled. 'Always wanted to be one of you guys. You might just come in handy.'

His secretary rang back a few minutes later. 'Mr Bergman will be pleased to help your enquiries any way he can. Two pounds ten shillings an hour plus expenses.' Phillips thought again. 'Maybe I'm in the right business after all.' He closed the file for the time being and reached out for another. There was never any shortage of work, and if Mr Bergman was any good, there could be plenty more for him.

Betty Wilson stared in disbelief as the police search team seemed to winkle their way into every nook and cranny of her normally well kept home. Nothing was safe or sacred as her personal effects, as well as Bill's, came under scrutiny. They became excited when blood stained clothing was reclaimed from the waste bin outside the kitchen door. Everything was carefully placed into separate bags and marked 'evidence.'

Betty's mind was in turmoil. She wanted to scream at them, 'Get out of my house,' but could only stand and stare in constant disbelief at the nightmare unfolding before her eyes. She wondered whether her home would ever be the same again; whether it would ever regain its sense of privacy and individuality. It was almost like being raped. She was the victim and there was nothing she could do about it.

Betty was not an habitual drinker but there was always something in the house for special occasions. Once the search was over and the team had gone, she went to the glass drinks cabinet, selected a bottle of Bells whisky and helped herself to a larger than usual shot.

'Better not have any more.' Realising that she was talking aloud she put down the empty glass, then sat for a moment, staring into the bottom of it. So far, the thought that she might be married to a killer had not entered her head. A single tear slowly turned to a cascade as she felt the full force of her helplessness.

'For God's sake Bill, what have you done?'

CHAPTER 8

Mary Donovan was in the last throes of her divorce. It had been a long drawn out affair, due mainly to the fact that she frequently missed appointments with the solicitors as well as the courts. Mary drank too much and knew it, but was no longer able to control the situation. It had begun with depression and become a way of life. Too weak to fight the demons lurking within her tired brain, it seemed easier to drown maudlin thoughts in drink. Now it no longer mattered where or how it all began. All that was left was the present and the next drink.

Sitting in the lounge of The Lion she was oblivious to the attentions of a man who stared across from time to time as if he knew her. Guinness was her favourite tipple. She had been born into a house where men drank little else. Sometimes these days she could out-drink them. She looked at the black and white face of the clock on the wall, recalling the days when such clocks were deliberately kept ten minutes fast to ensure that all alcohol was consumed within the time allowed by law.

Tomorrow she was due back in court for the final judgment over the matrimonial home, a bungalow in Upholland, five miles east of Ormskirk. Even through the veil of alcohol she could see that Jack was trying to do his best to protect her, mostly against herself. Somewhere in the back of her mind Mary knew that Jack only wanted to keep the property in his name so that she could never use it to fund her habit. He would never ask her to leave, much less try to force her out.

The barman came to her table collecting the empty glasses. 'It's time to go home for your tea Mary. I'll keep your seat warm till you get back.' He winked at her. She wasn't much of a problem so long as no-one upset her.

Mary stared at him; 'I suppose cos' I'm Irish, you think I'm going home to a pan of bloody stew.' She stood up. 'Well I'm not. Today I'm having breast of lamb, roast tatties and all the trimmings. Good-day to you mister barman.' She handed him the empty glass. Slowly, purposely, Mary walked outside into the late afternoon air, paying no attention whatsoever to the figure skulking in the background.

Pascoe went ahead. It wasn't far and he knew every inch of the route by heart. Slipping quietly into the bushes at the back of the bungalow, he took up his usual position. Mary didn't keep him waiting long. Fumbling for a moment with her keys she managed to get the door open. She disappeared inside and suddenly reappeared in the bedroom window for a few seconds dragging the curtains together but ignoring the wide gap down the centre, just as he knew she would. Pascoe trained his binoculars.

Mary's routine never varied much. She stripped, dropping the various items of discarded clothing to the floor before walking naked into the bathroom. Ten minutes under the shower seemed to help her recovery for a short while at least. Pascoe watched and waited. He had no fetish about a middle aged woman undressing. It wasn't about Mary. There was something about a female, any female, undressing before him that brought about exciting urges taking him to the peak of self gratification.

For a heavy drinker and a woman of middle years, she had managed somehow to preserve a figure which might once have been the envy of her friends. Pascoe concentrated on the binoculars anxious not to avoid any detail. He found it even more exciting that less than half an hour ago she had been close to him, fully dressed and now this.

Reaching for the camera, Pascoe carefully set the telephoto lens precisely. Almost on cue, Mary opened the curtains wider to allow more light, either forgetting or not caring that she was naked. She seemed to be looking for something on the window ledge. The staccato click click of the camera recorded her every move. For a few brief moments her breasts seemed larger and more precise as she bent forward to search for the missing item.

Pascoe's excitement was short lived as Mary disappeared once more from his sight. He waited for five minutes; still no further sign. On a sudden impulse he decided to investigate. It was risky but the thick hedges afforded good cover from the bungalows on either side. Keeping low he crept up to the window and peeped inside. Mary lay across the bed, still naked, facing towards the ceiling. Pascoe couldn't see whether her eyes were open or not but she didn't seem to be moving. Sure that she was asleep, he reached for the camera, taking a number of shots in rapid succession.

A black and white cat sitting on the fence meowed loudly before jumping down and ambling slowly towards Pascoe, with its tail erect, ready to make a friend. He retreated towards the gap in the bushes which had been his previous shelter. Suddenly Mary's face appeared at the window. The black and white cat jumped up to greet her, but her gaze was fixed further away towards the bushes at the end of the garden.

'You bastard. You feckin' bastard'.

Mary opened the window to scream her obscenities in the direction of the now empty bush. Pascoe breathed a sigh of relief as he reached the sanctuary of his car and rapidly departed.

'Lives on her own. Divorced, likes her booze, if I remember rightly.' Sergeant Lloyd looked down at the entry in his record book and frowned. 'This is the second time this week she's called us out.'

Drink fuelled imagination, or truth, it still had to be entered in the Station log as a complaint from a member of the public and investigated. He turned to the woman police constable.

'Go down to the call room and tell the operator to send a message to Tango 5. Tell them to get round to Mary Donovan at 83 Bridge Road and check her complaint about a peeper.' He hesitated for a moment. 'A watcher to you, and don't come back without two nice mugs of tea. Two sugars for me, please.'

Lloyd watched, amused, as she disappeared down the corridor without waiting for a second invitation. She reminded him in an odd sort of way of his own daughters. Five minutes later she was back with two steaming mugs. He reached for his cup at the same time pointing to the desk log.

'Don't forget to make your log entry young lady.'

The two patrol officers were still involved in friendly banter when they arrived at 83 Bridge Road. A couple of nights ago they'd searched the whole area for an hour following the previous complaint but found nothing. She was the worse for drink but insisted someone was looking through the bedroom window of her bungalow. They concluded that Mary was definitely under the influence and most probably seeing shadows. She was quite well known to one of the officers, having demanded assistance on a number of occasions following complaints alleging assault by her former husband. And locking herself out of the house. She had also received a caution after being found drunk and incapable.

In response to continuous ringing of the doorbell, Mary Donovan finally opened the door, wearing only the bath robe which had been thrown across the bed earlier. She was obviously naked beneath the garment. Mary confronted the two young officers. Unkempt hair and an absence of cosmetics only made things worse. She was a sorry sight.

'Well, have you'se caught him yet?' It was a simple question, soaked in booze. 'I'm after telling you right now. The filthy feckin' swine wants lockin' away.'

'May we come in for a minute Mrs Donovan?'

'I suppose so, if you must.' Mary turned her back, walking towards the dining room without waiting to find out whether they were following or not.

'Now, in your own words, just tell us what happened.'

Mary stared at them. 'For Chrissake!' She had a distinctly Southern Irish accent. 'I had a shower and then lay on the bed for a few minutes to cool down. I heard a funny noise outside the window and that's how I knew he was there. He's been here before, y' know.'

The younger officer looked at her. 'What did he look like Mrs Donovan?'

'How the hell would I know what he looked like?' She stared at him in disbelief. 'Sure, I don't go opening the bloody curtains when I've got no clothes on and there's a man outside, do I now? Sure, I only heard him. I didn't go looking for him. Bejesus, I know what a man sounds like when I hear one. You're all clumsy buggers.'

The two men exchanged looks, trying not to grin. 'OK, we'll take a look and make sure he's not still here.'

'Thank you lads. Would you'se like a drink?'

'Thanks, but no thanks. Not while we're on duty.'

'A cup of tea if that's what you fancy?

'Er, no, we're fine.'

'Oh well, suit yourselves.' She stood aside and watched them walk down the hall and out through the front door.

They began a search of the area around the bungalow.

'Arrest that cat!'

They both started laughing as the bewildered animal leapt over the fence into the next garden.

In a more serious tone the other responded; 'If I was a watcher , I'd be using binoculars from behind those bushes opposite the window.'

They walked down the garden towards the gap left by the intruder.

'Could be anything. Maybe a fox or dog chasing the bloody cat. Doesn't seem very big for a man. Mind you, he'd be stretched out.'

After a further bit of poking about they walked back to the car. The radio crackled as they called the Station. 'Tango 5 to Base.'

The call was transferred directly to Tom Lloyd.

'Hello Sarge, Constable 9200 here. We're at Bridge Road now but there's nothing happening. A black and white cat has just gone over the fence Do you want me to PURR-sue it?' He carried on without waiting for a response. 'I think the lady's had enough to drink for one night.' A few seconds later he signed off and turned to his partner.

'Sarge says to tell her to phone in again if she has any more problems, and we've got to keep our eyes peeled.'

If anyone had been watching Mary they could hardly have failed to see the blue flashing lights of the police car and the two athletic young men wandering about the place.

'We'll give you a call later Mrs Donovan, just to make sure you haven't got a man in the house.' The officers sniggered as they walked back to the patrol car.

Mary was not so amused. 'Bloody kids trying to do a man's job. Couldn't catch a feckin' cold.' She slammed the door in disgust.

Sergeant Lloyd was standing at the desk when the officers arrived back at the station for their tea break. 'Don't forget to call back to Bridge Road before you finish the shift tonight lads.' He knew they wouldn't let him down, despite the laughing and banter.

At precisely nine-forty-five, the policemen returned to Bridge Road to carry out a last check before their evening shift ended. The football arguments had been done to death. Thoughts now turned to the possibility of a well earned drink if they could make it before Last Orders was called. Provided the shift ended on time, they might just about manage it.

The bungalow lights glared out at them through gaps in the curtains, big enough for any interested party to peep through. There was no response to their persistent ringing. Both men walked around the property, torches flashing, checking for any sign of forced entry, but found nothing suspicious.

'Guess she's sleeping it off. Wasn't dressed for going out. She'd had more than enough earlier on. She was only waiting for us to go before starting again.'

They decided to leave well alone. It was only a courtesy call anyway, neither man feeling that Mary was in any danger, except from the inside of a bottle, but not from a watcher. They turned back towards the station, ready to sign off as their shift came to an end. Two eyes peered intently through the now tiny gap in the bedroom curtains. The black and white cat was back.

'Last Orders if you please.' The barman could be heard clearly above the loud droning sound of his customers voices. Blazers, adorned with military motifs indicated an association with the Parachute Regiment. The two off-duty policemen had arrived with time enough to spare for two pints of best bitter. The first glass was raised.

'To Mary, the new love in your life', each pointing towards the other.

'Let's fight for her! Better still, tomorrow we're back up there and let her choose.' Their laughter was infectious.

At the station, Lloyd finished writing his notes before handing over to the nightshift sergeant. He breathed a sigh of relief as the men paraded without any absentees. Reaching for his dog tooth jacket, he assumed his role as a civilian and walked out into the night air, ready for supper and bed.

The two night patrol men had been warned about the possibility of a prowler in the Bridge Road vicinity. The street lighting, casting its long shadows, sometimes provided shelter of the wrong kind. Stray animals, cats and dogs mainly, created warning noises to those who couldn't sleep, and the occasional crashing of a dustbin-lid caused by a domesticated fox was more than enough to wake anyone. One house, though, number 83, stood out, lights blazing through front and side windows. A black and white cat perched precariously on the bedroom window ledge. As the two officers approached, it jumped down and ran off into the bushes.

'I'll bet that's the bloody culprit. Someone's having a late night. Plenty of light but no noise.'

The second officer thought for a second before responding.

'Hang on a minute. I know this woman. I've been here before. She threw her husband out last year, then tried to get us to lock him up for attempted murder.'

His partner nodded as the event was recalled. 'Yes. That's right. Then gave us a load of grief. I think we'd best keep moving. There's no-one around here.'

The police car moved off into the night. The officers had other things to do, other places to go. Mary Donovan was too drunk to go anywhere. By the time they returned during the early hours every house was in darkness except for 83 Bridge Road, standing as brightly as a lighthouse on a winter's night. Without anything to report they carried on past.

Dawn finally broke through a fine drizzle and the first sounds of the day began to filter into the dreams of the sleepers. A milk float, its glass bottles jangling their familiar wake up call, trundled its way along Bridge Road. Guided by a firm hand and propelled by a small whining electric motor, it was always the first visitor of the day.

The old folks and the early risers awaited its friendly rattle and a brief greeting from the driver. An hour later the postman clanged the letterboxes, soon to be followed by the noise of car engines grinding through their gears, revving loudly with chokes fully engaged.

Mary Donovan sat upright, screwing up her eyes to avoid the bright light which blazed down from the ceiling. 'Jesus, I'm going to be late.'

Scrambling to her feet, ignoring the suede moccasin slippers, she scuttled towards the bathroom. Without a sideways glance the housecoat and nightdress were discarded. Stepping into the shower and turning the switch, she stood, head bowed under the spray bringing herself back to life.

Fifteen minutes later Mary walked naked into her bedroom, towelling herself. From the edge of the bed, she smiled ruefully at her mirror image.

'Sure, now, whatever happened to your beautiful friend? The one used to sit here and smile back at me.'

It was half an hour before she finally emerged from the bedroom and made her way to the kitchen. Black coffee, two rounds of toast and three Paracetamol had become a daily routine.

'Bejaysus, it's raining.' Mary went back inside to search for her umbrella, before stepping out once more to face the world. There was no queue at the bus stop, the last of the early morning commuters being long gone by this time. Shortly after ten o'clock she entered the Queen Elizabeth 2nd Law Courts. It was precisely ten-fifteen when Mary stepped out of the lift and straight into the arms of her solicitor. A smile of relief spread across his face.

'Hello Mary. Almost on time.'

'Top of the mornin' to you Mr Bingham.' She checked her watch. 'Sure now only a couple of minutes. Lady's privilege, you know.'

He let go of her hand. 'Let's find somewhere to chat. I'm not going to fight with you in the corridor.' Quickly ushering her into the first available conference room, he offered her a seat before taking up a position opposite. 'Now let's see what we have here today.' He opened his file of papers, making a pretence of studying documents with which he was already familiar.

'Been up half the night. Had the police out twice.'

The solicitor looked despairingly over the top of his glasses.

'Police? Oh God Mary not another assault charge, I hope. What was it about this time?' He had previous experience of Mary's fantasies and wondered how much this little adventure was likely to cost the tax payers. Usually she blamed her ex-husband, Jack Donovan.

Mary tried to return his steady gaze. 'Bloody Peeping Tom again. Staring right at me through the bedroom window, he was. The dirty swine.'

Bingham listened patiently. 'Given his description to the police, have you?'

'I've told you before Mr. Bingham, the police in England are bloody useless. Bejaysus, they send a couple of kids to my house, barely out of school. I felt like asking if their mothers knew where they were at that time of the night. Remember last year, when himself tried to kill me? What did the buggers do about that? Nothin', absolutely bloody nothin.'

The lawyer intervened quickly before the situation got out of hand. He knew precisely what Mary could be like once she started on her hobby horse. Somehow he had to avoid confrontation at a time when negotiations between the parties were on a knife edge and she wasn't making it any easier. The police had accepted Jack's version of events last year when Mary made the complaint. She was too drunk to make a statement and his explanation that he was merely defending himself seemed reasonable. But Mary didn't see it that way and no amount of persuasion was going to make it any different.

'Now, let's try to keep focused on today's business, otherwise we'll be here again next week and we really don't need that, do we?'

An hour of serious negotiation followed which resulted in a deal being struck between the parties. Mary left the court with a Consent Order allowing her to remain in the former matrimonial home for as long as she lived or until she remarried or took a common law husband to live with her. If ever her circumstances changed the property could be sold and the proceeds of sale divided between the parties. At least she would now have a roof over her head, no matter how much she drank. The tension of the court was dehydrating. She needed a drink.

Not wanting to take the lift, Mary walked down the wide staircase from the third to the ground floor. The Trials Hotel was conveniently situated opposite the court entrance. Looking neither right nor left she marched straight across the road and into the lounge bar. It was just twelve o'clock and Mary had the whole day ahead of her. 'Bloody solicitors. Money for 'owl' rope'. She settled into her first drink. It was late afternoon before she finally arrived home.

The phone rang. Mary tried to ignore it but the caller was refusing to give up. 'Hello. This is Mary Donovan now what d'youse want?' She listened for a moment. 'Bejesus, you can't come now I'm only after getting' home a few minutes ago and I've not had me tea yet.' She hesitated for a second. You'll have to call again.' Mary replaced the receiver and walked into the bathroom. 'Cheeky buggers think I'm at everyone's beck and call. That's the second time.'

Lloyd glanced at his watch. It was just coming up to eight o'clock and still two hours before the end of the shift. It was one of those quiet evenings which sometimes erupted into a flurry of activity five minutes before the shift ended, often preventing him from getting home on time. Tango 5 called. They wanted to know whether to follow up their previous calls to Bridge Road. He thought for a second, before responding.

'Yes, lads, better to be sure than sorry. Leave it till the end of the shift and make sure they're all tucked in for the night and don't bring any stray cats back with you.'

The two patrolmen had their orders. Eventually around nine-thirty they approached Bridge Road, still bantering. 'Remember, when we get there, no monkey business, or you might end up having to marry her.' Still enjoying the comedy of the situation, they arrived at number 83. The doorbell could be heard ringing loudly inside the house, but failed to get any response.

'Don't tell me she's drunk again.'

There were no lights showing anywhere in the vicinity. The curtains remained open despite the evening darkness. The jokes died away while they walked around the back of the property. The kitchen door, strangely, was slightly ajar. Pushing it gently they stepped inside and switched on the light. The place had a very neglected look about it. Dishes and linen waiting to be washed seemed to bear testament to Mary's way of life and the direction in which her priorities lay.

'Hello Mrs. Donovan! It's the police, just checking to see if you're alright.' The two officers proceeded into the hallway, switching on the second light. 'Hello Mrs Donovan! Are you home?'

They stepped into the lounge, switched on the light. Mary Donovan lay sprawled across the arm of the settee, half sitting, half lying. Glazed eyes stared at the two officers and a blackened tongue protruded grotesquely from the side of her mouth. Scarlet patches, now starting to darken, covered the back of the settee while a pool of congealed blood had soaked into the carpet. It all appeared to have come from the back of her head. Mary's normally untidy hair was now thickly matted in red clots. What looked like slivers of bone showed through.

The officer caught his breath, trying to control his stomach muscles, as his eyes and brain struggled to cope with the scene. No need to check her pulse, Mary was quite dead. His partner, attempting to put on a show of efficiency moved about the bungalow to make certain the killer wasn't still on the premises. On the table lay an open bottle of Scotch and a half filled glass, some unopened mail and a court summons indicating Mary had been in court earlier in the day. But no sign of a weapon.

He ran out to the patrol car. 'Tango five to base.' His voice wavering. 'Sergeant, we're at 83 Bridge Road now.'

There was a pause. Instinctively, Lloyd knew there was something wrong. The young officer's voice was shaking as he struggled to regain his composure.

'She's dead Sarge. Mrs Donovan I mean. You're going to need the Murder squad. There's blood everywhere'

The sergeant swung into action. Orders were automatic, to be obeyed, not questioned. He knew well enough that the first people at the scene of a crime can often cause havoc by touching or moving a body just to see if there were any life signs. His instructions were specific; touch nothing, do nothing and let no-one near the place until the CID arrive. It was standard procedure but had to be repeated. The young officer was on the verge of panic. It was his first murder scene and no amount of training could have equipped him to deal with the shock and trauma of it all. Lloyd continued as if to remind him, repeating his instructions slowly and precisely.

'OK Sergeant.'

The young officer tried to sound convincing but was already beginning to lose the battle with his retching stomach. The sight which had confronted the two men as they walked into the Donovan household might have been a scene straight from a Hammer film. Crime scene photography could be pretty gruesome at times but this was real life.

Tom Lloyd pressed the extension button marked 'CID'. Harry Jones was about to leave. 'Just taken a call from one of my beat men. Looks like a murder job at 83 Bridge Road.'

At Mary Donovan's bungalow the patrolman tried again to survey the scene from the hallway but could contain himself no longer. Running outside into the garden and grasping the downspout, he leaned over the grid as his stomach gave way to the shock of his discovery.

CHAPTER 9

Deakin prodded an approving fork into his favourite meal of tender fillet steak, medium rare, surrounded by onion rings, mushrooms and French fries. Raising his head slightly he glanced across the table. 'Anything nice happen today?'

Laura gave him a sly wink. 'Gregory Peck called. Took me to lunch at the Adelphi in his new Rolls. We shopped at Boodles for the usual stuff; a couple of brooches and a diamond necklace with matching earrings. Nothing special.' Rummaging amongst the finely chopped lettuce leaves of a Caesar salad, she continued to nibble nonchalantly.

'Oh, my God.'

'What's the matter with you?' She poked her fork in his direction.

'Should have taken your curlers out before he got here.'

She put the fork aside for a moment. Feeling gingerly round the back of her head she detached a single roller hanging loosely by her collar.

'Trust you to ruin my dream. What a pity you didn't notice my new dress.'

'I did, but it looks so expensive I'm frightened to ask!'

'Actually,' she said, ignoring his remark. 'I've been busy all day, washing, ironing, cleaning and polishing this place till my fingers nearly dropped off. Not that you'd notice.'

'That's why I picked you out from all the rest.'

'Cheeky devil. You never picked me. I picked you. God knows why. But I did.' The last piece of white cheese was stabbed, lifted into the air and popped carefully into her mouth, ending the friendly joust. 'Rang Mum and she was fine but getting ready for her pensioners luncheon club, so I stayed in and watched a film.'

Deakin couldn't remember Laura ever sitting down and having a lazy day. She polished brasses and furniture until he could see his face in them.

'Which one?' The question was asked out of curiosity. It would need a very special film to captivate Laura for a whole two hours during the daytime.

She smiled coyly at him. 'Beloved Infidel. And Gregory Peck was gorgeous. Remember? It was the life story of Scott Fitzgerald, the American writer.' Lips slightly parted as if she was about to kiss, her eyes wandered heavenwards, savouring the moment. 'Deborah Kerr played the part of Sheila Graham, his mistress. I'd have played her role for nothing.'

His eyes barely left the plate. 'Just can't win, can I? Still, I'm glad you're on my team. Don't suppose you'd work here for nothing, would you?'

Now it was her turn to laugh. It was a curious giggly sort of laugh that occasionally rose to a crescendo. 'Married you, didn't I? For better, for worse, the man said.'

She still excited him after all these years. That giggle was a sort of signal. It meant she was happy. Placing his knife and fork together on the empty plate he straightened up. 'You only married me because Pecky Boy couldn't afford you. But if you promise to behave, I'll let you stay a bit longer.'

She rose from the table and began to collect the plates. Two minutes later she returned smiling triumphantly and carrying a single portion of bread and butter pudding. He deliberately looked puzzled. Fillet steak and bread and butter pudding usually meant Laura had something to tell him.

'Not my birthday. Our anniversary's in the summer isn't it? Haven't booked a world cruise or something like that have you?'

Laura took it all in her stride, appreciating the unspoken compliment. 'Actually I made it for Greg but he couldn't stop for tea. Said he might pop around one evening next week.' Puddings were not her favourite dish at the moment. She helped herself to a cup of black coffee without sugar.

'Really enjoyed that. Mind if I drink my tea in the other room? I'll see what's on the television.'

Leaving the table, he wandered into the lounge putting the drink carefully on to a glass-topped coffee table. While waiting for the picture to settle he spread himself comfortably against the arm of the settee, removing his shoes and pulling on a pair of favourite well worn slippers.

It had been a day of endless argument and counter argument. There was that constant fear of overlooking some small detail, which might just turn out to be vitally important. Home was the only place where he could really relax after a good meal and in a quiet atmosphere. It was like a tonic and, at times like this, the only normality in his life.

A high profile murder case would keep him in the public eye and subject to constant scrutiny by the press. Everyone was waiting to see whether he was some sort of super sleuth, or whether the investigation would just fizzle out and die of old age without anyone being caught. It was rarely, if ever, out of his mind and would stay that way until he was satisfied that everything in his power had been done in the search for the killer. As far as he knew, Catherine Wilson was a decent, ordinary young mother, extremely close to her daughter, never deserving to die. Neither did anyone have the right to kill her.

Laura walked into the lounge, quickly crossing in front of the television to reach her favourite armchair. Having sat in front of the screen for most of the afternoon, it was time now to solve her crossword puzzle. She glanced across as his head settled into a cushion, making himself more comfortable. Given ten to fifteen minutes he usually managed to nod off. Ignoring the news and sport, Laura began to concentrate on the first clue. She looked appealingly at him. hesitating long enough to give the impression that the answer was on the tip of her tongue.

'Lazy, Crazy, but with burning potentiality. Two words, five and five.'

'What did you say?'

She repeated it for his benefit, waiting to see whether he knew the answer.

He was still working on it when the phone rang. Laura reached out a wary hand. They weren't expecting any callers, or visitors this evening. In a single look of resignation, her face reflected a feeling she had experienced many times before. It was sergeant Lloyd.

'Hello Tom. How are you? Good. I'm fine thanks. Want to speak to the boss? He's right here sitting next to me.'

Deakin sat up. 'What's the problem?'

'It's that Peeping Tom job chief. The lady who made the complaint has been found dead and the lads say it's definitely not accidental.'

'Remind me. What's the address again? Make sure they touch nothing. I'll be along shortly.' Replacing the receiver, he reached down to pick up a shoe.

Laura looked at him with a tinge of both sadness and acceptance. 'Well, at least you've been fed.'

He nodded. 'I'll be fine. Just make sure you lock up before going to bed, if I'm not back.'

She stood to kiss him as he prepared to leave for another long session.

Opening the front door, he suddenly turned back. 'Need to make a quick call.' In the lounge he picked up the phone. 'Sergeant, will you get on the blower and see if you can raise Dr. Hayes for me and ask him to join us at Bridge Road? Tell him it's urgent.' Heading back to the front door once again, he slowed down, turned towards her and smiled. 'Nutty slack, love.'

'Pardon?'

'Your clue, Sweetie.' He leaned forward to give her a quick kiss.

'Nutty slack.'

'Of course,' was all she could think to say. 'Take care Sam, you're all we've got you know.'

'Safe as houses love. Back as soon as I can.' He moved out into the night air and drove away, leaving Laura watching, as the rear lights blazed red before disappearing out of sight.

Once inside the house she locked the door and returned to the lounge. Another long wait was just starting. She tried to concentrate her mind on the crossword puzzle, writing in the words nutty slack.

'Sam Deakin, you're like a prize butterfly. Just when I think I've got you all to myself you flutter away again.'

'Evening Mr Deakin, sir.'

The young policeman had managed to recover some of his dignity and was now standing to attention by the front door of 83 Bridge Road. Deakin looked at his pale face, guessing what had caused it and recalled his own first experience of violent death. 'Hello constable, was it you who found the body?'

'Yes sir.' He continued almost to chatter his report. 'We've been here a few times lately, sir, following calls about a, er, watcher sir. We were on a routine visit this evening and came across this situation.' He stopped to catch his breath.

Deakin took note of the pallid complexion. 'Are you feeling alright?'

'Yes, thank you sir. It was a shock when I saw the lady. It was just that I saw her alive only yesterday and spoke to her about the complaint.'

'What did she have to say?'

'Well, not a lot, she'd been drinking heavily but thought she saw a man's face looking at her through the gap in the bedroom curtains.'

'Could she describe him?'

'No sir. Said he ran off when he knew she'd rumbled him.'

Leaving the constable to his guard duties Deakin entered the house. The short hallway had two doors to his right and a kitchen facing at the end. On the left hand side there was a bathroom and separate toilet and what seemed to be a second bedroom. Deakin continued towards the light shining brightly through the lounge doorway. The furniture had seen better days and there was a general atmosphere of untidiness rather than dirt. From the arm of a settee Mary Donovan stared at him through lifeless eyes. Her tongue protruded, as if desperate to speak. He hadn't known the woman, although he knew of her. The fracas in which the police had been involved a year ago might now have some bearing on her death.

It would be all too simple if that was the case but you had to start somewhere and this was the first avenue of investigation.. Deakin looked closely at the wounds, attempting to decide the degree of similarity with the previous killing. There was an ominous familiarity about the deep indentation under the jawbone.

As he studied the scene, two possibilities sprang to mind. Mary might have answered a knock at the door and allowed her visitor to follow her into the lounge before being struck from behind. The alternative was that someone walked straight into the house uninvited and murdered her. Deakin recalled the two patrol officers had entered through a partially open back door. If the blow to the head hadn't killed her instantly then certainly the strangulation marks suggested the killer was taking no chances. There was no obvious evidence of theft and from her sitting position Deakin assumed that there had been no sexual assault. Someone wanted Cathy Wilson dead, and now it looked as if someone, maybe the same someone, wanted Mary O'Donovan dead as well. And yet they couldn't have been two more different people.

Deakin couldn't fail to notice the blood spattered table lamp standing on a small table at the end of the settee. Above his head, on the ceiling, there were other spots which looked like minute blood stains. They would have come from the instrument being withdrawn from the skull as the killer pulled his arm back after the initial blow. The first strike would certainly have crushed her skull, discharging cranial fluid and severing a network of fine veins. The heart would have been still pumping blood at the rate of two hundred pounds pressure to the square inch during her dying seconds thus causing the spray effect. This certainly would account for the state of the lampshade. Deakin stood up and adjusted his position, trying to work out exactly where the killer must have stood prior to the attack.

Only a small amount of blood had soaked into the wildly patterned carpet, at the front of the settee, indicating that possibly the killer may have absorbed some into his clothing. Blood on his person would raise the question of whether he lived alone or possibly had some place to go where he could clean up before going home. The small amount of blood was also a clear indication that the victim had died very quickly.

If he was correct then Mary could well have been walking ahead of her assailant from the front door. In other words it was someone she knew or was expecting, someone she trusted. Maybe she was right all along about the peeper and if so, she'd paid a terrible price. He considered the thought. Surely the killer must have been invited on to the premises otherwise he would have killed her in the hall and probably face to face.

Jones walked into the room.

'Evening chief.' He looked around the crime scene without waiting for a response and stared down at Mary Donovan as if expecting her to answer him. 'I know this lady. We had her in court last year when her husband was supposed to have tried to kill her.'

Deakin rubbed his chin thoughtfully. 'Yes, I remember the case. Anyone know where the husband is?'

The young patrol officer interrupted.

'Excuse me sir. She was due in court today on some matrimonial business.'

'How the hell did you know that?'

'There's a summons on the table sir with today's date on it. Saw it when I was looking around the place, just in case anyone was still here when we arrived.'

Deakin walked to the table and picked up the document. It was a summons for a property adjustment order and maintenance claim against her former husband. Suddenly things began to fall into place. His memory was his filing cabinet, and somewhere deep down inside a voice was shouting *I'm in here*. Now the details came flooding back. He recalled how unconvinced he was that the husband had done anything wrong. There was nothing that could be supported with real evidence. The case was passed down the line to Jones. No evidence was offered by the prosecution. He had met the husband only once, but sufficient for him to recall the face.

He turned to the detective sergeant. 'Get a couple of lads down to the canal and see if there a barge still moored near the Seven Stars pub, might be called Reflections or something like that. If there is, you should find

Jack Donovan aboard and I'd like to have a few words with him.' Changing the subject, he continued,' Doctor Hayes has been called, I hope.'

'I'm here, chief inspector.' Hayes had been standing quietly behind Deakin waiting for him to finish giving his orders. Jones lifted his hand in salute, and without waiting for a response, went outside to instruct the squad members, leaving the Doc with his boss and the late Mary Donovan.

'Good evening. What have we here then?'

The pathologist was already pulling on his surgical gloves. 'Christ, nothing for ages and now two in no time at all. Is the world going completely mad?' Hayes took up a kneeling position and began.

Deakin with two officers in attendance, stood watching as Hayes gently but firmly raised the head just sufficient to be able to view the deep laceration which had caused the deadly fracture. Blood dripped from the wound on to his rubber gloves, while the matted hair stood stiff as straw.

The young patrolman reached again to cover his mouth as the body belched, expelling the gases now accumulating within. The doctor moved his hand gently over her eyes and for the first time that day Mary seemed to be at rest. Finally he stood up, turning towards the chief inspector.

'You mentioned a barge man. If he's your suspect he can't have got very far; she's only been dead a few hours, three or four at the most. A high percentage of rigor mortis remaining yet.'

'She was in court earlier today. I can soon find out the exact time she left and maybe we can tie this one down tightly.'

Hayes was concerned about other matters. 'There seem to be similarities between this one and the Catherine Wilson lady.' He continued; 'The blow to the back of the head, followed by an attempt at strangulation and no evidence of self defence. I'll be able to tell you more once we get her back to pathology.'

The zip racing along its track to close the body bag was the only sound in the room. Yesterday Mary Donovan had given them a hard time but today a deep atmosphere of sadness hung over them all until the body was removed. Suddenly everyone had a job to do.

The fingerprint experts began to dust the area, the photographer busied himself with extra shots of the room, then the entrance hall, and finally, the outside approaches. The forensic team started their own inch by inch search with the determination of well trained gun dogs. Deakin took a last look around before going outside and calling for his sergeant.

'Get as many statements as you can from the neighbours and make sure they include positive or negative references to the Peeping Tom.

Jones couldn't resist the temptation to mention the Wilson job. 'What do you think Chief?'

Deakin kept his own counsel for the moment. 'Let's hear what Jack Donovan has to say for himself first. He might just solve the case for us.' As if by way of terminating that part of the enquiry he added, 'Anyway, I'm not much in favour of coincidence but that doesn't mean to say it can't happen, so we'll just have to wait and see.'

One by one the flashing blue lights were extinguished gradually allowing Bridge Road to assume its more normal rural appearance. The property was cordoned off with thick red and white tapes and two officers positioned to prevent any unauthorised access to the premises.

'I'm going back to the station. Give me a call when you find Mr Donovan.'

Deakin climbed into his car and headed back.

Lloyd was still on duty having doubled with the night sergeant in case any extra help was needed. Deakin stopped long enough in the reception area to let him know that everything was in hand and he was free go home.

'Before you go, will you give my missus a ring and tell her I'm back here if she needs to call me for anything, otherwise I'll be home in a couple of hours.'

Deakin busied himself studying the similarities between the recent Wilson death and the events of this evening. On the face of it, there had been a case to prosecute against Bill Wilson for his ex-wife's murder, but it beggared belief that he would go out and commit another knowing he was on police bail and still a prime suspect under investigation. He picked up the internal phone.

'Where's sergeant Lloyd?'

'He went home over an hour ago.' It was the night sergeant.

Deakin glanced at his watch, surprised to note it was already after midnight. 'Any chance of a coffee? And see if you can find D.S. Jones for me. Tell him I want a word.'

He put the phone down and waited for the hot drink, still concentrating on the Wilson file. With all the events still fresh in his mind, he struggled to try and find some thread, remote or otherwise, which might connect the two killings. Two women, both divorcees, living a few miles apart; one a drinker with no kids and the other a normal mother with one teenage daughter. Each of them squabbling with ex-husbands over property and money.

One 'Ex' has a new wife and we don't know about the other yet. Both attacked from behind with a blunt instrument, using excessive violence and followed by attempted strangulation. Neither offered any resistance, suggesting that the killer was either known to them or else they felt there was nothing to fear from him.

The Peeping Tom, if he existed, had an advantage in Mary's case but really it was only throwing up the possibility that it might just turn out to be a copycat killing. Could the peeper have been following both women? The ringing phone broke his concentration.

'Deakin.'

It was Jones. 'We've traced Jack Donovan. The lads are bringing him back now.'

The black and white cat jumped on to the window ledge outside Mary Donovan's bedroom. Orange eyes peered through a small niche in the curtain seeing only a dark and empty space.

CHAPTER 10

Jack Donovan stepped ashore into the cold night air, casually dressed in a warm polo neck sweater and slacks. There was no need for his reefer jacket. The Seven Stars pub, with its welcoming log fire, was only a short walk from the barge. Clean shaven, hair neatly combed and a slightly ruddy complexion from time spent on the canals, he looked relaxed and confident. Donovan was the type of person who attracted interest. Wherever he went, people seemed curious to know more about a man who travelled alone, and although civil, tended to mind his own business. A broad shouldered man, over six feet tall and weighing around fifteen stones, was hardly likely to go unnoticed, especially when unaccompanied. There was no obvious reason why a stylish female wasn't hanging on to his arm.

Eating at the waterside restaurants and pubs two or three times a week had become a habit. Nothing extravagant, he enjoyed well cooked plain food. It helped to break the solitude of the boat and kept him generally in touch with day to day events in the local areas. The buzz of conversation around him, and the occasional pub pianist, all helped to maintain an air of normality. He wanted to be neither a recluse nor a misanthrope but wasn't ready to move on yet. In any event a canal barge was unlikely to impress someone used to all the comforts of home, even if it was well equipped.

The barman raised his head as the two detectives entered. Instinct told him they were on business. Sometimes they just called in for a pint. The Seven Stars was not only a regular haunt for locals but also played host to boat people passing through the area.

'Evening lads. What can I get you then?' His meaty, calloused hand poised on top of a pump.

'Evenin' Ted. Two halves of mild please.' One of the detectives leaned forward to speak in confidence. 'We've been over to the barge by the bridge but the owner's not on board. Don't suppose you'd know if he was in here?' He stepped back and waited.

Ted nodded towards a corner of the lounge.

'Gentleman with the newspaper. Think that's him. Came in for dinner earlier and stayed on.' He spoke quietly.

'Thanks. Have one yourself.' The change from two half crowns was left on the counter as to the two men walked over to where the stranger was sitting. It was a handsome tip for a few seconds work.

'Mr Donovan, is it?'

Looking up from his paper, he seemed surprised that anyone could refer to him by name in this place. 'Yes. Should I know you?'

'Mind if we sit down a minute? Jack isn't it?'

'How do you know me?' He felt apprehensive but also curious, never forgetting his previous encounter with the police when they arrested him on suspicion of attempted murder and put him through hell before dropping their enquiries. He could do without a repeat of Mary's drunken antics.

'We were told you were on a barge by the bridge, and when we got no reply, this seemed to be the most natural place to look.'

He stared at them. Alarm bells must have started to ring and yet he didn't seem to know why. 'Well, you've found me. Mind telling me what this is all about. I take it you are from the CID? I'm sure as hell not in debt!'

A warrant card flashed in front of his face, giving him little opportunity to study it. 'We have some bad news for you Jack. Sorry to say your ex-wife has passed away and as far as we know you're still her next of kin.'

They watched in silence for a moment at the colour draining from his face.

'What do you mean? I was in court with her only this morning and she was on good form then alright.'

The detectives both looked at him, obviously searching for a telltale sign, some slip of the tongue or mannerism which might give him away. 'Jack, we need you to identify the body and we also need a statement from you detailing your whereabouts over the past twelve hours. Would you mind coming back to the station with us? It will be much easier and quicker to sort things out from there.' It was hardly an invitation.

'What's happened to Mary? She been in an accident?' Covering his eyes, the big man suddenly began to weep, as shock overtook him. 'Sorry lads,' I know she was an alcoholic but we did have some good times in the early days you know.' He dropped his head forward to wipe his eyes. 'She wasn't always like that, you know.'

No-one interrupted him. They wanted him to speak, to give whatever information he wished. Sooner or later it would all knit together.

'She got very depressed after a couple of miscarriages and that was when the drink began to take her over. One tiny baby was all she really wanted. She would have been a great mother.' Donovan's chest heaved as he struggled to regain control of his emotions He dabbed at his eyes, submerged in a sea of sorrow. 'Only today I agreed she could keep the house for as long as she lived, and now this happens.' Suddenly it began to dawn on him. How did she die? Nobody so far had said what happened. Clutching the handkerchief tightly in his fist, as if trying to wring out the tears, he looked from one to the other. 'What happened? An accident, a heart attack or what?'

'Sorry to say Jack, we have reason to believe she was unlawfully killed. That's why we need to talk to you and to have her identified as soon as possible.'

'Unlawful killing? You mean she's been murdered?'

Both detectives continued to search his eyes for any sign of a good actor, but there was nothing to be seen, only disbelief. 'If you've finished your drink we'd like to get moving. There's a lot to get through and it's already very late.'

Leaving his drink on the table, Donovan rose to his feet matching both men for height and physique. It would have been offensive to the memory of Mary to have carried on drinking. The drive to the police station took only about fifteen minutes with very little talk or scenery at such a dark hour to lift the depressive atmosphere. On one side of the road the nightshift crews could be seen walking through the gates of the new Birds Eye Frozen Foods factory. Huge neon signs blazed down from its sides only to be followed by the inky blackness of their less illustrious neighbours. Further along the road, spaces between the factories told their own stories of the devastation caused by the bombing during the war and still not remedied twenty five years on. On arrival at the police station he was taken directly to the interview room.

'I need to see the pathologist before interviewing Donovan. There's a few things which need to be discussed,' said Deakin.

Jones was quick to respond. 'Right Chief I'll do the first interview and hang on to him until you get back.' The two men parted company.

Deakin made his way to the mortuary grateful that Julian Hayes had offered to stay back and get on with the job. He knew how important it was to the detective. At this early stage there was always the chance of something turning up while the trail was still hot. 'Morning Doc or is it evening? I seem to be losing track of the days.'

Hayes nodded.' I recognise the feeling. Anything interesting turned up?'

'Well, I've got the ex-husband at the station and need to interview him shortly. But I wanted to speak with you first, just in case you've picked up on anything.'

Despite his tiredness, Hayes remained thorough. 'I'm praying that this is not the beginning of a developing pattern. She was quite drunk at the time of death which might have been a blessing in disguise. Loaded with whiskey and probably Guinness.' Pausing only for a second, 'Nothing to eat for possibly twenty four hours before death and drinking at that rate was almost enough to kill her anyway. Liver and kidneys in a shocking state and in my view she probably had less than twelve months to live.'

Deakin shook his head. 'You're telling me that the husband had no need to kill her if he knew she was doing it to herself.'

Hayes took a single pace backwards from the mortuary table discarding surgical gloves into a hygienic metal container. 'I'm more concerned about the method used. I've looked at my records from the Wilson case and there are too many similarities to ignore the possibility that you might just have a multiple murderer on your hands this time.' He was beginning to fuel Deakin's worst fears. 'Just let me say that in both cases we have a right handed killer, of average height, using a similar sort of blunt instrument and victims with almost identically sized bruises on the neck, in almost identical positions. My opinion is that both women were killed by the same hand. Neither of them needed to be strangled. They were already within seconds of death anyway, if not already dead. It's as though someone wanted to witness the actual moment of death. Anyone in mind?'

So far Deakin had managed to keep the possibility of a copycat killer to himself and for the moment he wanted to keep it that way. Oddly, he found the idea preferable to the thought of a multiple murderer being somewhere out there on the loose. He rubbed at his chin for a moment. 'I thought the Wilson matter was going a bit too smoothly, and now this one. Where the hell do we go from here? Two almost identical domestic murders in pretty quick succession is hardly believable.'

Hayes interrupted.' We know for certain that the killer is right handed because of the angle of entry on the skull. we also know that the weapon was some sort of cylindrical bar about half an inch in diameter, because of the blood tracks. Don't discount your suspects from the Wilson case just yet. Now let's see what your scene of crime lads can come up with.'

Deakin looked down at Mary Donovan. Hayes careful but probing examination had necessarily involved even further violation of this tragic woman. Her body must have suffered untold insults in the search for truth and motive, and hopefully, justice. Finally Hayes was able to give her back some dignity as he drew the white sheet up to her neck, leaving only an ashen grey face exposed, eyes closed as if in sleep. It was the least he could do in the circumstances.

'Can I go ahead with formal identification?' It was a job Deakin hated because it often involved highly emotional scenes and hysterical outbursts from people ill equipped to handle the sudden death of a loved one. But it still had to be done. He wanted to get Donovan down here as quickly as possible and also to study his reaction when he came face to face with Mary.

'Certainly. Anytime it suits you.'

Deakin checked his watch. It was already after two o'clock in the morning. Laura would be fast asleep now. 'Her ex husband can be brought here right away, if that's OK with you.' Hayes was already resigned to losing his night's sleep. Another hour wouldn't make much difference. 'I'll get on with my report till you come back. Maybe catch some sleep later.'

Wasting no time, Deakin went back to the station and straight to the interview room. He couldn't help noticing the surprise on Donovan's face as he walked through the door. 'Hello Mr Donovan. Chief inspector Deakin. I think we met on the canal bank recently. I'm looking into the cause of your former wife's death and need your help.'

Donovan looked baffled as he struggled to recall the incident for a moment. 'Yes, of course, the fisherman.'

Deakin nodded. What would he give to be somewhere else right now with his rod and line, anywhere rather than here. 'Mr Donovan, I wonder if you will be kind enough to go with me now and tell me whether you can identify the body which, I believe, may be that of Mary Donovan, your former wife?'

Before he had time to answer Deakin continued, 'You see Mr Donovan, early identification is essential if we are to make real progress. I'll take you to the mortuary now and then I think it would be a good idea if you keep your boat moored for the time being at the place where we met. That is, until our enquiries are complete. I will need to see you again and I need to know where I can find you without searching the whole canal system.' He turned to Jones. 'A word please sergeant.'

The two men walked outside leaving Donovan to his thoughts for the moment. Jones was the first to speak. 'He's not hiding anything. I'm pretty sure. Alibi seems solid enough: shopping locally at the time of death and witnesses available. He had dinner at the Seven Stars and then went into the lounge bar to read his paper and enjoy a few pints. I don't think we have a problem with this man.'

Deakin felt inclined to agree.

'OK. Sort the lads out and make sure the property is kept sealed until we get back there tomorrow. Then get yourself off home.'

Jones looked pleased getting an opportunity to catch up with some sleep.

Deakin turned his attention back to Donovan, leaving Jones to pass on his instructions to the night men. The two men left the station, heading for the mortuary.

Hayes stood ready to greet them. 'Good morning Chief Inspector.' The detective returned the formal acknowledgment and introduced his companion. They walked together into the medical area where several figures lay covered in sheets, the two men following close behind. Hayes stopped by one of the metal tables, gently peeling back the sheet to reveal the ashen grey features.

Jack Donovan started, shock and disbelief showing in his face. There was no doubting it was her. 'Oh Mary, what have they done to you?' He followed the line from her shoulder trying to touch her cold lifeless hand.

Deakin stepped alongside him. 'Mr Donovan, is this lady your former wife?'

Donovan barely whispered 'Yes.'

The detective and the doctor stood back, allowing him time to gather his thoughts and pay his respects in his own way. He kissed two fingers and then leaned over touching them on to her forehead. 'It's been a long time since I kissed you old girl. Not since before we went our separate ways but God knows I never wished any harm on you.' Tears streamed down his face as the big man turned away and walked slowly back to the doctor's office.

'What do you want me to do Mr Deakin?'

'I'll take you back to your boat now and tomorrow we can decide the best place to keep it moored until my enquiries are complete.'

'Anything you say. Anything at all.' Donovan turned his attention towards the doctor. 'Was she raped, doctor?'

Hayes wasn't surprised at the question. Deakin nodded his agreement to an answer. 'No, Mr Donovan, most definitely not. She died as a result of haemorrhaging from a fractured skull.'

'Did she die in agony, or was it quick?'

The pathologist held his gaze. 'I think I can assure you that she would have known nothing and not even felt anything from the first impact to the time of death which would have been an extremely brief period, possibly even instantaneous.'

'Thank you, doctor. I just couldn't bear the thought of her lying somewhere dying slowly and me not being able to do anything about it.'

Deakin stopped to thank the pathologist before leaving the building. Hayes held out a glove free hand.' We must have that lunch sometime Chief Inspector.' Nothing, it seemed would put this man off his food.

CHAPTER 11

The silhouette of Reflections stood out against the weak light of early dawn as Sam Deakin pulled off the road, parking halfway between the Seven Stars pub and the canal towpath. Once out of the car, the two men walked down to the water's edge, where the boat lay in her berth. The only sound was a gentle lapping of water against the steel hull. Deakin wondered why the boatman had bothered to move the vessel such a short distance upstream from its previous mooring near to the Old Bridge. It seemed a bit odd.

'Welcome aboard Mr Deakin. Cup of tea?'

He stood aside, allowing the detective to walk across the short gangplank bridging the gap between hull and bank.

'Thanks. I could do with a drink right now.'

A surge of boyish excitement swept through him as he climbed down to the lower deck level to begin the tour. Despite years of fishing on the bank, this was his first invitation to go aboard one of the steel giants of the waterways.

Squeezing past the detective, Jack Donovan led the way, pointing out various features as they gradually proceeded towards a lounge at the forward end of the boat. At the rudder control he had noticed two small lockers, clearly labelled 'Wet' and 'Dry,' which were intended to act as wardrobes for any cumbersome clothing which needed to be discarded outside the confines of the living accommodation. He was surprised to discover that beneath his feet, under detachable boards, lay a powerful engine and four relays of heavy duty batteries, together with large fresh water tanks. Donovan explained that the barge could carry sufficient water and fuel for up to two weeks of cruising depending on the number of passengers.

Off the long narrow corridor, was an entire house in a straight line. Two cabins provided sleeping accommodation for four people, preceded by a dining area with table and two bench seats which also converted into beds. Next came a toilet, separate shower and kitchen with hot and cold water, refrigerator, cooker and wooden cupboards. Deakin was fascinated. Finally they reached the forward area with its cottage suite, fitted bookcase, radio and record player. A squat stove, its black chimney pipe leading out through the roof, gave an air of warmth and welcome.

Studying the photographs displayed on the walls, before taking his seat to await the arrival of the tea, he couldn't help noticing the pretty young woman, her easy smile and bright eyes. There was no doubting Mary Donovan, for much of her life, had been attractive. *If only you could speak to me now.* His thoughts were interrupted by the return of his host.

'There you are Mr Deakin.'

He took the mug of tea gratefully, still looking at the photograph. 'A very pretty woman.'

Donovan's smile was tinged with sadness. 'Once upon a time, a real beauty and good fun as well. She had a wonderful Irish sense of humour.'

'What made you move such a short distance upstream?' Deakin changed the subject quickly.

Donovan explained there was no reason to stay by the Old Bridge after the court case finished. He had decided to move on towards his eventual destination at Brighouses Basin but changed his mind, deciding to have a night off and a few drinks at The Seven Stars before moving north again.

Deakin broke the silence which followed. 'Strange world we live in today. Last time we met you and I were busy minding our own business, getting on with our lives and now this has to happen.'

Donovan looked at him as though trying to take the measure of the man. They were both were exhausted. Despite the stress of the evening's events he exhibited no animosity towards the detective. His original gut instinct when they'd passed the time of day with each other on the towpath stayed with him. Deakin was a straight man, probably a very good copper. 'This time last week I was busy trying to figure out how to keep a roof over Mary's head and keep myself afloat, if that's the right expression.' A thought came into his head. 'Was she wearing her ring? The Claddagh ring I mean. I bought it years ago and she never went a day without it even after we fell out.'

'Her personal jewellery might have been removed by the pathologist in which case it will be in a sealed bag which should be returned to me with his report. I'll let you know. What did you call it?'

Donovan looked shy. 'It's a Claddagh ring. They come from a fishing village of the same name in Galway. It's a tiny heart clasped in two hands and can be worn in three different ways. On the right hand with the heart pointing toward the finger tips means that the wearer's heart is free. Pointing toward the palm means that the heart is not available for romance. Worn on the left hand the wearer is married. It's one of those things young people do and somehow becomes significant at different times during their lives. More tea Mr Deakin?' He stood, ready to go back to the galley.

Out of the window the first rays of daylight were beginning to show through billowing clouds. 'Better not. I must get back and catch some shut-eye before lunch time. Things are pretty hectic at the moment.' Deakin rose to his feet ready to take his leave. 'Once the body is released, will you be making the funeral arrangements, or is there someone else we need to contact?'

Donovan nodded. 'I'll be dealing with everything. Mary has a couple of sisters in Ireland. I'll need to speak to them before they read about it in the press or maybe even see it on the news.'

Deakin turned to leave then hesitated.' You won't forget what we agreed about not leaving the area?'

'Don't worry. I won't be leaving this place until Mary's killer has been caught and put away for life. In any case I'll have to clear the house and deal with the sale eventually.' He thought about it for a second or two. 'I'll go back to the Old Bridge. It might be more convenient for everyone.'

Deakin was satisfied. 'That's fine. We'll need to speak again soon, but if anything at all comes to mind, call me.' Deakin left the barge. He'd eliminated the first suspect and had no idea where to start looking for the next one.

Jack Donovan sat down, elbows resting on the dining table, staring into yet another mug of steaming tea. 'Who could possibly want you dead Mary? God knows you were just a sick woman.' Tears began to roll uncontrollably down his cheeks. Reaching into his pocket he pulled out a handkerchief. The letter 'J' embroidered into one corner stood out. Mary loved to embroider. He even had shirts with the breast pockets bearing the same initial. He dabbed his eyes. It was almost as if she was touching him again. 'Just a tiny baby was all you ever wanted.'

Sleep was beyond him as, red eyed, he watched the dawn bring in a new day. From the side drawer of a small bureau he pulled out a card index box, flicking through it until he came across the address and phone number of Mary's younger sister in Mallow, in the south of Ireland. Ten minutes later he was inside the telephone kiosk next to the car park by the Seven Stars. Feeling in his pockets for loose silver, he carefully spread it across the top of the call box, separating out the silver into sixpences, shillings and florins in order to make sure he put the correct amount into the slot when the operator instructed him. The ringing tone seemed to go on forever before a sleepy voice answered and tried to connect him. 'Put your money in now caller.' The operator held the call for a few seconds until the five shillings had been inserted. 'You're through now Caller, thank you.' The operator's line closed.

'Hello. Is that you Kathleen. It's Jack here.' He brushed quickly over the greetings. 'I'm fine, thank you, but I'm sorry to call you at such an odd hour. Hope I'm not being a nuisance.' Kathleen was always the sensible one in the family. She'd know how to handle it. 'Kathleen, I have to tell you Mary passed away last night.'

A loud gasp followed a short silence. 'Oh my God, Jack. Why didn't you say she was ill. I'd have come over and given a hand.'

Donovan's lips tightened. 'She wasn't ill Kathleen. She was just found dead.'

'A heart attack was it then?'

'We're not sure what it was but the police are looking into it. there'll have to be an inquest.' Donovan changed the direction of the conversation. 'Kathleen, I'm wondering if you would like me to bring Mary back home to her family once the inquest has been dealt with.?' In his heart he already knew the answer.

'That would be nice Jack. You'll remember our little churchyard in the village. She'll be back among friends and well tended. I promise. You're a good man, Jack. I'm sorry Mary didn't always do right by you.'

'One minute left, sir.' the operator cut in on the conversation.' Unless you have more coins to insert.'

'Sorry operator. I've no more change until the shops open.'

'Just one minute left then.' She politely cut herself out of the conversation.

Donovan turned his attention back to Kathleen. 'Sorry about this. I'll call you later from the house. But don't worry about anything. I'll be staying here until everything is sorted out and I'll call you with any news.'

'Jack. is there something you're not telling me?'

There was a click as the line went dead. Kathleen would have to wait.

Donovan replaced the receiver, pushing the kiosk door open with his foot.

'God Dammit, you fool.' He spoke the words aloud, realising that no-one could contact him. The only phone was at Mary's house. Suddenly he felt exhausted. According to his watch, it was more than twenty four hours since he last climbed out of his bed.

Deakin finally appeared at the station shortly before two o'clock. Five hours sleep was as much as he could spare himself. After a long hot shower, followed by one of Laura's special breakfasts, he was back on his feet. Looking down at a desk, littered with notes, mail and statements, he wondered where to start. A knock on the door distracted him for the moment.

'Thought you'd like a drink before you start, sir.'

He accepted it gratefully. 'Thanks young lady. You'll make a fine wife for someone but for God's sake don't marry a copper; they're never home.'

'Not the marrying kind, sir.' She smiled back at him. It was an open friendly face. She seemed a happy sort. He watched with a look of calm appreciation as the neat blue clad figure slipped out through the door.

Retirement was still a few years away for Deakin, although there were times lately when he felt it couldn't come soon enough. As long as crime was still Britain's fastest expanding industry there was no possibility of an early pension. For a moment his thoughts wandered back over the years as he recalled how neither of his parents had lived long enough to enjoy retirement. They'd died when he was a teenager, not too long before the outbreak of the war which had plunged his life into further turmoil. 'Maybe it's just as well we don't know what's in store for us.' He turned back to the job in hand.

Dozens of statements already taken, had been studied in unrelenting detail. Anything looking remotely like a coincidence was double checked. Meetings, updates, further decisions, left nothing to be taken for granted. Lists of sexual perverts and mental patients out on licence, not forgetting men on parole, all had to be screened for the slightest connection. So far all this had yielded nothing of any consequence.

Donovan's statement told a different story. Not yet old enough to retire, he was existing on the profits from the sale of his tool-making business. When things turned sour with Mary he'd felt unable to continue living and socialising in the local area. Buying a canal boat had been a risk but he enjoyed the experience so much that he decided to live on it for a year or two, before putting his roots down elsewhere. Hopefully, by that time things would have sorted themselves out with Mary. There was no other woman in his life, not even on the horizon.

Jones poked his head round the door. 'Afternoon chief; managed some shut eye then?' He still appeared weary but, like his boss, had learned the hard way to take things in his stride, being fortunate that he had no-one to please but himself.

'Yes thanks; not much but it'll do for now.' He glanced again at the paper mountain. 'Any new developments?'

There was some news, not much but helpful. 'One witness claims to have seen a white car outside the Donovan house around the time of the murder. Didn't see the driver but thinks it was there for about a quarter of an hour. Next time she looked it had gone.'

Deakin couldn't blame the woman for any lack of perception. She could never have known or even guessed that she might be looking at a murder scene. It was often the way with bystanders. But sometimes the combined evidence of two or three people might just produce that bit extra.

'Check the statements from the rest of the neighbours with special reference to the car and if necessary go back and ask again. It's worth a try.'

The sergeant took himself off to the CID office to give his instructions and grab two coffees at the same time. Ten minutes later minutes later he was back. 'Lads are on their way chief. There's nothing else in the earlier statements, but we'll give it a go.'

Deakin picked up the phone. 'See if you can get me Doc Hayes at Pathology.'

The response was instant.' Sorry sir, but Dr Hayes is not back till tomorrow. There should be a note on your desk.'

Deakin frowned. It wasn't like him to miss something like that. 'Call him first thing. Tell him I'd like a word when he can manage it.'

Tomorrow was almost here anyway and he didn't blame the good doctor for wanting to spend a day in bed. He sometimes wondered how Julian Hayes ever managed to sleep after working on the victims of crime and various other types of unexplained sudden deaths, day after day.

Turning his attention to more routine matters, he pushed the empty cup to one side, making space for himself and Jones to start work on more of the statements taken by the squad members. Something else kept nagging away at his tired brain. It was strange that Mary Donovan had complained several times about a watcher or peeper and yet none of the neighbours had reported anything unusual. One patrol officer had even suggested that the villain was no more than next door's cat which had taken a fancy to her bedroom window ledge.

'There has to be a connection with the Wilson job, Chief. They've got too much in common.' Jones was pretty adamant.

'OK, tell me who and why someone wanted both these women dead, because they sure as hell have nothing in common. At least nothing we know about yet.' Deakin was struggling with the problem. 'If you want to go down that road, then you need to find the connection soon, otherwise we've got a random killer on the loose in the area, which doesn't bear thinking about. But for God's sake keep an open mind.'

'Well Chief, Cathy Wilson might have been murdered by appointment. Her ex-husband denies phoning her, despite what his loving daughter says, and if he didn't then someone did, and she went at that person's invitation.' He paused for a moment. 'Mary Donovan seems to have admitted someone into her house willingly and maybe, just maybe, she was expecting him, or even her.'

Deakin took it on board. 'Fortunately, in both cases we can be reasonably certain of the actual times of death. We've also established the times of the victims' last movements and therefore it follows that we've narrowed the killer's window of opportunity. In other words, there was a reason for him to kill at certain times, one being in the late evening and the other much earlier. Has that got anything to do with his job, the availability of the women or some other eventuality?' The questions were posing other questions rather than answers. It was all about argument, counter argument and elimination.

Jones intervened. 'The attacks and instruments used are too similar to be coincidental, especially in such a short space of time.'

Deakin was inclined to agree but still not fully convinced. There was always the possibility they were seeing some sort of copycat killing. More importantly though, the case against Bill Wilson was starting to come apart.

'While I remember.'

Jones paid attention.

'As soon as you have a few minutes to spare I'd like you to call at the teacher training college along St Helens Road. There's a few hundred young ladies there and I think that they ought to be warned about being out alone and they'll need to keep an eye out for that peeper in case he decides to have a look at some of them.'

'Tell you what Chief, they've got a few hundred hulking young males to chaperone them and a lot more volunteers down town.'

Deakin had already moved ahead. 'Call Mr Wilson's solicitor. Tell him that we are going to re-interview his client. He'll want to be present.' He thought for a moment, convinced that there were still questions which needed to be answered, probably by Bill Wilson.

The phone rang. 'Excuse me sir. DC Thompson, the Scene of Crime Officer would like a word.'

'OK, put him through.' He pressed the phone to his ear. Thompson was a keen young man. He had a knack of finding fingerprints in the most unlikely places. Recently, in an unrelated matter he had discovered how a premises, apparently secure had been entered by using a flat steel support from a lady's corset.

'Afternoon chief.' The southern accent sounded out of place in Lancashire. 'Just confirming there are no fingerprints and no sign of forced entry. Whoever came in was admitted freely. No scuff marks on the back door but there are stains, some blood smudges, on the edge of the mortis lock. Looks to me as if he was admitted through the front, closed that door behind him and then walked out from the back of the house wearing blood stained gloves.'

Deakin listened carefully as the officer continued. The information would be accurate. He knew that much already.

'Obviously, he took his gloves off after he left. It's amazing that no-one seems to have seen anything. Nothing to report from the outside yet.' The report was concise but sufficient for the time being. 'It seems clear enough that Mary Donovan invited someone into her home, obviously not knowing or even realising he, or she, was there specifically for the purpose of murder. Therefore, it had to be either someone she knew and trusted, or at least someone whom she felt no reason to fear. The question is; who comes into that category?'

The only person presently fitting into that category was Jack Donovan. But he'd have to be a natural actor. Deakin sat back to review it yet again. More coffee, more statements and no answers was proving to be an exhausting process, but there was no other way. Bill Wilson's home phone had not been used at all on the day in question, but that didn't bar him from using any of the telephone boxes dotted around the town area. The problems seemed endless.

'Sorry to disturb you, sir. Your news conference is due in ten minutes. You did ask me to remind you.'

It was Alison the pretty red-haired trainee being efficient, obviously relishing her close proximity to the action. Deakin glanced at the clock, then at Jones, wondering where the days were going: each one seeming to merge into the next. 'Let's go and speak to the gentle-men of the press, before they hang us out to dry.'

The briefing room was neither comfortable nor welcoming. The white neon lighting was harsh and the chairs hard. But no-one seemed to notice or care. All eyes were fixed on Deakin, pens held poised for his every word. Tomorrow he would be reported, mis-reported and criticised by a press hungry for success. Journalists having no idea how the investigation was proceeding would likely make up their own version of events. There was a story to tell and murder is always a best seller.

Deakin took his place at the centre of a long table, flanked by Jones and a competent looking secretary. He looked into the sea of faces. 'Good evening, members of the press. Most of you know me but for the record I'm detective Chief Inspector Deakin and the gentleman to my right is Detective Sergeant Jones. This meeting will have to be brief because we are in the early stages of a murder investigation and have a great deal of work to do. We will however be happy to keep you informed of any progress as our enquiries proceed.'

A hand went up. It belonged to Don Reading of The Mail. Deakin inwardly breathed a sigh of relief. He respected Reading as a principled journalist who told it as it was, without unnecessary embellishment.

'Two murders in such a short space of time, both of them similar in method suggests that you must be look-ing for a maniac.'

Deakin felt uncomfortable. He felt inclined to agree but this was not the time to say so. 'At the moment we are still following up certain lines of enquiry and it would be remiss of me to say anything which might prej-udice them.'

Reading looked at him. 'Then you're not ruling it out?'

Deakin returned his gaze. 'I'm not ruling anything out at this time.'

Another hand was raised. It belonged to a stranger. Deakin nodded towards him.

'Johnson, Telegraph.' There was nothing friendly about him and he didn't seem to be communicating with his fellow professionals.' It seems to me Chief Inspector that you are clutching at straws. What are you going to tell us that we can print for our readers and help them feel safe in their beds?'

Deakin felt the hairs on the back of his neck stiffen slightly. 'Well Mr. Johnson. For the record let me say that this is not about selling your paper, or pleasing the public. This is a murder enquiry being investigated in an orderly and, I hope, professional manner. Many statements have already been taken and there are more to come. Forensic scientists are involved and everyone is working flat out. Perhaps you will be kind enough to print that.'

Johnson glared at him. There was something almost malevolent about the man. 'I might just say that despite your best efforts nothing much is happening.'

Another hand was raised. Deakin nodded in the direction of the voice. It was a fresh faced cub reporter from the Advertiser.

'Is there any possibility of an early arrest and prosecution in this case?'

Deakin almost smiled at him The youngster had inadvertently taken the sting out of the situation. 'In this type of case an arrest might be imminent but the slightest leak of information could lead to the guilty party being given time to flee or even set up a false alibi. We can't be too careful. I'm also aware that murderers aren't always caught, despite the best efforts of dedicated policemen. But I'm sure we will find this person. It's only a matter of time'

Realising he was becoming slightly morbid, he decided to bring the meeting to a close. But before he could do so, Johnson spoke again. 'Was the victim raped or sexually assaulted? And if that is the case then shouldn't you be putting every woman in the area on her guard?'

'No Mr Johnson, she was not sexually assaulted or raped.'

'I hope you're not going to tell me you're looking for a hit man, Chief Inspector?'

'I think you are quite capable of answering that question yourself.'

Johnson glowered. 'I've got my headline. As a matter of fact I already had it before I came here today.'

Deakin terminated the meeting before any further questions could be put to him. The press could always make up their own story until something concrete came along. The audience trooped out of the tiny room all of them charged with the responsibility of trying to satisfy the insatiable hunger of their reading public. Deakin eyed the group wondering who might speak in his favour, knowing too well that they would all exaggerate the truth. It helped to keep them in a job and sell papers.

Jones made his exit and headed for the college, with DC Gray as an observer. It would be a good idea to get to the students before the press releases.

The approach from the main entrance gave it the appearance of a stately home. A long straight, wide road leading to the main building, was surrounded by immaculately trimmed, sweeping lawns. He remembered the students being evacuated to Blackburn during the war and the college being converted for use as a military hospital. He couldn't help thinking that it must have seemed like paradise to those poor sods who had been shot to pieces and brought here for recuperation.

'Pardon.' Gray looked at him, as if he had made some monumental announcement.

'Nothing. I was thinking aloud. This place used to be a military hospital during the war. The old prefabricated wards are all still behind the main building.

'I never knew that.' Gray seemed surprised at Jones' local knowledge.

'Well, you wouldn't. You're not from round here, are you?

'That's true but why the history lesson?'

Jones never took his eyes from the road. 'After the war they brought their young ladies back and started over again. A few years ago they decided to take in the male of the species and doubled their numbers. But not due to the birth rate,' he added as an afterthought. The car came to a standstill and the two men got out. A revolving door with two glass side doors gave the main entrance a deceptively large appearance. Once inside they found themselves only a few paces from a horseshoe shaped reception desk. Within seconds they were being ushered along a corridor towards the administration offices.

The sign on the door, written in gold lettering announced 'Margaret Cox, College Secretary.' Underneath was another less auspicious notice telling all and sundry to knock and wait. Jones obeyed the sign, standing like a nervous schoolboy outside the head's office.

'Come,' the voice had one of those accents which was difficult to place. Jones couldn't help wondering whether that was what Roedean girls sounded like. Probably just London, with a touch of the middle classes. He entered, Gray close on his heels. 'Good afternoon Miss Cox. I'm Detective Sergeant Jones and my colleague is Detective Gray. I believe you are expecting us.'

A clock somewhere nearby struck the hour. Miss Cox returned his gaze.

'Well it is afternoon now Mr Jones. Your timing is very precise. Would you care for some tea?'

'Thanks but no. We'll be getting our lunch shortly.'

'Very well. Please be seated and the perhaps you'll enlighten me as to the reason for your visit.'

Jones was used to creating pen portraits of people he met in his line of business. Some he would never forget. She was an impressive woman. The starched blouse, with its little black lace bow at the neck, seemed to be having difficulty containing her ample figure. The space between two buttons was being pulled apart and a small area of pink flesh was exposed. Once golden hair now peppered with grey, was immaculately groomed, as were the long slender fingers with their neatly trimmed nails. He tried to guess her age. Forty five, maybe. Not married either. Jones sat down as he was told. Gray sat next to him.

'We are investigating two murders which occurred not too far from here and my superiors feel that you ought to be warned about possible danger to your female students.'

'You're not suggesting that one of our male students may be the killer?' Her eyes held him with a directness that was impossible to avoid.

'Miss Cox. We're not here as part of an ongoing investigation.' It was as much as he could do, not to blush.

Gray cut in. 'We're worried in case this person strikes again and we need to impress on your young ladies how careful they need to be. They must not be allowed to go out alone or with strangers for the time being.'

'And how long may I ask, is that likely to be?'

Gray thought for a moment. 'Well, until we catch the killer. I would have thought.'

Miss Cox looked amused at his reddening face. 'Well, er, detective Gray, I think you said.'

'Yes Ma'am, that's correct.'

'I have in excess of five hundred young ladies living on these premises, on one side of a six foot barbed wire fence and a like number of red blooded males on the other. They are all strangers Mr Gray. Now what do you want me to do? Shall I get the ladies to a nunnery until your enquiries are complete?'

Jones interrupted. 'We already have two bodies in the mortuary and I don't need any more.'

Miss Cox switched her gaze.' Very well sergeant. In what way can I help?'

'I'd appreciate your co-operation in calling everyone to assembly at the earliest opportunity and then, either you or we, can address them and advise on security. I think I should also tell you that there's a Peeping Tom operating actively in this area.'

'Goodness me, Mr Jones, you have got your hands full. Would you like to be here tomorrow morning before nine? I'll have the entire population of Edge Hill waiting to greet you.' She smiled at him. But there was something in the smile which suggested that underneath the veneer of academia there still lurked a real woman.

'Might come here one day, myself.' Jones stepped into the car. 'Bet she could teach me a thing or two.'

'What would you study?' Gray was keen to know.

'Womanhood my dear Watson. Womanhood.' For the first time in days the tension was broken.

Deakin made his way to the car park. If anything important cropped up he'd soon get to know. Fifteen minutes later he arrived home to the enticing smell of lamb chops sizzling gently under the grill and surrounded by a ring of tomatoes and mushrooms. Next to them a pan simmered with new potatoes, while Deakin's favourite, bread and butter pudding, lay in wait in the oven. Laura greeted him with a quick peck on the cheek and a warning to keep clear of the kitchen, dinner was about ready to be served. He barely managed the headlines in the evening paper before dinner was ready. The man from the Telegraph flashed through his mind. *God knows what he'll get up to in his column tomorrow. Not a very nice character.*

Laura watched patiently as he prodded the chops. They were lean and tender. They were always lean and tender but he still had to prod them. She smiled across the table. He never let her down. Deakin was a creature of habit, except of course he didn't know it.

'Why would a woman, an ordinary woman like you?' He stopped, and started again. 'Sorry, I didn't mean it to come out like that.'

Laura laughed. 'Sam darling, I am an ordinary woman. Now what are you trying to say?'

He started again. 'Not from where I'm sitting. you're not. Hair permed, smart red dress, gold buckle. I don't know how you manage to do it all on a copper's pay. But you were never meant to be ordinary.' He felt sufficiently exonerated to continue. 'Anyway, let's leave that till later. What I wanted to ask was simply what might cause two ordinary women to go voluntarily to their deaths? What would cause them to more or less invite someone to kill them?' It was one of those rare occasions when he was so concerned about a case he was still working on that he felt justified in seeking an opinion.

Laura held her knife and fork steadily while considering the question.

'I can think of a dozen reasons why a woman might invite some person into her home during the daytime. But I can't think of a logical answer to why she should go to a remote place at night willingly, unless of course, she was having an affair, or maybe even being blackmailed.' She hesitated for a moment.' There's always the possibility that she had joined a lonely hearts club and didn't want a strange man to know where she lived on the first date.'

Deakin frowned. 'Do you think she would do such a thing so close to her ex-husband's new home?'

'Might have added a bit of spice to the occasion. Some women are capable of anything.' Laura continued with her meal, leaving him to think things through in his own way. Ten minutes later she walked into the kitchen with the empty plates and returned with the steaming hot pudding.

Deakin's eyes lit up. 'If they were all as ordinary as you, I'd still pick you anyway.'

'I don't know why you go chasing after criminals when you get away with murder all the time! You're just an old charmer.'

Almost reluctantly Deakin rose from the table. 'That was a great meal and by the way, you've got the job for life.'

'Job! Paid galley slave you mean. And don't forget, we're at Mum's tomorrow, so you'll be spoiled again.' Laura walked behind the armchair to tuck in a cushion at the back of his head. 'Ruined by women that love you.' She picked up her knitting bag and settled down on the settee. Mum's cardigan would have to be ready in time for her birthday no matter what. Plain white, cable stitch, warm pure lambs wool. Just the way Sally liked it.

Laura glanced towards Deakin. The newspaper lay on the carpet next to him while he slept soundly. Laying the knitting aside for a moment she crossed the floor and pressed a button on the television. Coronation Street was about to start. Settling back into her seat with the knitting, Laura looked forward to half an hour of idle gossip.

CHAPTER 12

The constant murmur of voices mingled with occasional loud laughter signalled the beginning of another long weekend at The Ram's Head Inn. By Sunday night the staff would be exhausted, the stocks depleted, and the world's politics sorted and laid to rest for another week. Life in the village didn't vary much though there had been an influx of city commuters in recent times. People enjoying success in business, life in the town, and the more sedate country style pleasures at weekends. The best of both worlds.

Keith Taylor glanced at his watch before walking into the hotel restaurant to book a table for two. The beamed ceiling with its imitation hanging lanterns gave the room a quaint and warm glow. A vibrant orange décor blended with a chocolate brown carpet added a touch of luxury. It was their favourite nightspot and perfect for the occasion. Tonight was special.

The restaurant manager, busy at his tiny podium checking and double checking the evening list of diners, looked up and smiled, holding out a welcoming hand in recognition of a good customer.

'Gooda evening Mister Taylor.' His strong Italian accent, bright eyes and broad smile seemed to have been designed specially to put even the most nervous person at their ease, at the same time guaranteeing to flutter more than a few female hearts. It was all part of his stock in trade and Janet just adored the way he fussed around her whenever they came for a meal.

'Hello Max. I need a table for a special occasion tonight. What can you do for me?'

Max broadened his smile, genuinely delighted they had chosen his venue. He had watched the relationship blossom over many months. He knew instinctively it wouldn't be long before it became permanent in every sense of the word. An intimate window table, a flower spray and a flickering candle would be far more appropriate than a dimly lit corner which might make it look as if they were trying to hide from the world.

'For you, my friend, everything will be very nice, I promise.' Max pored over the evening's booking chart. Table twenty one looked good. 'Eight thirty is a good time for you, I think, maybe?'

'Yes, of course. Thank you. See you then.'

Taylor walked back towards the lounge, stopping in the hallway to make a call from the public telephone, the last step in preparation for what he prayed would be a long and wonderful evening, a night to be remembered.

'Hello sweetheart, it's only me,' he paused for a second. 'Everything OK?'

The warmth of Janet's voice always made him feel good. He smiled as if she was already there, standing next to him. 'I've managed to book a table for eight thirty, if that's alright with you.' Of course it was.

'If you're late, I'll eat both dinners, and leave you the bill.'

The conversation was cut short by Janet's promise to get out of the house as soon as he got off the phone. She was almost ready to leave. Taylor was reluctant to hang up. 'It's not too late to cancel. I can call around with a take-away if you fancy a night in.' It was easy to picture Janet giggling on the other end of the line. There was a certain undeniable mischief in her voice.' See you shortly.' He hung up.

Squeezing his way to the already overcrowded bar Taylor patiently waited to catch the barman's eye. The arrangements were now complete and in a short while the unsuspecting Janet would walk into his little love trap.

'Bitter please.' A minute later he was silently raising his glass to the continuance of a long and loving relationship. Tonight was the first anniversary of their meeting. He wanted it to be memorable for more than one reason. Janet was special, a happy sensible young woman, with a sense of humour. A refreshing change from the growing cult of groupies and crazed, wildly dressed pop music followers. Tonight he was hoping to put the seal on their relationship.

Seated at her dressing table mirror, Janet Stone gently touched the tips of long eyelashes, putting the final touches to make-up which was hardly necessary but added something extra to the already soft, gentle lines of her features. Her rule was never to leave the house looking anything but her best. Womanly intuition told her that something special was about to happen in her life. She'd read it in her stars as well. 'Good news for Geminis,' the forecast had said. 'This week ends on a high note, particularly if you have agreed to a romantic meeting.' Janet read her horoscope every day, treating it as a bit of harmless fun, not to be taken too seriously. *I've got my romantic meeting arranged, so how's that for ending the week on a high note? Let's wait and see my girl.*

Keith was usually a pretty laid back sort of person, but there had been a faint touch of excitement in his voice, and it was the curious way he'd spelt out the timing of their meeting. Normally he would just say something like *See you when you get here, or I'll book the table when you arrive.* He definitely was just a bit on edge.

She emerged from her bedroom, looking as if she had stepped straight from the catwalk, in high heeled evening shoes and a pure silk shimmering dress with diamante butterfly broach. Janet knew she had that *look good, feel good factor* mentioned this week in *Woman's Own.* It wasn't only personal pride at stake but just as important that Keith should be proud of her as well.

She was about to reach for her coat when the phone rang.

'Double five two five.' Janet paused to discover who was calling. Maybe Keith had forgotten to tell her something. *If you're not Keith you can buzz off. No woman needs a lengthy conversation when she is about to go out for the evening.* Her voice and expression became tense, and business like. She listened intently.

'No, not tonight I'm afraid, I have to go out.' Janet hesitated, checking her watch. 'I'm late for a dinner appointment at The Ram's Head and I'm actually leaving the house right now.' The caller was not so easily put off. After a minute of persuasion Janet responded.

'What kind of car did you say? Thanks, see you in ten minutes then.' She replaced the receiver feeling annoyed at the intrusion. Tonight of all nights. Stepping outside into the cold night air, wrapped in a soft suede jacket, her final touch of luxury, Janet set off towards The Ram's Head. The first encounter should only last a couple of minutes. The second might just mark the beginning of something wonderful. She had a good feeling about it.

Most of the commuter traffic had disappeared. Quickly reaching the junction at St Anne's parish church she turned right towards Preston. Heading down the hill towards the by-pass she turned left on to a long straight stretch.

The sleek Austin Healey sports car swept on to the already crowded car park at the Ram's Head, headlights searching for a space. The car was her pride and joy, her symbol of success, not to be parked anywhere it was liable to be scratched or damaged. Janet avoided parking too close to other cars particularly when visiting pubs. After a few drinks people could be careless with handbags, umbrellas and walking sticks, or opening doors.

For a moment she hesitated, undecided whether to slip into the pub and announce her presence to Keith before the meeting. She clutched her handbag while locking the car door carefully. Three short headlight flashes attracted her in the direction of a car now standing in an unlit area. The driver had parked alongside the entrance to the beer garden. It was only open in the summer months when there would be coloured lights around the perimeter, with rustic benches and tables and candles floating in oil. Janet had visited it many times. She screwed up her eyes as she walked down the beam of light to the spot where the driver was standing. Shivering slightly in the cold night air she wondered whether it was a touch of nerves or just getting out of a warm car. *This meeting had better be quick. It was not the weather to be standing around.*

'I'm Janet Stone.'

The hand that gripped her throat gave no warning. Every woman's worst nightmare was coming true. An attack so sudden that resistance was impossible. Rape! Murder! She wanted to cry out but was unable to utter a word. The hand momentarily released its grip, as if to spare her life. For a split second Janet might have believed the assault was ended, as she leaned forward now struggling to breathe, to live. A powerful blow to the back of the head sent her reeling forwards and downwards. Blood gushed in a fountain spray from the fracture wound, saturating her fawn suede coat. Eyes locked, wide open, Janet's face took on a grotesque appearance as her matted, blood soaked hair, now became sullied with a mixture of dirt, oil, and surface gravel. Seconds later the assailant disappeared into the night.

Janet Stone was dead, and yet her lifeless body continued to make low moaning noises, as if refusing to die. The last air she breathed took its leave almost obscenely, refusing Janet any final vestige of dignity and being replaced only by a coldness which indicated the early signs of rigor mortis. The expensive jacket, no longer able to protect the wearer from the night air slowly discharged its unwanted cargo of blood. Brain and bone fragments clung to the pale green dress, creating a hideous mismatched pattern. Her watch had stopped, as she crashed to the ground, at eight twenty five precisely.

Taylor put the glass down on the bar counter, fumbling nervously in his pocket before pulling out a small leather covered box. A solitaire diamond, in a platinum setting, flashed brilliantly as it caught the glare of overhead lighting. God. He would die if she said No or didn't like it. But this was what surprises were all about wasn't it? Confidence slowly ebbed. He wondered whether to risk one more drink before she arrived. Staring at the lounge entrance, wishing Janet would walk through the door, he found himself fiddling again in his pocket, wanting to check the little box and its treasured contents.

'Glass of bitter, please.' The barmaid pulled at the pump handle. 'Late is she? If she's not here by closing time you can have me instead.'

He laughed at the idea, 'Might just keep you to that. If she doesn't turn up.'

Max walked briskly from the restaurant into the lounge, picking out Taylor for his personal attention. 'The table is ready whenever you are. Your good lady not here yet?' He looked around.

Taylor shook his head, unsure whether he was worried because Janet was late, which was unusual, or whether big night nerves were beginning to have some effect on him. 'Sorry about this Max. She did say she was on her way when I spoke to her about half an hour ago. Must have been delayed. She should be here any minute.'

'Don't worry my friend. I keep the table for you.' Sensing agitation he added;' She don't come don't worry. Plenty more fish in the sea.' He nodded towards the high stools along the bar and laughed. 'Some very beautiful fishes at the bar right now, eh?'

Taylor looked across at the group of women who had just arrived for a hen party. They were very loud. Everyone talking and no-one listening. Obviously some sort of office party. Maybe someone leaving to get married and enjoying a last fling. At least they sounded happy. 'Where are you?' He whispered under his breath.

At eight forty five Taylor's concern was beginning to deepen. His call remained unanswered despite the continuous ringing tone. It satisfied him for the moment. *Thank god you're on your way at last.* Staring long and hard at the entrance, he willed Janet to come breezing through it with her usual radiant smile. His hand strayed once more to the leather box, as if for reassurance.

Shortly after nine-fifteen a decision had to be made, either to order food or cancel the table. Last orders in the restaurant had to be placed by nine-thirty. If Janet turned up and had to walk into the room on her own, everyone would know she was late and that would be embarrassing. Suddenly he realised the significance of his thoughts. What did he mean by If she turned up? Why shouldn't she turn up? Surely there must be a simple answer?

Max appeared at his elbow. 'No lady eh?'

Taylor was no longer smiling. 'I'm worried Max, I think I'll have to go and look for her.'

Max frowned, realising for the first time that things were not as they were intended.

'Don't know where she could have got to. She told me that she was leaving the house over an hour ago and it's only five minutes away.' He searched the manager's face as if expecting him to offer an explanation. 'I'd like to give her another ten minutes and if she still hasn't arrived, I'll pop up to the house and make sure she's alright.' Instinct screamed at him to go to the house right now. It was only a few minutes away. But the fear of missing her somewhere en route held him back. It would be awful if she were to walk in and not find him waiting. Maybe she had met a neighbour or someone at the door and stood chatting.

'Don't worry, I keep the table till last orders.' Max was understanding. He'd known them long enough to appreciate their eating habits. Janet was never one for arriving late, certainly not this late. 'When she arrive, let me know and I fix something for you both.'

Taylor sat back, depressed, with the remains of a drink he no longer felt able to enjoy, any more than he could put up with the constant shrill noise of the all-female party. They seemed to be getting even louder. At nine thirty he left The Ram's Head, failing to notice the Austin Healey sports car, obscured by a van. Taylor drove directly to Janet's home.

Her car was missing. 'God, I hope you've not broken down and been left waiting for the RAC man to come.' That couldn't be the case, otherwise he would have seen her somewhere along the route. The house stood in darkness but he rang the bell anyway. It was more in hope than expectation. 'Jan, where the hell are you?' He spoke out in frustration. Pulling a crumpled envelope from his pocket, Taylor scribbled a note: 'Darling, waited till nine thirty. Gone home. Please call and let me know what happened. Love you, Keith.'

Pushing the note through the letterbox, he climbed into his car and drove back to the Ram's Head. There seemed little point drinking alone and his appetite had diminished. Leaving his car outside the entrance, he stopped briefly to apologise to Max for the cancellation. The all-female party was now in full swing, everyone chattering and no-one listening. Shrieks of laughter rang out. Taylor looked around the lounge for the last time. Still no sign of Janet. Max would have told him immediately if Janet had phoned the hotel. Taylor made his way home dejectedly.

At midnight, he rang the Ormskirk Cottage hospital. The receptionist was polite but uncommunicative. Nobody by the name of 'Stone' had been admitted or even treated for a minor injury. By one o'clock he had fallen asleep without having eaten and knowing what had happened to Janet. Taylor woke with a start calling out her name. He realised it was a dream. The phone stayed silent.

'Hello, 6283.' Deakin picked up the phone without switching on the light to try and avoid disturbing Laura too much.

'Jones, Chief. Sorry to trouble you but we've got another one on our hands.'

'Oh, Christ. No.'

'Afraid so, chief. Young woman down by The Ram's Head. You know the place. It's along the Burscough Road.'

Whatever Deakin's thoughts might have been when he answered the call, they were instantly dismissed, as he came fully awake, reaching for the light switch. 'Where are you now?' He might have known. 'Give me half an hour and I'll see you there.'

Laura rolled over, resting an elbow on the pillow. 'Can I make you a drink before you go?'

How many women would put up with this abnormal way of life and still be willing to get up in the middle of the night to make him a hot drink?

'You get back to sleep lovely, I'll be back in a couple of hours.'

Switching off the bedside light he vanished, carrying a jacket, tie and shoes, leaving Laura to try to get back to sleep. Within minutes he was on his way. Deakin knew the Ram's Head quite well as a popular public house with an excellent reputation for its food and beer. It was an old country inn, laden with character, a short drive from Ormskirk on the Preston Road. In the summer time they opened a beer garden at the side and rear which was proving popular. The small snug was still very much a private members' club reserved for the elders of the village. Strangers would be very quickly frozen out. However, it now boasted a modern restaurant with an excellent standard of cuisine. Laura enjoyed the occasional meal and clearly enjoyed the fuss made by the Italian manager. They probably would go more often if it weren't so crowded at weekends.

The blue flashing lights of the Incident Unit stood out against the darkness of the night as he approached the car park. Temporary lighting was still being erected by some of the murder squad team at the far corner. As he came to a standstill, Deakin was able to see Harry Jones standing with the remainder of his team.

Red and white warning ribbons surrounded the area where the body lay. Jones was busily organising a fingertip search of the lighted zone and at the same time trying to keep the wider area intact until dawn. Only then would they be able to carry out an inch by inch search of the area. He already had yet another team securing the patch of ground at the rear of the public house in case any poachers were wandering in the vicinity. It was another area which might produce something useful in daylight.

'Sorry to drag you out Chief but I knew you'd want to be here.'

The pub customers had left the area hours ago but a small group of young men, probably from The Hesketh Arms, had stopped on their way home out of curiosity. They were becoming noisy. 'Been an accident has there, constable?' someone shouted. They looked like a bunch of students from the Edge Hill college with their long trailing scarves and regional accents. He sometimes wondered if they just came here to learn about drinking.

'Move that lot away sergeant.' From Deakin it was a polite and simple order that called for instant obedience.

Jones left the forensic team and walked across to the group. 'Any of you lads see anything happen here tonight.' There was a general murmur of 'No.'

'Right, off you pop then. There's nowt here for you lot.' He stood his ground as one by one they moved away, still muttering. 'Keep moving lads unless you want to be out all night.' Their noise drifted slowly down the road.

Turning his attention to the body, Deakin knelt down to take a closer look. Despite her dreadful appearance, made worse by the onset of rigor mortis, he could see that she had been a good looking young woman. He estimated her age in the early thirties. There was something precise about the remains of her mascara and make up which told him she was a woman who had paid attention to detail. 'What is it?' He looked up.

Jones, though tired and worried, was not a man who gave in to his emotions in the middle of an investigation but Deakin couldn't fail to notice the strain of recent times was now beginning to creep up on him. They could both do with a rest, but not yet.

'Notice the similarities with the Wilson, and Donovan cases and this one, chief? We're looking for a maniac alright. The same one for all three.' He continued to stare down at the body knowing that one day he would surely come face to face with the person who took the life of this once pretty woman. Jones never used the word *maniac* lightly. The enormity of the problems now looming would hardly bear thinking about.

Deakin studied the wounds to the back of the head. There were also the tell tale marks on the throat, just as they had been with the others. A wide pool of blood, both around and beneath the figure, was sufficient to confirm that death had taken place on the very spot where she lay. Most certainly, she had not been brought to this place and dumped. 'Identification?' he enquired.

The sergeant didn't need his notebook. 'Janet Stone, 15 Victoria Road. There's someone on the job there now chief.' He was a good sergeant, and would deserve his promotion, whenever, if ever, it came to him. Somehow he always kept himself busy on days when promotion was under discussion.

'Hello Sam, we've really got to stop meeting like this.'

Deakin recognised the voice, and nodded his recognition.

'Hello Doc, looks like more of the same I'm afraid.'

Hayes knelt down next to him and opened his black leather Gladstone bag, reaching inside for his surgical gloves. Deakin moved out of the way to make more room for him. After a few minutes the pathologist climbed to his feet. 'Got ourselves a madman alright.' The tone in his voice left no room for error. 'Cause of death without doubt the blows to the back of the head. And the strangulation wasn't necessary.' Having already checked the body temperature, he glanced at his watch before making a swift calculation.

'Time of death probably between eight and nine o'clock last night.'

Deakin looked at him and then towards Jones before posing the question. 'Why would any woman walk to the darkest corner of an unlit area, and almost invite someone to kill her? A private argument perhaps, maybe starting in the pub and ending out here?' A much more troubling thought was already forming in his mind.

Jones intervened. 'We found a set of keys close to the body and they fit the Austin Healey parked near to the entrance. She might have been meeting someone on the car park, leaving her car behind, and going off somewhere else.

'Possibly, but then she would have known her assassin.' Deakin had to keep an open mind. Why did this woman walk across the car park to the darkest corner? The thought seemed to be lodged in his brain. Surely she would never have taken such a risk for a complete stranger? 'Or be cajoled into doing something she would never normally do. No sign of a fight, or even a scuffle. No robbery. Keys on the ground, and she was dressed for a night out.' He stroked his chin thoughtfully. 'This lady had plans and somehow they were thwarted.'

Hayes was about finished with his electronic notebook. He turned towards Deakin. 'I'll be off now Sam. See you towards lunchtime at the mortuary.' He'd forgotten it was Saturday until it was mentioned. 'I'll come in anyway. This is important and I've got nothing special on this weekend. See you later.'

He walked quickly to his car without a backward glance.

The photographer stood waiting to see if there were any further instructions. Deakin wanted a picture of the car park from the point at which the Austin Healey was parked to the spot where the body was still lying. He also wanted an exact measurement of the distance walked by the victim before she was struck down.

Jones was the first to break the silence. 'We've got two others who seem to have behaved in a similar manner, so what are we saying now? That they all have something in common? A divorcee, a drunken divorcee and this one.'

'Excuse me sir.' The young DC stood respectfully alongside Deakin.

'What do you want lad?'

'We've traced the car and it belongs to a Miss Janet Stone. She lives about five or ten minutes away.'

Jones' theory was being blown apart. But he had another idea.

'Maybe something as simple as a lonely hearts club.'

Deakin sighed. 'You been chatting to my missus?'

CHAPTER 13

The pathologist was still engaged in the final stages of the examination when Deakin arrived. There was never a good time to visit the mortuary. He looked around at the impressive array of stainless steel neatly and precisely set out. Used instruments, bloodstained scalpels, bright steel probes and saw blades waited in a sterile solution to be fully decontaminated before they could be used again. A bag marked 'Soiled gauze' lay next to them, sealed and ready for the incinerator. Once more, he found himself having to fight the feeling of nausea.

Glancing over the top of half rimmed gold magnifying glasses, Hayes nodded, without interrupting his dictation into an overhead microphone. It seemed to be hanging by a thread above the stainless steel table. Deakin could only stand and admire not only the way the pathologist went about his work, but particularly his great care and respect for the deceased.

The autopsy came to an end, with one final comment, as he removed his surgical gloves. 'Make sure this report is typed and delivered as soon as possible. It is very urgent. Thank you Elizabeth.' He switched off and turned his attention to Deakin.

'Do you ever sleep?'

Deakin shrugged. It was a question he had been asked many times over the years. 'If people only committed murder at ten in the morning on bright sunny days, you and I would probably be redundant. Thanks for checking this one so quickly. I do appreciate it.' He waited for the pathologist's observations on his examination. There was something, but probably not what he wanted to hear.

'Cause of death is beyond doubt. Brain damage due multiple skull fractures. The back of her head was smashed like an eggshell. She was hit with tremendous force.' The staccato sentences seemed to add weight to his remarks.

Deakin had no need to take notes. But he listened intently to the pathologist, already knowing, or guessing, much of what he was about to be told. He was still hopeful of that something extra, which, on occasion, Hayes was able to produce.

'Time of death around eight thirty last night, now confirmed.' He waited in case Deakin had a question. 'No sign of recent sexual activity, and no violence other than to the head, face, and throat. Contents of the stomach indicate a partly digested snack, probably about four thirty. No alcohol in the bloodstream.'

Deakin interrupted. 'She definitely never came out of the pub then? More probably never went into it, so what the hell was she doing on the car park?'

He stared at Hayes as if expecting him to answer the query.

The pathologist carried on. 'The marks on her face were, without doubt, caused as she fell to the gravel surface. Not the slightest indication of resistance and no skin under the nails; no knuckle bruising. For the avoidance of doubt, I am sure this is the work of a psychopath. It's not a domestic killing. Whoever did this must really hate women, all women.' Hayes found himself looking straight into Deakin's eyes. There was not the slightest sign of a flicker, no room for doubt.

'This report is almost identical to the others that I prepared on Catherine Wilson and Mary Donovan. Thumb marks on the neck of each one of them indicate a left handed person, someone very powerful, and in each case crushing blows delivered by the right hand, holding a blunt instrument, like a round steel bar of some description.' Hesitating only to gather breath he concluded, 'Only a psychopath would violently confront women in this way, without apparently intending rape, or even torture, simply death.'

Deakin knew he was right but it was a hard pill to swallow. Murder without motive has always been the toughest test for any detective. Deakin, however, believed that nobody kills without reason, no matter how improbable that reason may be to an ordinary sane person. Sooner or later it would become apparent, then he would have his day. Hayes might be endlessly involved in searching for medical and scientific evidence but Deakin had to find the killer. Each of them was locked into his own brand of investigation and both in a common cause.

'How does he choose his victims? Random or selective?' Deakin was thinking aloud. 'Once we solve that little conundrum, we'll know where to start looking.'

'Any ideas?' Hayes was curious to know what the detective could possibly have in mind.

'I don't know but maybe a salesman of some sort or a debt collector.' Deakin was well aware how many theories end up in a waste paper basket

'Possible, I suppose.' Hayes nodded. 'Thought about calling in a criminologist?'

Deakin had heard it all before. It was like grasping at straws. Killers always make mistakes, no matter how much they plan or how carefully. His job was to find the mistakes and too much talking was as bad as too little.

'No disrespect to any criminologist but I already know a lot about the character we are looking for, and I'm not so sure whether background speculation will take me much nearer to finding him.'

The two men stood facing each other. The victim lying between them was the only person who knew all the answers but couldn't tell.

Deakin pondered over the idea. 'Might try one meeting just in case we've missed something.' The discussion came to an end. There was nothing more to be said at the moment.

Jones was already waiting when Deakin got back to the office. 'We've found the boyfriend. Shall we go and see him or do you want him brought in?'

Deakin kept his coat on. 'Let's go.' The two men walked out of the police station and got into an unmarked, dark blue, Ford Cortina GT. To an unpractised eye, it was a smart, sleek looking car The only clues to its real identity lay in the standard issue police radio built into the lower half of a dashboard packed with instruments. There was also a portable blue flashing light clipped to an inside panel, ready to be jammed on to the roof should a chase become necessary.

Their route was via the High Street and between rows of busy shops. Neon signs seemed to be springing up all over the place, in bright gaudy colours, giving the town centre a bright and lively, if American, appearance. Sales and promises of huge reductions invited people into every store. The butchers shops, and grocers had their own style of white, hand painted window advertising, which had to be washed away and rewritten every morning to suit the moods of an increasingly demanding public. A set of traffic lights loomed ahead, marking the end of the main street.

Deakin looked out of the passenger window, wondering whether he might get a glimpse of Laura coming out of one of the department stores. Occasionally, when he was out on a job, he would catch sight of her, scurrying about, always on the lookout for bargains. Shirts, ties, socks, cufflinks and handkerchiefs filled his wardrobe in silent tribute to her shopping tenacity. He smiled to himself. She was a good one.

Ten minutes later, they swerved on to the forecourt of a block of privately owned flats. For a brief moment, the two men stood and admired the completely unbroken view across the hills towards Parbold and Ashurst Beacon. In the distance they could see barges chugging their way along the canal towards Preston Brook and cars climbing the hill on the far side of the valley. Somewhere behind them, a tractor could be heard grinding its way round a field.

'These look like a good investment,' Jones commented. 'Nice outlook.'

Deakin was not so impressed. 'Not much of a one for flats really. I'd rather have my privacy. It's worth the extra. Wouldn't mind the view, though.'

The lift doors opened allowing the two men to step out into the second of three floors. Facing them was a long, narrow, white walled, corridor, fully carpeted in high quality Wilton, and complimented by subdued overhead lighting. It had an air of peace, and decorum. Each white painted front door carried a brass number plate and matching brass doorbell with small nameplate inscribed with the surname of the occupier.

Jones looked along the corridor. 'Fancy coming home to this place after a night out with the lads. You could end up in anyone's flat. They're all the same.' He read the nameplate alongside the front door. 'Taylor! This is him.' He pressed the button and waited. From somewhere inside the property the sound of tubular bells could be heard giving out their melodic warning. But no-one answered the door. 'Friedland. Latest thing in novelty door bells.' He rang again as if to demonstrate its pleas-ant features. There was no reply but within seconds a head appeared as if by magic from the flat next door. An elderly lady, wrinkled but still powdered and rouged, looked the two men up and down before deciding whether to bother speaking.

Deakin took the initiative. 'Good afternoon madam. Do you happen to know whether Mr Taylor is out shop-ping? If so, what time's he usually home?' He gave her his Max Bygraves smile.

The woman stared hard before deciding that at least he looked honest. 'Mr. Taylor works on Saturdays till about six o'clock. But you'll need to be quick if you want to catch him. He's in and out again to see his young lady over the weekends.'

Deakin stepped a little closer as if to take her into his confidence. 'Don't suppose you know where he works?'

The old lady smiled. 'Yes I do actually he sometimes comes home in one of the company vehicles and it has the name painted on the side.'

Deakin waited patiently, breathing in her lavender water. Then the answer came.

'Can't remember the exact name but it's a plastics factory on the other side of the valley, near the power station. Something to do with 'Sun Visors' or something like that.'

He returned her smile. 'Thank you madam, You've been a big help.'

She stood her ground. 'Anything I can do?'

The last thing Deakin wanted to do was discuss murder with an elderly lady. 'No thank you. But I'm most grateful for your help.'

The Ford Cortina cruised its way comfortably across the winding country road towards a water tower in the distance. Eventually they reached the entrance to a small industrial estate. Jones got out of the car to study the board where the names of the companies on the site were displayed. 'That'll be the one,' pointing to a name. 'Super-Visors,' and in brackets underneath, 'Specialist Plastic Injection Moulding.'

'How appropriate. If you excuse the pun.' Deakin permitted himself a wry smile as the Cortina moved on towards its destination. There were only a handful of vehicles on the car park and no-one on duty in the white walled, open plan, reception area. A brass bell standing on the reception desk had a small card propped against it which read 'Please ring for attention.' Somewhere in the distance Deakin could hear the buzzing noise, and a few seconds later a man appeared from the rear of the reception area.

'Can I help you gentlemen?'

Deakin spoke first. 'Would it be possible to speak to Mr Taylor?'

The man seemed unimpressed. 'May I ask who wants him?'

'Yes, indeed. I'm Chief Detective Inspector Deakin, and this gentleman is Detective Sergeant Jones.'

'I'm Taylor, perhaps you had better come into the office.'

The two detectives followed him into a sparsely furnished office, containing only the barest of necessities and obviously not intended for board meetings. A large desk covered in technical drawings, and surrounded by three upholstered commercial armchairs on castors just about filled the room. No pictures adorned the walls; just skeleton outlines of various commodities in plastic.

Keith Taylor sat down opposite the two detectives, waiting for one to speak.

'Do you know a Miss Janet Stone?' Deakin watched him closely.

'Oh God, don't tell me she's had a smash' The words shot out. He corrected himself and toned down his local accent.' I'm sorry. Yes of course I know Janet' We've been keeping company together since last summer.

Deakin studied the man now facing him across the desk, as if to confirm an opinion already forming in his mind. Clean shaven and smartly dressed in a jacket, shirt, and tie, the uniform of middle management, he looked to be in his middle thirties. A slim but powerfully built man, around six feet tall, with light brown hair, neatly combed, and a pleasant though serious face. Nothing that might suggest he was anything other than what he seemed. No sign of nerves or agitation.

'Mr Taylor, I'm sorry to be the bearer of bad news but I have to inform you that Miss Stone is dead. And, it is my unpleasant duty to have to make enquiries into the circumstances surrounding her death.'

There was no way of avoiding or even trying to water down the truth. The fact was simply that Janet Stone was dead and not by accident. He allowed a moment for the information to sink into Taylor's brain. The face before him turned pale, lips tightening. Grey, bloodshot eyes glistened.

'Dead?' The voice was reduced almost to a whisper.' What do you mean? An accident?' That local accent was back and thicker than ever. 'We were supposed to meet for dinner last night but she never arrived. I went to look for her, even rang the hospital, but she just didn't turn up.' His head now sank into his chest as he struggled to maintain some dignity.

Deakin gave him only a moment's respite. 'It was no accident Mr Taylor. Your friend was found dead in a corner of the car park of The Ram's Head during the early hours of this morning.'

Taylor looked on the verge of collapse.

Jones leaned towards him. 'Can I get you a drink or something?'

The man was too distraught to answer and just stared ahead.

Deakin had to override his natural sympathy and pity. This was never going to be easy. 'Just for the record, would you mind telling me where you were last night between say eight and ten?'

Taylor shook his head as though trying to clear it, and get some sense into the situation. A terrible thought seemed to strike him. 'Surely to God, you don't think I killed her?' Deakin interrupted his tormented thoughts. 'I don't think anything at the moment but it is very important that you answer my question.'

Though Taylor looked at him, he failed to focus. 'I went to The Ram's Head to book a table for dinner at about eight o'clock and then phoned Janet to confirm that everything was OK. She told me that she was almost ready to leave and we were supposed to meet at eight thirty. Like I said, she never turned up and eventually I went to her house around nine thirty to see if something had happened. She wasn't there. I left her a note and then I went back to The Ram's Head, cancelled the table and went home. Later on, I even called Casualty at the cottage hospital.'

Jones cut in. 'When you spoke on the phone, how was she?'

'She was on top form, Sergeant, laughing, giggling; she had a great sense of humour, you know.'

Jones didn't know but accepted the answer anyway.

The importance of the words which he had just spoken seemed to finally dawn on Keith Taylor. He could hardly believe that he had just consigned Janet to history. He'd said 'She was' when he ought to have been saying 'She is'.

Jones broke into his thoughts. 'There's a gap of about fifteen minutes which is all we need to cover really.'

Deakin decided it was time to terminate the interview. He stood up and offered a friendly hand.

'Mr Taylor, we'll need to speak with you again and one of my lads will have to take a statement from you shortly. I trust you'll be willing to make yourself available?'

'Of course. Janet was the best thing that ever happened to me inspector and now she's been taken away.'

Reaching into his pocket, he pulled out the small leather box. The solitaire diamond in its velvet case had never got the chance to work its magic. At last the tears came. Holding his head in both hands, Taylor sobbed uncontrollably.

The two detectives walked outside, hardly noticing the twinkling lights now springing up across the walls of the valley. The red warning light at the top of Parbold Hill stood out like a homing beacon. Dusk was beginning to close in all around them.

Deakin posed the question, 'What can be purer than the driven snow? What do we really know about Miss Stone?' Then correcting himself, 'More likely it's what we don't know about her that's more important.'

The Cortina engine roared into life, shattering the silence of only a moment ago. Jones slipped it into gear.

'The lads have been to her house and made some local enquiries. I understand she never married, yet obviously enjoyed the company of men. It seems that she was courting strongly some years ago but gave it up to nurse a widowed mother. She seems not to have bothered much until about six or eight months ago when she met our friend Mr Taylor.' He waited for questions. 'Has a brother somewhere but no-one seems to know anything about him. Taylor will probably volunteer to be her next-of-kin if we can't find anyone else.'

Deakin now interrupted. 'Younger or older brother?'

'Younger, I think. He wandered off after the death of the mother and only kept in touch occasionally. I've got someone trying to trace him.'

'Anything else?'

'Not really Chief; she was a cashier with the local Building Society, with a good reputation for honesty and integrity, an excellent timekeeper and seldom absent. But that was only obtained by phone.'

Deakin grunted with dissatisfaction. 'Why would anyone want to kill the perfect woman?' He glanced again at the sergeant. 'That's what you are telling me; isn't it? She was the perfect woman. Wasn't she?'

The Ford Cortina cruised back across the valley towards the distant lights of Ormskirk. Deakin decided to take another look at the exact spot where death had occurred. 'Do you mind? Only take a minute.'

Jones nodded, and turning left on the edge of town drove straight to the Ram's Head. It was almost dark when they arrived, and the section of the car park reopened to the public was already full. An officer stood on duty at the edge of the crime scene. He recognised the chief inspector and saluted smartly. 'Evening sir.'

'Hope you're not thinking of sneaking in there when we've gone, Constable?'

'Very tempting sir. But I can resist it.'

Deakin looked around the car park, before gesturing. 'She parked over there,' indicating a lighted area. He turned about. 'And she walked to that place, which is in total darkness.'

Jones was well aware of the situation but failed to see any particular significance. 'Where does that take us?'

Deakin persevered. 'If she was meeting someone she knew, then why not park near to them? We know that this is the least used area because of the lack of lighting and the beer garden isn't open in the winter. Wouldn't it be easier to park here than to drive into one of the other spaces alongside the wall, and then have to walk all the way across?'

Jones was still at a loss to follow the logic of Deakin's mind.

'Think about it. She parked against the wall, near to the entrance, because she was intending to go into the pub, which fits with what Taylor said.'

'Supposing she was already in the pub and came outside with someone?'

Deakin dismissed the suggestion. 'There were enough people in the pub who knew Taylor and Miss Stone. If they were together, then Taylor is in serious trouble. I think she stopped to speak with someone she could never have been able to identify at that distance, and in darkness.'

Jones stared at him, still not convinced. 'Someone who knew she was on her way to the Ram's Head. It still could have been Taylor then? Only two people knew she was going to be here, Taylor and Max, the restaurant manager.'

Deakin ignored the discouraging remark and hurried on. 'It's not a random killing sergeant. It's selective.' He sounded almost relieved. 'If it was random, then she would have been attacked getting out of her car, not forty or fifty yards away in the opposite direction to the pub entrance.'

The two men climbed back into the Ford Cortina and headed towards the police station. Deakin settled back in the passenger seat deep in thought. At times like this Jones was wise enough not to disturb him. Something else would now be gnawing away in the back of Deakin's mind to be revealed when he was ready.

'You look tired sergeant. Get yourself off home and have a rest.'

Jones needed no second invitation.

Deakin had a couple matters which needed attention.

Sergeant Lloyd was at the desk when they arrived.

'Haven't you got a home to go to either?'

He smiled at the chief. 'My wife and daughters are out shopping today. Doubt if I have still got a home to go to. They've probably sold it'

Deakin managed a grin. 'Don't know why I'm asking you. I don't even know if I'll get in tonight.' Something else was niggling away in the back of his mind.

Chapter 14

Laura heard his key in the front door and turned to greet him. The welcoming smile froze. She stared in disbelief. Deakin could sometimes be a little forgetful if he was busy on something important. But this was ridiculous.

'Sam, I know you're run off your feet but for God's sake.'

'What's the matter. What have I done? I'm not even in the house yet.'

'You were supposed to collect Mum three quarter's of an hour ago and bring her here for dinner.'

'Oh God, I'm sorry love. Completely slipped my mind. I'll go now.' A look of genuine alarm spread over his face. 'Hope I've not spoiled the dinner. Will you give her a call and say I'm on my way, please?'

Laura stood in his path. 'If you're really that tired, Sam, we can cancel mum for tonight, or I'll go and fetch her and you have a rest.'

'Not at all. She'll be sitting on the edge of her chair. I'll be as quick as I can.' Neatly side-stepping Laura he headed for the door. It was as much a damage limitation exercise as anything else. 'Back shortly.'

Laura watched him drive away before returning to her chores. There was still plenty to be done. She turned the heat down leaving the potatoes to simmer. Next there were the roast potatoes in the oven and the lamb to check. She picked up a knife and began to chop the fresh mint. She liked to put a teaspoonful into the peas, saving the rest for mint sauce. Things were beginning to move along nicely again.

Deakin knew nothing of the wildly negative thoughts that went through her mind when he was late. Occasionally he had to visit people to inform them of the sudden death of a loved one. Her worst nightmare was that someday it might be her turn for such a visit. It wasn't just about being forgetful, late, or even a dinner being over cooked. It was about her state of mind. Policemen didn't seem to be commanding quite the same respect these days, as they did when she was young.

'Hello Mum.'

The old lady leaning rather heavily on her stick, stood to greet him. 'Hello Sam. Thank you for picking me up but I could have got a taxi, you know.'

He laughed at the idea. 'Two drivers in our house, and you want to call a taxi. Being a bit extravagant aren't you?' She accepted the outstretched arm, still using the stick to prod at the floor. He made sure the door was shut and locked before leading her to the car. Climbing into the front seat, Sally was delighted to be able to spend a few moments alone with him.

'Bought you a little present today.' She sounded a bit coy.

It was easy for him to play her little game, waiting to see what was in store.

'Mum, I keep telling you not to waste your money on me.'

Opening her handbag, Sally produced a small parcel, neatly wrapped. She thrust it into his hand 'Not very extravagant, I'm afraid.'

'Do you want me to open it now, or at home?'

'It's yours. Do what you like with it.'

He opened the small package before starting the engine, then kissed her lightly on the cheek. 'Thanks Mum, just what I wanted, a reminder of my dubious past.'

Sally beamed her satisfaction as he examined a porcelain model of a policeman, complete with helmet and truncheon. 'Thought you might like it.' She settled back. Sally loved the front seat.

'Takes me back some years,' he said wistfully. 'They were good days, Mum. Thank you.'

Arm in arm the couple walked into the house, Deakin praying that Laura was not still out of sorts with him. She had already seen them through the kitchen window, laughing together.

'Look what Mum bought us today.' He handed over the ornament.

Laura looked at it. The price tag was still on the base.

'For goodness sake Mother, he doesn't deserve it. You almost didn't get here tonight.' She glanced at the little ornament again, casually peeling the label from under the polished boots. 'Might have taken the price tag off it.'

Sally smiled back at her. 'Don't suppose he would have noticed anyway.'

'No mum, there've been a few things he's missed lately.'

Deakin quickly retreated to the safety of the dining room looking for some spot where his new image could stand. Throughout dinner he remained preoccupied with more important matters. Both women knew the signs well enough and made their own allowances. The conversation finally focused on holidays.

'Sam and I were thinking of taking the car down to the South of France and staying at a place called Frejus. It's not far from Monte Carlo and Nice. It's supposed to be very good. We hope to rent one of those new static homes.

They're like caravans except much bigger and without the wheels.'

They had already reached an agreement about holidays for this year. Later in the year they would get to spend some time alone. The holiday home was big enough to take six people so baggage really wasn't a problem. Mum was no trouble at all. Deakin had always treated her as if she were his own mother anyway.

'Now don't you two start worrying about me again. I'm fine, just get on and enjoy yourselves. I only slow you down when we're all out together. In any case you need a break from me. It'll do you both good.'

Deakin tried to reassure her, but Sally was having none of it. 'Maybe when you come back we could manage a weekend in the Lake District. You know that's my favourite place.'

Laura interrupted. 'Tell you what Mum, there's no need to rush, we'll delay the bookings for a week or two in case you change your mind. We can take you to the Lake District any old time. Compared with the South of France, it's only around the corner.'

By ten o'clock Sally was ready for her bed. Deakin now had the task of running her home and making certain the house was secure before leaving.

'Want me to come with you for company?'

'No. You can start the dishes if you like and I'll give you a hand when I get back.'

'Don't forget to come home this time.'

Deakin soon had Sally home and settled for the night. No matter what, she couldn't go to bed without a cup of Horlicks. He waited patiently and made sure the cooker was switched off the minute the milk boiled.

'Don't bother coming to the door Mum. I'll lock it on the way out and then I know you're safe.'

Ten minutes later he was back at the house and in time to catch the late film. 'The Loneliness of the Long Distance Runner,' starring Michael Redgrave, and Tom Courtenay. He recalled seeing a couple of years ago at the cinema with Laura, but was happy to watch it again in the comfort of his own home.

Laura looked up from her crossword puzzle, interrupting his viewing. 'There's a clue here I just can't get.' She paused to make sure he was paying attention. 'Tamper with a lordly racehorse, six letters.'

Deakin barely moved his gaze from the screen. 'Try nobble.'

Laura looked at the puzzle and started to giggle. Everything was back to normal. Ten minutes later he was snoring. His coffee had been left to go cold, and the film was now without an audience. Laura closed the doors on the TV cabinet before waking him and coaxing him into getting himself to bed.

Sunday dawned without any emergency phone calls, and Laura was able to get herself ready undisturbed before calling for her mother, and taking her off to church. Deakin was messing about in the shed sorting out fishing tackle, before going down to the canal. It was only for half a day but he enjoyed it, and he had some thinking to do.

'Lunch at three OK with you?' Laura asked him, knowing perfectly well that it would be fine.

Deakin nodded his approval. Half an hour later he was at the canal bank, and seated in his favourite spot. Still in winter clothing, he was prepared to face the cold of early morning. Armed with two flasks of coffee and a large umbrella, Deakin began to set up his rod for the first cast of the day. A hundred yards or so upstream he noticed Reflections still at its mooring down by the old bridge.

Jack Donovan had been free to move on for almost two months now but had insisted on staying local as long as possible in the hope of seeing Mary's killer caught. Apart from accompanying Mary on the journey to her last resting place in Mallow in Southern Ireland, he hadn't budged from the area. It was late morning before he showed himself and spotted Deakin along the towpath. He waved an acknowledgment and shortly afterwards walked down to pass the time of day.

'Good morning. Not just catching fish, I hope.'

Deakin smiled. 'Hello Mr Donovan, how's things with you?' He sensed that an opportunity to question him was about to be seized. Progress on the case was slow. The team was still busy cross checking statements against information already received. It was all a process of elimination. Laying his rod to one side he stood up to face him. Despite all he had gone through in recent times and having to bury his ex-wife in Ireland, Donovan looked to be in reasonably good condition. Possibly due in part to the relaxing nature of his surroundings.

'Sorry to take up your personal time Mr Deakin but I was wondering if there'd been any new developments.'

Deakin shook his head. 'I'd like to be able to give you some good news but our enquiries are still ongoing. We're doing the best we can. But I promise we'll get to the bottom of it no matter how long it takes.'

Donovan seemed satisfied with the response, given in a civilised and friendly manner. 'Thanks. It's hard just sitting and waiting day after day, not knowing what's happening and not being able to do anything about it.'

A thought came into Deakin's head. 'If you want to help, think about what Mary might have had in common with two other women who she never knew or met. However small the link, it was enough to get her killed.' He watched. 'I'm not sure I should be telling you this, but we are looking to see whether there have been any similar murders elsewhere outside our patch in case there's a wider pattern forming.'

Donovan looked puzzled. 'I wouldn't know where to start with that one. Mary picked up friends and dropped them on an almost daily basis but they were mostly the same drinking fraternity.'

One thing was certain. The killer was no habitual drunk. Deakin turned again to Donovan. 'Was she in some sort of lonely hearts club or a member of some oddball group?' He felt almost ashamed at having to ask the question, but was also certain that there had to be an out of the ordinary sort of answer.

'I think it's safe to say that Mary had no hobbies or interests in recent years. No interest in men whatsoever, although after a few drinks she'd talk to anyone.' He added; 'After the divorce I had very little contact with her. She was always after more money and I knew she just wanted to drink herself into oblivion. I suppose it's possible she formed some sort of association I don't know about. But I doubt it.'

Deakin listened carefully. 'I'm not looking for a drunk. I'm looking for someone who knows exactly what he's doing and plans it very carefully.'

'Care for a coffee?'

'I want to do some fishing and I'm expected home for lunch. I'd better not.' The two men parted company. An hour later it was time to put away the tackle and make tracks for home.

Laura laid the table while Deakin showered and changed. Mum was lunching with the senior citizens today at the church hall. They had prospect of spending an afternoon and evening alone. 'You never know girl. You just never know.' She started laughing to herself.

Deakin took his seat and started to prod away at the lunch. 'I investigated your theory. The one about the lonely hearts club.'

'And what happened?'

He grinned at her. 'Well let's put it this way; don't give up the day job.'

'At least it was worth a try,' she said.

CHAPTER 15

The tiny, one bedroom flat, was located at one end of a poorly lit passageway on the first floor of an old terraced property. A cheap attempt had been made to create a galley kitchen in one corner of the living room. Hardboard sheets pinned to a wooden frame barely managed to hide an old gas cooker and porcelain sink with its wooden draining board and single brass cold water tap. The bathroom and toilet, at the other end of the passageway, were shared by mutual consent with the other tenants. But, whatever its shortcomings, it offered Katie Hopkins, and her offspring Michael, a precarious foothold on an independent way of life. It was their kingdom.

Close to the junction of Wigan Road and Moor Street, Ormskirk, the house was no more than ten minutes walk from the town centre. For Katie it meant a start, and everyone has to start somewhere. She wasn't complaining. Things could always be worse. But she was determined to make the most of her opportunity.

Baby Michael looked in the direction of her voice. 'One day my little bunny, you and I are going to live in a palace, with servants, and lots of money.'

She smiled down at him, at the same time thanking God he had no apparent resemblance to his father. 'Wonder if those eyes will stay blue for ever? Hope so.

Don't want you looking like him, do we?' The baby's lips parted as if he were about to give her a broad smile. The sharp blue eyes sought out her face. Was he really smiling? Or was it just wind? Katie looked proudly down at the gentle, gurgling little form. 'Come on Bunny,' she cooed at him. 'We've got things to do and places to go, today.'

With the baby safely tucked into his buggy, Katie left the flat and set off along Wigan Road towards the town centre. Within minutes she turned into Derby Street West, stopping several times, but only to window gaze. An abundance of mini-skirts gazed back at her, and in one shop a selection of micro-minis was enough to almost take her breath away. 'Now there's some real fashion if you've got the money.' She looked in another window, immediately spotting some baby-doll pyjamas. Katie sighed to herself as she pushed the buggy away from the window and moved on towards her destination. 'One day soon, maybe.' She bent down to adjust his woollen bonnet. 'You'll buy me nice things, when you grow up. Won't you?'

Mother and son continued past the end of the row of shops and began to enter the business area. Number 81 was an early Victorian building. Modern brass plates welded to enormous pillars on either side of the entrance listed the occupiers and their professions. Overhead, a larger single sign simply said Imperial Chambers. Katie looked down the list and found what she was looking for. Howard Phillips and Partners, Solicitors, 3rd floor. 'This way, bunny. Wonder if you'll be a solicitor when you grow up.'

Michael gurgled his own happy response.

The concertina gates on the old lift banged noisily as they slammed shut, leaving it to whine and groan its way to the third floor. It wasn't the most pleasant of rides. Dragging the gates open, Katie breathed a sigh of relief, almost rushing into the corridor, pushing Michael before her. She walked nervously towards a door marked Reception. Having to face a solicitor and pour her heart out was an embarrassing and daunting experience. But matters needed to be dealt with and Katie was not about to duck the issue any longer. 'I've an appointment with Mr Phillips,' she said to the receptionist.

'Miss Hopkins. is it?' the receptionist smiled at her. 'Eleven o'clock. I'll tell him you're here. Take a seat please.'

Katie sat down, pulling Michael reassuringly close to her in his buggy. She heard her name mentioned on the phone, and look towards the desk.

'Mr Phillips will be with you in a couple of minutes. He says, if you like, we'll mind the baby while you're talking to him. Might make things easier for you. She smiled again, stood up and walked across to the buggy. Michael gurgled at her. 'Blue for a boy eh? What's your name little man?' Michael garbled his response. The phone rang. 'Mr Phillips is ready now.' She opened the office door and stood between Katie and the buggy. 'He'll be fine. If not you'll probably hear him anyway.' She ushered Katie through the door.

Katie had no idea whether to sit down or shake hands or what the protocol was. Howard Phillips stood up to greet her and offered a large welcoming hand.

'Let's start at the beginning, shall we?' he said. 'Just tell me what you want and why you need to have it and we'll see what can be done.'

It seemed all too simple. Katie blushed. Mr Phillips sounded competent and reassuring. There was no doubting that. *He must be familiar with cases like mine. Must see them all the time. Does he know how embarrassing it is for me though?* 'I met this lad last year.' Her voice suddenly dried up and she began to croak.

'Would you like a glass of water, or perhaps a warm drink?' Phillips was well used to dealing with nervous clients.

'No thank you. I'll be alright in a minute.' Her mind went back instinctively to that first meeting with Martin Richards, and his awkward attempts to impress her. A tall young man, slimly built and with a shock of light brown hair, being three years older than herself, he seemed anxious to display the extra knowledge he had gained, which he believed had taken him from youth to manhood.

'His behaviour was pretty normal at first.' Memories, which she had fought to repress, began to crowd back into her brain. She could feel her hands beginning to tremble. She wanted to lift them in front of her face and hide. 'We dated a few times but I suppose I always knew it was going nowhere. He was too pushy, too domineering.' Katie thought for moment, trying to get her facts into the right order. 'Also, I soon found out he had a jealous streak and that worried me.'

Did she really have to tell the solicitor about the way Martin would try to take over her conversations with friends, constantly bragging, and making offensive remarks, before dragging her away? How much did he need to know? Steeling herself, Katie felt her nails dig into the palms of hands now tightly clenched.

'I told him to stop interfering between me and my other friends and stop showing off all the time. He took no notice. He never took notice of anything I said. After a bit, I just couldn't take any more.' The truth was she had tried to end the relationship in a quiet and friendly manner but Martin was having none of it and simply ignored her requests for a cooling off.

'I decided to call it a day and told him it was over. At first he was angry but I suppose I half expected that. Finally it dawned on him I really meant it. Then he started calling at all hours of the day and night.'

She broke away from her story for a moment to explain about the phone; coin operated, and located on the ground floor in the hall, it was for the benefit of all the tenants, with absolutely no privacy. 'It was a nuisance because people on the ground floor were always shouting for me to come down and answer the thing. I told Martin to stop calling. He took no notice and began to annoy everyone in the house. Finally I had to threaten him with the police.'

She recalled only too well that her complaint was treated extremely casually. The officer simply took the view that it was a couple of youngsters quarrelling and they'd soon make up.

'When did you first visit the police station?' Phillips interrupted her flow.

'That's easy,' she said, rooting through her handbag. After some rustling and shuffling, she pulled her hand out like a magician with a rabbit and produced a diary. The pages flicked over exposing the daily events of the relationship. She had even noted her distress at having to face the other tenants and apologise for the inconvenience being caused to them by his bizarre actions.

'It really got me down. Finally I wouldn't answer any more calls. I was praying he'd give up and go away. But, not long after that he came round to the flat. I answered a knock on my door and found him standing there. One of the other tenants must have let him in.'

The memories of that night still haunted Katie, but somehow she had to find the inner strength to bring everything out into the open, if ever she was to get her life back on track.

'He said he knew I had another man in the flat and barged his way in. He threatened to kill him.' What happened next would remain with her for the rest of her days. 'He grabbed hold of me and dragged me into the bedroom. I tried to push him away. He punched me with his fist, full in my face. I fell backwards across the bed and he began dragging me around by the hair, pulling at my clothes and hitting me in the stomach and chest at the same time.'

Tears began to roll down her cheeks as the awful memory of that night came back in all its graphic detail. Phillips offered her a tissue, watching as she dabbed her eyes. He delayed matters until he was certain Katie was able to continue.

'I'm sorry,' Katie sobbed. 'But it was horrible.'

'It takes a great deal of courage to relive an experience like the one you've described, particularly to a complete stranger. But now it's in the open we can start to put things right for you.'

'I didn't mean for that to happen.'

'Don't worry. You're doing very well.'

'There was blood everywhere. My lip was split. That only seemed to excite him even more. He was like a madman. I thought he was going to kill me.' She paused for a moment to gather her thoughts, and then chose her words carefully. 'He stopped hitting me.' Katie hesitated again, not knowing how to finish the sentence.

Phillips spoke up. 'I doubt whether you're going to tell me anything I haven't heard before, but I need to hear it from you, otherwise I could be accused of putting words into your mouth.'

Katie looked straight at him. 'He ripped my dress and my underwear. Then forced himself on me.'

She wept openly. 'You see, I'd never been with a lad that way before. But there was nothing I could do to stop him. I thought I was going to die.' At last it was out in the open. She had spoken to someone about it for the very first time since that terrible night.

Thank god Michael can't understand any of this, she thought to herself, and then, dabbing gently at her eyes, she went ahead. 'He behaved like an animal, and afterwards, got up and just sneered at me, saying I was his and no-one else wanted me anyway.' She recalled his warning that he'd be back and she'd get more of the same, whenever he felt like it. 'I soaked myself in the bath for ages. I just couldn't get rid of his smell. I was still sitting there after the water went cold.'

What the solicitor must now be thinking of her? Would he understand how, for a long time, she blamed herself?

'I was too frightened to go to the police again. I'd heard stories of what happened when other girls complained about being assaulted. I thought about leaving the area. But where could I go with no money and no job? Going back home was out of the question. My stepmother would have made a meal of it.'

'The problem was sorted for me. I'd had indigestion for weeks. I thought was nerves. because of everything that was happening in my life. I wasn't able to eat or sleep properly.' The next part of her story was embedded in her mind forever. 'I dosed myself with all kinds of things, but nothing seemed to help, so I decided to take myself off to the doctor.' She stopped briefly. 'For a while, finding I was pregnant kicked the bottom completely out of my world. It was like I was being punished. All these thoughts were inside my head. How was I ever going to stand the shame of being an unmarried mother? Where would the money come from? Where would we live?'

Phillips nodded kindly.

'I had peace until after Michael was born. Then it all started over again. Martin trying to pretend to be a proud father was just a joke. It was another way of getting at me. That was the last straw as far as I was concerned.' The whole story had now tumbled out, even the most intimate detail, and she felt a tremendous sense of relief. There were hidden reserves of strength left in Katie Hopkins, as Martin Richards was about to find out.

Phillips picked a set of Legal Aid forms out of a tray and handed them to Katie. 'Sorry to trouble you with these, but even I have to get paid, you know.'

Katie signed the forms, handed them back and waited.

Phillips picked up his Dictaphone, speaking rapidly. 'Open a new file, Hopkins versus Richards. We act for Kathleen Hopkins, the plaintiff. Mark it Urgent, Domestic Violence.' His instructions were fairly simple and straightforward, given with a quiet air of confidence. The work on Katie Hopkins case had started in earnest. 'Phone the Area office for an emergency Legal Aid Certificate, and get a hearing date for an Interim Injunction from the court.' He turned to Katie with a reassuring look.

'We'll call you later this afternoon and see you in court tomorrow. Your case should be in the twelve o'clock list. You know where the courts are?'

Katie had never actually been inside a courtroom in her life but she knew of the Law Courts. They were near the station, in the town centre.

Phillips explained briefly that emergency applications were dealt with during breaks in routine cases or by judges who were not actually sitting in open court. Temporary Injunctions, he went on to explain, were frequently awarded by the court pending a full hearing of the complaint and it was not unusual for anyone breaking the Court Order to be sent to prison, which usually turned out to be the best deterrent of all.

'See you tomorrow then Miss Hopkins.' Phillips stood up and shook hands, following her outside into the reception area, where Michael was enjoying the full attention of everybody in the typing pool.

'Good-bye, and thanks very much,' Katie pushed Michael back to the lift.

Phillips picked up his intercom. 'Phone Mr Bergman and ask him if he can call round and collect the summons as soon as I can get it issued. It should be ready just after lunch, so he'll have all day to call on Richards. It's important that we get it served as soon as possible.'

Katie crossed the road and walked back down the opposite side of Derby Street West, heading towards Wigan Road once more. For the first time in ages she stopped outside The Music Box. Huge posters of the Beatles, The Who, and The Rolling Stones gazed down at her. Katie looked at Michael and sighed. 'Maybe not a solicitor, eh? Looks like these fellas are making a fortune.' She smiled wistfully to herself. 'One day little Bunny. One day.' But he was already fast asleep.

Back at home, Katie left Michael to sleep while she prepared his bottle, saving a drop of warm milk to soak into a little rusk. He was nine and a half pounds when born, and already looking for something more than milk. During the afternoon they both rested. The tension which had built up inside her was now releasing itself and being replaced by an overwhelming feeling of tiredness. The room gradually descended into darkness. It was dusk when Michael woke with a gentle whimper. Katie jumped up quickly, not knowing the time, but relieved to see it wasn't yet six o'clock. Within a few minutes he was pulling hard on the teat of his bottle. She left him propped against a pillow while she made herself a cup of Nescafe. She had already got into the routine of eating her evening meal after he was bathed and ready for bed.

A voice called out. 'It's for you Katie,'

Checking to see that Michael was safe, she ran down the stairs and picked up the receiver. It was Richards. This time Katie had some confidence. For a minute she was tempted to boast about him having to be in court tomorrow but thought better of it. He probably wouldn't turn up anyway. She decided on another ploy. 'I've been to the police again today and taken out a summons against you. They're coming to see you tonight and I'm going to tell them about this call as well.' Banging the receiver back on to its cradle, she went back upstairs, being careful to double lock her door, just in case he was stupid enough to try again. Katie had no sooner lit the gas under the kettle, than she was called to the phone again. Now she was angry. She stormed down the stairs, and grabbed at the receiver. 'I'm ringing the police right now, and I'm going to ask them to lock you up tonight.' She stepped back in horror, hardly recognising the sound of her own voice, and deeply embarrassed. The voice on the other end of the line wasn't his.

'Sorry if I frightened you Miss Hopkins.'

Blushing deeply, she explained about the previous caller.

'Don't worry, we'll put a stop to his tricks tomorrow. Sorry to be ringing up so late but it is very important. Now if you will be kind enough to meet me at eleven thirty, we'll have time for a conference before meeting the judge.'

'Alright Mr Phillips, I'll make sure I'm there.' Replacing the receiver more gently, as if continuing with her apology, Katie then ran back upstairs to Michael. Lifting him carefully out of his cot, she kissed him. 'This is our Kingdom, little Bunny. We rule here.'

CHAPTER 16

A single track overhung with dense foliage provided a well disguised rear entrance to Edge Hill Teacher Training College. Pascoe parked his car on Ruff Lane and walked along the pathway until he reached a clearing from which he could see into the Eleanor Rathbone hall. The camouflage was ideal. No-one at his back, and plenty of long grass ahead. He settled down to wait.

The sound of voices nearby broke his concentration. They came nearer and louder. Pascoe turned on his side and curled into a ball, pretending to be asleep. If they spotted him, it would look like he was a tramp sleeping in the woods. The receding autumn light worked in his favour. The young couple, arms locked around each, faces almost touching, passed almost within touching distance without noticing his presence. The voices stopped a few yards ahead. Raising his head slightly, he was able to see them more clearly. They were kissing.

Pascoe watched as the young man began to unfasten the buttons on the girl's coat. His hand moved underneath her sweater then upwards to her breasts. She kissed him harder as he massaged her gently. They bent down together and stretched out in the long grass to the side of the path, oblivious to their unwanted guest.

Pascoe's excitement mounted. Determined to see what was about to happen, he raised his head even higher, oblivious to the risk, The girl was on her back while the boyfriend lay face down, snuggling up to her. Now she was seeking him out. At the same time his hand moved downwards. Pascoe had never been this close-up before. He could hear every word.

'You do love me don't you?' Her voice was trembling

'Yes, of course I do.' He sounded breathless.

'We are going steady, aren't we? I mean, I wouldn't do this for anyone else you know.'

Pascoe guessed what was coming and steeled himself not to make a sound.

'Grown up aren't we. So do it for us. You know it's what we both want.' He was trying to sound confident.

Pascoe stared as if mesmerised while the girl arched her back and the final garment was removed. The young man impatiently shoved her skirt further upwards.

Pascoe could contain himself no longer. The warm wet sensation on his leg was telling its own story as the pair began to make love in earnest.

'Oh God darling. Tell me you love me. Please.'

'Course I do. Is it good for you?'

'It's wonderful.'

Minutes later they fell apart, exhausted.

'Do you still love me Charles. I mean, you haven't lost your respect for me. Have you?' She sat upright.

Pascoe flattened himself into the long grass.

Charles remained confident. 'I've already said I love you. What else do you want me to say or do?'

Suddenly she was in a hurry to dress herself and re-gain her composure. Now standing, she put her arms around his neck, kissing him passionately. 'Tell me you love me again.'

Charles put his arm around her waist and began to propel her away from the scene. 'God, how many times do I have to tell you?'

Pascoe's excitement only abated when they were out of sight. No photographs, no binoculars, but that wasn't important this time.

Joy waited until after ten o'clock but there was no sign of Pascoe. She decided to go to bed and made her way upstairs. Supper was on the table for him if he wanted it. Shortly after eleven he arrived. After a couple of minutes she heard his footsteps on the stairs. Fear gripped her. She could smell the alcohol before he got anywhere near.

'Don't crack on you're asleep. I know yer' not.'

She didn't answer.

'Look at me when I'm fucking talking to you.' Grabbing her by the shoulders, he forced Joy to face him.

She felt herself being dragged towards his side of the bed.

'My fucking wife aren't ye'? Know what that means do ye'?

She knew better than to respond when he was in drink.

'I'm entitled to have you any time I fancy. Like now.' He pulled her legs over the end of the bed before forcing them apart. The minutes that followed seemed like hours as he forced himself into her and persevered in his drunken way. 'Fucking useless bitch.' He pushed her to one side and climbed into bed. In no time he was snoring.

Joy slipped out of bed quietly and made her way to the bathroom. Tears streamed down her face. 'Can't take much more of this. I'll have to do something about it,' she sobbed to herself. But what? Eventually she found her way back to bed, praying that sleep would come soon. At six thirty she was downstairs making his breakfast. Pascoe came down late and seemed unusually angry. Joy never questioned him. She knew better.

'You seen my wallet anywhere?' he snarled

'No. You know I don't touch your things.'

Ignoring her reply, he searched the dining room, then the kitchen. 'Oh Christ!' He left his breakfast on the table untouched. Picking up his donkey jacket, he walked quickly out of the door, slamming it behind him.

Pascoe's car made the journey to Ruff Lane in minutes. Parking once more by the single track, he jumped out and hurried towards the spot where he had lain the previous night. Suddenly he spotted the black leather wallet half covered in the long grass. Breathing a sigh of relief he bent down to pick it up.

'What you doing 'ere mate?'

For a moment Pascoe panicked. But it wasn't a policeman. It was a security man. *Must have seen me coming towards the women's buildings.*

'Er, nothin' pal.'

'Don't you know you're trespassin? This is private property.'

'I was doing a spot of rabbitin' 'ere yes'day, and lost me wallet. So I come back to look for it and 'ere it is.' He waved it.

'I have to warn you not to come again. Trespassin' is a criminal offence y'know.'

Pascoe began to feel confident. 'Arright mate. I heard yer' He turned and walked back down the path. The security officer followed at a discreet distance. Pascoe got into his car and drove quickly away from the scene. But not before his registration number was noted.

Once out of sight, he breathed a sigh of relief. *Need to be more careful else I'll be gettin' collared. Better get a move on, else I'll be late for work. Should just make it with a bit o' luck.*

Lunchtime couldn't come soon enough. Pascoe hurried down to The Lion.

'Pint o' bitter an' two cheese cobs.' He never said *please* to anyone. No words of welcome or acknowledgment were exchanged between customer and barman. A couple of two shilling pieces were shoved across the counter. There was no change and no tip. He took a bite, nearly choking as someone brushed past him, catching his elbow.

'So sorry,' the voice said.

Pascoe had never heard her speak before. She sounded real posh.

'Arright.' It was all he could think to say.

'Hello John. The usual, please.' She was smiling at the barman.

'Hello Mrs Topping. I'll bring it over in a moment.'

Pascoe could smell her scent. It was powerful. He turned away from the bar. His eyes followed the woman, step by step into the lounge. She sat down at her usual place. She seemed to be staring straight at him. He quickly averted his gaze. *Stupid bastard. It's the barman she's looking for to let him know where she's sitting. What the bloody hell's up wi' me today?*

He watched as the barman poured a glass of Nuit St. George, then raised it to the light to ensure there were no particles of cork floating around, before taking it into the lounge. 'There you are Mrs. Topping. Can I get you a sandwich?'

'Thanks John but I'm alright for the moment. I daren't eat anything. I'm going to dinner with a friend later.' She handed over a ten shilling note. 'Help yourself to a drink.'

The barman took the note. 'Thank you very much. I'll get your change.' He headed back to the bar.

Pascoe watched the whole performance. *If only you knew what I know. You wouldn't be sitting there smirkin' all over yer face, with that fancy drink. I'll sort you out later missus.* He looked up at the clock behind the bar. *Time I wasn't here.* Swilling the last of the drink in one gulp, Pascoe put the glass down on the counter and walked outside.

The security officer at Edge Hill was completing his incident report before going off shift at two o'clock.

'Everything OK.?' The relief man enquired. It was more of a greeting than an actual question.

'Tell you the truth I'm not so sure. Spotted a fella. Early this morning it was. Looked like a tramp, except he had a car. He was nearly at the back of The Eleanor Rathbone block. Said he'd been rabbiting last night and lost his wallet. Came back this morning and found it.'

'What's wrong with that? Sounds OK to me.'

'Well, I took a look around after he'd gone and no snares had been set anywhere in that area. Used to do a bit m'self once. Know what it's about.'

'D'you reckon he'll come back?'

'Don't know, but you'd best keep an eye out. Just in case.'

Pascoe was torn between two choices. Taking another look at Mrs Topping or going back to Edge Hill, risking the security. He felt sure that the young lovers would be back. They were both enthusiastic. Might be an easy target or even the back of the Eleanor Rathbone at a push. It was doubtful he could fit both in during the evening. There wouldn't be enough light for that. The boutique lady won. He could still smell her scent and it excited him.

The phone rang in the CID office. Gray picked it up.

'Good morning. May I speak to sergeant Jones please?'

It was a familiar voice but he just couldn't place it for the minute.

'Sorry, he's not here at the moment. Can I take a message and get him to call you back?'

'Is that detective Gray? This is Margaret Cox from Edge Hill.'

'Yes ma'am. It is.' Gray was embarrassed to find her powers of recall to be sharper than his own.

'I thought it was. Perhaps you will be good enough to tell Mr Jones that we had an incident here the other day which might interest him.'

'Certainly ma'am. I'll get him to call you the minute he arrives.' Gray replaced the receiver. *Wonder if maybe she's got a bit of a crush on our Harry. Wouldn't be surprised. She was looking at him a bit funny. She's nice though.*

Jones knocked and waited.

'Enter.' It was the voice of authority.

'G'morning Miss Cox. Hope you don't mind my calling. Thought it might save you having to go through everything twice.'

'Most considerate of you sergeant, and Good morning to you too. Please take a seat and thank you for being so prompt. I just hope I'm not wasting your time.'

Jones had already made up his mind. It was a Somerset, possibly Devon accent. It didn't matter which. She still sounded like a lady. He looked a bit sheepish. 'That depends on what you have to say. But I'm sure you wouldn't waste your own time and I did say you should call if anything happened.' His mind was diverted for a moment. *Wouldn't mind wasting a bit of time with you on the back seat at the Roxy some Saturday night.*

'Care for a cup of tea sergeant?' Without waiting for an answer she reached for the phone. 'Helen, can I have tea for two please? Thank you.' It was ordered before he had the chance to refuse.

'A curious incident was reported yesterday but only came to my notice this morning. I apologise for any delay.'

'That's alright, Miss Cox. I wouldn't expect you to drop everything unless it was serious, of course.' His mind was again temporarily diverted. *On the other hand miss.* The very thought could get him into trouble.

'No sergeant. It may be something and nothing. I just thought you ought to know. One of my security officers came across a tramp in the woods at the back of the Eleanor Rathbone hall yesterday morning. He challenged the man who then said that he had been poaching on the previous evening and dropped his wallet. He said he had come back in daylight to look for it and indeed had found it.'

'What did the security man think?' Jones needed to know.

'Well, my man was really astute. He followed the tramp out of the woods to Ruff lane and was surprised to see him getting into a car.'

'It may not be too unusual for a poacher to have a car. Don't suppose it was a new model anyway.'

Miss Cox was not finished. 'Ah. Yes Mr Jones. But, you see, the security man knows something about snaring rabbits. He went back and searched the area but could find no evidence of poaching, and in fact, no rabbits anywhere near the place.'

'Don't suppose he got the registration number of the car, did he?' Miss Cox seemed to be warming to the challenge but was stopped in her tracks by a knock on the door.

'Enter,' Her voiced sharpened slightly. Helen came in with a tray of tea.

'Thank you.' She turned back to Jones. 'Shall I play mother?'

Jones nodded. *Thank God for an in-house detective.* 'Er, Yes please. Have you got the vehicle details to hand?' It was easy to see that she was enjoying her cameo role. She was almost teasing him. Playing with him. *I wish.* The thought had crossed his mind more than once.

Miss Cox handed him a sheet of paper. The detail was already neatly typed and signed by the security officer. Jones read it through. *Wouldn't mind having you on my team anytime.* A faint smile crossed his lips.

'Something wrong Mr Jones? No spelling errors I hope.'

'Not at all. Just a passing thought.'

'Dare I enquire what it was about.

'Well, if you must. I was thinking, I could do with a few more like you on my team. The report is very impressive.'

'I'm always open to offers, Mr Jones. Provided of course the salary is commensurate.'

I bet you're on more than our chief constable. Jones thought better than to speak his mind. He came to his feet. 'Thanks a lot. I enjoyed the tea and our chat. I promise we'll look into it very soon but if anything else crops up in the meantime please call me, day or night. I really don't mind.'

'I have a feeling that may be sooner than you think sergeant. Womanly intuition you know.'

'So long as it's in a good cause, I'm happy to oblige. Thanks for your time. I really do appreciate your efforts.' He didn't know what else to say. *Was she really coming on to him? It felt like she was. Maybe we'll get to the Roxy yet. If not, somewhere more comfortable.* Somehow he knew that next meeting wasn't going to long coming.

CHAPTER 17

There was always a damned queue waiting to squeeze in and out of the narrow entrance to the huge court complex. Howard Phillips waited his turn to claim a spot in the irritatingly slow rotating doors. A warm draught of air greeted him as he stepped into the reception area before starting the climb up the wide spiral staircase to the first floor. A barrage of signs and notices left no-one in doubt as to the route to their final destination. As he passed the entrance to the Court Restaurant the smell of fresh brewed coffee drifted into his nostrils. But he resisted the temptation and continued to follow the signs for the District Judges Chambers. Phillips stopped outside an immaculately polished oak door. The nameplate in gold lettering bore the name His Honour Judge Henry Swift. Beneath the title was an illuminated message: Now in Session. Do not enter until the green light shows. A bright red light acted as a secondary warning.

The Judge's Chambers, comprised furnishings which matched the light oak panelling set against a lush royal blue carpet. A large oak desk with matching table set against it to form a 'T' shape occupied the centre of the room. A miniature law library suited to his expertise lined the walls. The idea was to be able to dispense law without the need for ushers or official court attire. Occasionally, if the contest required more than six or seven people to attend, the judge would move the venue to one of the vacant open courtrooms, and declare it to be a Chambers hearing, to protect the element of privacy and informality.

In the waiting area, small circles of padded seats in groups of six were located outside each chamber. These afforded no privacy, only uniformity. Declaring his presence to the receptionist, Phillips chose an empty circle. Carefully, he placed his file of papers on the seat next to him and his coat on the opposite side, ensuring as much privacy as might reasonably be expected. He checked his watch. The case was due to be heard in about ten minutes. No time for coffee.

From his briefcase Phillips pulled out his copy of the Times crossword. It was a few days old but that didn't matter, because he rarely completed it anyway. Katie Hopkins was due any minute and there would be a couple of protocols to run through. At eleven forty-five he asked the receptionist to broadcast a call for his client, and a minute later he could hear her name resounding throughout the building. It was possible that she had got lost between the Crown Courts, County Courts and the District Judges. This often happened and sometimes caused havoc.

'Where on earth have you got to, young woman?' Phillips whispered under his breath. He stared into the distance, willing her to come into view.

The case was delayed for fifteen minutes. But eventually he had to face the judge, without his client being present. The first thing he had to do was offer an apology and make it clear that the client was fully aware of the fine detail concerning the hearing arrangements. The second was to seek the judge's indulgence.

Deciding to try and plead for the injunction, despite the absence of his client, Phillips put his case. On rare occasions it was possible to make such a plea, but the circumstances had to be special, often calling for affidavits of evidence to be produced in support of the application.

Judge Smith looked sympathetically at the solicitor. 'A very convincing argument, Mr Phillips, and I have no doubt, a very worthy cause.' He hesitated only for a moment, a slight smile seeming to cross his lips.

Phillips knew the old fox was on to him and waited.

'But, Mr Phillips, I have only one concern, and I'll tell you what it is.' He put his fingertips together as if in prayer. 'How are you going to positively identify your client to me?' Leaning back into his red leather armchair, he waited.

The lawyer fully understood the judge's position. 'I apologise for being unable to comply with your request. Of course if my client had attended.' He shrugged his shoulders. 'Well what can I say?'

The case was adjourned sine die, but with permission for it to be reinstated on twenty four hours notice. It was a fair decision and the best that could be made given the circumstances.

Howard Phillips knew when he was beaten but it had been worth a try. The judge also respected the fact that he was fighting hard for what he believed to be a good cause. Once the formal Legal Aid documents arrived, Katie would have to produce evidence of her income which would include any Social Security payments, and they in turn would include her National Insurance number which was acceptable as proof of identity. In any case, once in court she would be under oath and the judge could easily satisfy himself as to who she was. In the meantime, she could be anyone.

He returned to his office feeling slightly deflated. Katie Hopkins needed help. He was certain of that. He had had faith in this young woman and it looked as if she had just let him down, without any attempt to explain herself. He stopped in the reception area. 'Miss Hopkins never turned up at court this morning. Has she called in sick or left a message?'

'No, sir. No calls or messages for you.'

'Thank you. If she rings put her through right away.'

As he walked into his office he hardly noticed the mountain of post and documents awaiting his attention. Making space for the 'Hopkins' file he reached for the phone. 'See if you can reach Miss Hopkins on the phone for me.'

The switchboard reported no answer from the number they had for her.

Staring at the closed file in front of him, and wondering what had gone so wrong in such a short time, was worrying. If he were to believe his client, then she was at risk. Phillips had known cases where victims of violence had been held prisoner to prevent them from getting to court. Years spent in the legal profession had helped make him a pretty good judge of character and Katie Hopkins had impressed him with her sincerity and obvious determination to defend her baby whatever the cost. On impulse, he reached for a sheet of paper and scribbled a note. *'Dear Miss Hopkins, I am concerned about your non attendance at court today and shall be obliged if you will kindly contact me as soon as possible so that I can make new arrangements to go before a judge. I hope this note finds yourself and Michael well. Sincerely yours etc.'*

Signing the note, he folded it and put it into an envelope addressed to Katie. 'Get someone to take this round to Miss Hopkins flat right away please. Tell whoever goes to make sure that the address is correct and that she gets this letter in person.'

Within fifteen minutes a call came to the office from the payphone in the hall of Katie's home.

'Sorry, Mr Phillips, but I can't get an answer.' There was a pause, before the messenger added; 'Curious thing is,' he hesitated again, 'I think I can hear a baby crying inside. But there's no letterbox for me to look through.'

'Young man, stay where you are. I'll get a policeman to call. Ring me back as soon as you find out what's happened.' Alarm bells had already begun to ring in Phillips' head. He was well known at the local police station and for many years had enjoyed good relations with the desk sergeant, Tom Lloyd. 'Is Sergeant Lloyd on duty?'

'Is that you Mr Phillips?'

Phillips frowned at his own stupidity. 'Sorry Tom. I just wasn't paying attention. Wasting no time on pleasantries, he said; 'I have a client with a young baby, and she didn't turn up in court this morning. My clerk can't get an answer but says he can hear a baby crying inside. There's no letterbox for us to look through.'

'Give me the name and address and I'll get someone round there straight away.' He listened for a moment. 'The name rings a bell. I think she was in here recently. I remember the young woman coming to the desk, and seeing an inspector. We sent a couple of beat men to a local man's flat to warn him about the complaint.'

'Thanks Tom, I'm obliged to you. I'll wait for your call.' Satisfied he had done his best, all he could do was wait to find out whether his concern was justified. It was a while since he had felt so strongly about a client's domestic welfare; a clear indication that Katie Hopkins had made a deep impression on him.

Michael Hopkins was definitely not a cry baby; not without reason. What started as a whimper now began to reach a wider audience. The sight which confronted the two officers as the door burst open, under pressure from a powerful pair of shoulders, was bizarre. A small baby lying in a cot, stared towards the ceiling, crying loudly. He stopped the instant the strangers came into his view, looking at them with babyish curiosity.

Katie Hopkins lay a few feet away from the cot, her face half turned, eyes fixed in horror, it seemed, on the kitchen. A wide pool of congealed blood surrounded her head and shoulders. Walking carefully to the right hand side of the body and looking closer, the officers could see that the back of her head was shattered, leaving a black gaping cavity exposed through matted hair.

The young law clerk gazed at the scene for only a brief second before a wave of horror overtook his senses. A normally ruddy complexion turned to ashen grey, while his voice seemed to be jammed somewhere in the back of his throat.

The older officer stepped in front of him. 'Stand back son. Don't come any further into the room. This is a crime scene now.' He sent his partner hurrying back to the police car to report the situation to the CID office. Tom Lloyd took the call, noting the exact time, one forty five.

'Sarge,' the patrolman blurted out, 'the woman's dead. We broke in and found her dead, on the floor. She's been murdered. Head's been smashed wide open.'

Lloyd cut him short. 'Make sure you don't touch anything. Make certain no-one else gets into the flat, no matter who they are.' He was well aware that news-hounds frequently tuned in to the police radio channels, sometimes arriving at the scene of crime before the murder squad. Putting a finger on the phone cradle to cut off the caller, Lloyd cleared the line before calling the CID office.

In Katie's building, the law clerk come out of the toilet, grim faced and still trembling with shock. He made his way to the telephone in the entrance hall. His boss needed to be the first one to hear the news at the office.

Phillips immediately said, 'Get yourself off home, young man, and have a rest, but under no circumstances discuss what you have seen with anyone.' After warning the clerk that he would need to give a statement to the police at some stage soon, he replaced the receiver. The phone rang again almost immediately. This time it was sergeant Lloyd.

'Sorry Mr Phillips, I think your client has died.'

Phillips knew better than that. 'I think you mean my client has been murdered. Miss Hopkins was seeking an Injunction against a man called Martin Richards, on your inspector's advice. It seems Richards had beaten and raped her previously and is a pretty nasty character.' He added, 'I'm not sure whether I'm helping, but at least it's something.'

Lloyd knew about the assaults but was certain rape had never been alleged. He had young daughters of his own. It was something he would have remembered.

'No,' said Phillips. 'She was too embarrassed and frightened to mention it at that time, especially in front of other men.'

Lloyd had heard the same comments before. A growing number of women seemed to be complaining to the press lately about the indignities they had to suffer when making a complaint, particularly of a sexual nature. He replaced the receiver on its cradle, thought for a moment, then picked it up again. 'Message for DS Jones. When he arrives, ask him to have a word with me about this Hopkins matter.' He turned to the young constable standing in front of the enquiries desk. 'Where's the bloody tea then lad? Get your skates on. Don't just stand there. We're not in Madame Tussauds.'

Within the hour Richards was arrested on suspicion of murder as he was about to walk into the bookmaker's shop on Derby street. Despite his fierce protestations, he was brought back to the station and left locked in a cell until everything was set up and ready for that all important first interview. The verbal denials on his arrest now counted for nothing. Two hours of solitude had given him time to think. Time to create an alibi perhaps. Time to plead provocation, possibility even diminished responsibility.

It was four thirty in the afternoon when Harry Jones walked into the interview room, meeting Martin Richards for the first time. He knew the man's track record, which included petty theft, but more importantly, two counts of actual bodily harm. Richards was a violent thief by nature. Jones didn't like that. Two pairs of uncomfortable wooden folding wooden chairs faced each other across a small bare topped table. Despite the scant furnishings there was still hardly enough room for the brace of burly detectives and their prisoner. The hunched figure glared defiantly at the two men opposite.

'Your full name Martin Richards?' Jones' voice was curt.

'Yeah'.

Jones caught a glimpse of bad teeth. 'I'm Detective Sergeant Jones, and this is Detective Constable Gray, and I think you know why we're here.' He looked him over for a brief second. Sharp featured, Richards was wiry and slim. His clothes were ill fitting and in need of washing. 'You do know why you're here, don't you Richards?' The lack of response, prompted Jones to continue. 'You have been arrested on suspicion of the murder of Kathleen Hopkins. That's what we are here to talk about. It is my duty to caution you and remind you that you do not have to say anything, but anything you do say will be taken down and may later be used in evidence.'

The word 'murder' seemed to jolt Richards into life. Shock and fear gave an intensity to red edged eyes. At last he spoke. 'Dunno what you're talking about. I never fucking killed no-one. I keep telling you busies but no-one wants to listen. You can't have no proof 'cos I didn't do nothin.'

'Richards.' Jones almost spat the word out. 'We've already had you in here once for hurting that young girl, and it's a matter of record that you threatened to kill her more than once. So don't lie to me.' He glanced down at the file of papers which Tom Lloyd had sent through to him. 'Were you in court this morning?'

Richards looked surprised. 'Me, no, I wasn't in no fucking court.'

Jones closed his fingers tightly into the palm of his hand.

'If you were, and I'll soon find out, then God help you for lying to me. If you weren't in court then I want to know why. What's it to be?'

Richards looked surprised. 'Why would I be in court.?'

Jones was in no mood for games. His huge fist came crashing down on to the table, 'I've warned you Richards. Don't fool about with me.' The harsh edge to his voice rang out. 'You know damned well that Miss Hopkins was due in court because she laid a complaint about your conduct and threats to kill her and I think you went around to her flat to make sure she didn't get there.'

Richards pulled himself back into the chair as if trying to escape the awful stare. 'And I've told you. I don't know nothing about any fucking court case. I had a word yesterday and she just said you was fucking coming to see me again, that's all.'

Jones never blinked. 'You're lying Richards. And you damned well know it. All defendants have to be put on notice of any hearing, even if someone has to put a note through their letterbox.' The sergeant waited.

Richards was being brazen to the end. 'I keep fucking telling you. I'm not lying. Yeah, I know I threatened to kill her but that doesn't mean I done it. I don't know nowt about it. I want to see my brief.'

Jones sat back momentarily, allowing Detective Gray to continue with some mundane questions about times and places concerned with his alibi. If Katie Hopkins hadn't told him about the case and just used the ploy about the police to frighten him off, then it was possible that he hadn't visited the flat for fear of being arrested on sight. Maybe forensics might come up with some answers. Martin Richards was a natural born liar and would say anything to save his own skin.

'Just for the record, let's get a few things straight.' Studying the file, Gray continued. 'You, Richards, visited this young woman, uninvited. You bullied her, made her life hell, and beat her up. Raped her. All this before we caught up with you the first time.' He wasn't finished yet. 'As if that wasn't enough, you kept going back, making her life a misery, finally threatening to kill her. And you expect us to believe you?' He glared at Richards, who had no time to answer before Gray came at him again; 'I've been to the mortuary today and seen young Katie Hopkins. I saw a crushed skull, a bruised face, chest, and legs. And bite marks. Some new, and some not so new. I believe you caused all of them.'

Richards' eyes turned to slits. 'Rape? I never fucking raped her. She loved it a bit rough. Said it made 'er 'ot. We done it often enough. How's that rape?' A smile flickered as he looked at the detective. 'You know what it's like. Only with you lot it's the uniform ain't it? Makes them really 'ot, don't it? But I never fucking did 'er in.' Even the girl's death didn't seem to have touched him.

'What did you do with the weapon?'

The reply was automatic. 'Never 'ad no fucking weapon.' He failed to notice Jones rise from his chair as if to stretch his legs.

Gray was having none of it. 'Let's start again, from the beginning, shall we?'

'Never mind startin' again. What about my fucking brief. When's he comin'?'

Jones interrupted. 'I'm asking the questions now, and I'm not going to ask you twice to stop foul mouthing me.' It wasn't hard to imagine Richards' aggression turning to violence with a defenceless young woman.

Richards smirked. 'Rubber truncheon time is it now. 'ose pipe gang coming are they? He leaned backwards, supporting himself on two legs of the chair. 'I'm saying fuck all now till my brief gets here.' The blow that hit the side of his head sent him reeling from the chair.

Jones stood over his prostrate body. 'Oh dear. Mr Richards has fallen off his chair. I did warn you didn't I? I said you'd hurt yourself. Didn't I?'

Richards struggled to focus, his head spinning as he reached for the outstretched hand. Jones gripped him, crushing the very life out of his fingers. Pulling him to his feet, the two men came face to face. Jones, showed a crooked smile and looked straight into his eyes as his knee powered its way towards the unprotected groin. Richards fell back to the floor screaming in agony. Jones now dragged him to a sitting position in the chair.

'Let's start again shall we, Richards? Only this time without that filthy tongue of yours.'

Twenty minutes later the questioning came to an abrupt end. 'This interview is being terminated at eighteen thirty hours and the prisoner being returned to his cell for his evening meal, and mandatory rest period.' Turning his attention back to Richards, Jones towered above him. 'This interview may be over Richards, but I'm not finished with you. Not by a long way.' Leaving Gray to keep an eye on the prisoner, he walked along to the Custody Sergeant's office.

Gray had a look of forced sympathy about him. 'You shouldn't have upset the sergeant. He can be a real bastard sometimes. Perhaps I should have mentioned, he hates foul mouthed women bashers.' He looked into Richards eyes. The smirk was long gone.

Jones walked into the custody reception area. 'Richards is all yours, for the time being. If I stay in there any longer, I swear, I'll kill the bastard myself.'

'What d'you think?' Lloyd was curious to know his opinion.

'Circumstantial evidence by the ton, but nothing positive. It may be a coincidental killing. Somehow I just can't visualize him in the role of full time psychopath. He's just a cowardly thug really. It's what he did to that poor girl during the months before she was murdered that gets to me.' Jones needed a break. It had been a tough day so far.

'I'm off for a bite to eat. I'm sure the Chief will want to interview him first thing in the morning, but I don't think we need to call him back from his conference.' He left the prisoner to be escorted back to his cell. A very long day was beginning to come to a close but there was still plenty to do. Permission had to be sought to detain the prisoner beyond the initial four hour period to twenty four hours. Richards would also need to be represented.

Lloyd looked at the station clock, then at the young trainee officer. 'Early dart tonight, son. Just time for a cup of tea, if you get your skates on.' His eyes narrowed as he watched the smart uniform, and gleaming black leather boots disappear towards the kitchen. 'Don't know you're born these days.'

In his haste to oblige the sergeant, the trainee almost knocked Alison over as she walked out of the kitchen. 'Sorry,' he stammered. 'Er, Sarge wants a drink.'

She smiled at him. That flustered face made him look rather cute and innocent. 'Next time you rush in like that, make sure it's me you're running after, not a sergeant.' She winked before walking away, leaving him to gaze after a pair of well balanced hips.

CHAPTER 18

Deakin nodded his greeting. 'Morning Tom. How's things?'

'Not too bad, sir, thank you.' He looked up.

'Any news on our peeper,?'

Lloyd shook his head. 'I've got the lads on red alert for the next time he shows. Someone might recognise him or we may just get lucky.' Changing the subject. 'But we've had Martin Richards locked up since yesterday for the Hopkins job. Sarge Jones has interviewed him a couple of times but he's a tough nut to crack.' He waited for a reaction.

'I'll have a word later when Jones has finished with him, if it's still necessary. Let me know if the uniformed branch get anything on the peeper please. I need to eliminate him from other enquiries. Send my mail through, there's a good chap.' Deakin walked off, leaving the sergeant to get on with his work, pausing only to look into the CID office for Jones. He carried on to his own office, hardly reaching his chair before a bundle of mail was deposited on his desk.

'Morning sir.'

He looked up and reached out to take the correspondence.

'Coffee?' Alison smiled politely.

'Yes please.' Even though his mind was focussed else-where, Deakin couldn't fail to notice the starched cleanliness of the young woman. She was like a breath of fresh air, bubbly, alert, and a happy soul. It was almost like looking at a young version of Laura.

Deakin worked his way methodically through the correspondence. The Home Office seal stood out on a letter which was marked for his urgent attention. The report it contained caused him to reach for the phone.

'See if you can find Dr. Julian Hayes for me, at the Home Office Pathology Unit please, and say it's urgent.' It was only two or three minutes before his call was returned. The voice needed no introduction.

'Julian, glad I caught you. Just a few queries.' Questions were fired at the pathologist. To an observer it would have been obvious that Deakin wasn't getting the answers he hoped for. Thanking Hayes for his help, he put down the phone and leaned back into his chair.

'Has Sergeant Jones arrived yet?' he called out to Alison.

'No sir.'

'As soon as he arrives, I'll need a word.' For the next hour papers were shuffled and re-shuffled into trays marked 'Urgent' and 'Routine'. Shoplifters were separated from harmless drunks, car thieves from cranks, and decisions made or confirmed about whether to prosecute or caution, detain or bail. Even the most mundane enquiry had to be answered.

Deakin was never against delegating authority but always keen to draw a line between what was reasonable and what wasn't. Young officers had to be trained, and disciplined into good working practices which would stay with them throughout the whole of their careers. Good practice on the streets had to be linked to good administration. He was well aware that sloppiness, lack of attention to detail and poor quality notebook records could easily be punished by experienced barristers capable of exploiting the smallest loophole. CID officers were being sent on courses and taught by barristers experienced in the art of statement taking and evidence giving. The wind of change was beginning to blow in their direction at last. A knock on the door broke into his thoughts.

'Chief, you wanted me?' It was Jones.

Deakin beckoned him towards a chair. 'I wasn't here when the Hopkins case broke. Everything OK, is it?'

Jones looked at him through tired and depressed eyes. The tension built up over hours of questioning Martin Richards had taken its toll. 'To tell the truth Chief I'm not sure. Thought we had Richards over the proverbial barrel yesterday, but he insists he was never near the woman's flat on the day she was killed. He admits phoning her but nothing else. He's got an alibi, not exactly set in stone. But it is an alibi and might carry some weight in court.'

Deakin detected a marked reluctance to admit, even at this early stage in the investigation, that there was no sign of a breakthrough as far as hard evidence was concerned. So far, it was flimsy or purely circumstantial. There was an obvious suspect, with a record of violent conduct but that in itself wasn't enough. In any case, there was something terribly familiar about the crime scene. The superintendent boss might not be very happy with the idea of detaining Richards for a further seventy two hours without some factual evidence but his name was still the only one in the frame for the time being.

Deakin rubbed his chin thoughtfully before putting him on the spot. 'D'you think Richards was capable of killing Cathy Wilson, Mary Donovan, and Janet Stone, as well as Katie Hopkins?' His expression darkened.

'Because he either did all of them or none. Julian Hayes makes it clear enough in his report.' His fingers tapped on the document lying between them on the desk. 'It's all in here. There's no doubt about it. I've spoken to the Doc within the past hour, and he's positive.'

Jones wasn't really surprised. 'I doubt very much whether he could have killed them all. Richards is a thug but doesn't fit the psychopath pattern. He's too much of a loud mouth for that. If he killed Katie Hopkins, it would have been during one of his long bullying sessions, and that's clearly not the case with any of the others. But I still believe he was the only person who had some warped reason for wanting her dead.'

Deakin pushed the pathologist's report across the desk. 'Having a reason for wanting someone dead and carrying out the act are two different matters. Take a look through that lot while I rustle up some coffee.' He got up and walked out of the room deliberately leaving Jones to study the report alone. Within ten minutes he was back, armed with fresh brews.

Jones raised his eyes from the file as Deakin spoke.

'I don't think we have any choice. We've got to release Richards.'

The phone rang.

'Deakin.' He waited.

It was Lloyd from the front desk. 'There's a solicitor here, sir. Says he represents Martin Richards and wants to see his client.'

'Let him wait, and tell him we won't be too long. Someone will be along to see him shortly.' He had anticipated something like this would happen.

Jones stood up wearily. Hours of interviews had all come to nothing and they'd have to start all over again. 'Sorry, Chief. Feel as if I'm letting you down all the time.'

Deakin shook his head. 'No you're not letting anyone down.' There wasn't much point in asking Jones to think positive at this time. He was demoralised, full of tension, and exhausted. Deakin knew only too well how hours spent questioning suspects could affect the best of detectives. A major part of his working life was spent listening to lies and denials of even the most blatantly obvious facts.

'Go down to the Custody office and release Richards.' It was more of a request than an order. 'When you've done that, I'll be in the CID room.'

Jones was half way out of the room when suddenly he turned back. 'Almost forgot Chief. I was called out to the teacher training college at Edge Hill. Security man came across a tramp at the back of the ladies' accommodation. Thinks the fellow was lying about doing a spot of poaching. I'm having him checked out quietly. There may be something in it.

Deakin's ears pricked up. 'Keep on top of it. You never know. It might have some connection.'

'I wouldn't worry too much about the odd tramp. But this one had a car.' Jones often seemed to keep the best bits to the last.

'In that case you should be able to check him out without raising suspicion.'

Martin Richards swaggered out of the police station shoulder to shoulder with the solicitor, back to his old ways within seconds. The two men walked down the steps leading towards the town centre, and freedom.

'Shower of bastards,' he said. 'Think they could con' me into coughing for someone else's job? Not a fucking chance matey. Fancy trying to pin a murder rap on me. Cheeky bastards. It's them should to be locked up, not me.' Without a backward glance he waved two fingers in a V sign towards the entrance.

The solicitor pulled up sharply. 'If you hadn't bullied and beaten Katie Hopkins in the first place, none of this might ever have happened.'

Richards glared at him. 'Thought you were supposed to be on my side?'

The lawyer stood his ground. 'My job is to see that you're treated fairly, according to the rule of law. What would you know about treating people fairly Mr Richards?' Turning his back, he walked towards the car park, leaving his client standing at the bottom of the steps, to find his own way home.

Jones watched from the office window as the two men left the police station, seemingly engaged in deep conversation. Suddenly they split up and went their separate ways. Usually he would have expected them to put on a show of solidarity, at least until they were out of sight. They might have been expected to go back to the solicitor's office for a cosy chat. He permitted himself a wry smile and 'A lovers tiff,' spoken for the benefit of anyone who happened to be listening. It was time for the crime conference.

Deakin walked into the meeting without notes. He knew what had to be said. Most of the men were close to exhaustion. All leave had been cancelled following the latest incident. Statements had to be taken, read and filed according to their importance. He looked through a haze of blue smoke, picking out the old hands, cigarettes dangling from stained brown fingers. Smokers and drinkers maybe, but they were the backbone of his team.

Besides the occupants who shared the house with Katie Hopkins, every person in her road had to be interviewed. There might be information forthcoming about a stranger loitering in the area, perhaps even a peeping tom. There was always that slender chance. The meeting was intended to bring the squad together so that no hours were wasted by duplicating work. He looked around the sea of faces packed into the small office. There was only seating space for half a dozen but there must have been fifteen of them in the immediate group.

'G' Morning,' Adjusting his voice level, he said; 'I know every one of you is doing your best, so let me begin by reassuring you that every piece of information is being scrutinised. Nothing is being wasted. I can now say, with a degree of certainty that the 'Wilson, Donovan, Stone and Hopkins cases are closely linked. In other words we are only looking for one man.' He hesitated for just a moment. 'The pathology reports on all four make that quite clear.'

'The pathologist is satisfied the same instrument was used in each case and there are other similarities which needn't concern us today. But the point is that we know we're looking for a psychopath.' He let the impact of the word, psychopath, sink in. 'We're searching for a man who is able to gain the confidence of women to the extent that they either allow him to enter their homes or go to him willingly.' He now turned to the pathology reports, at pains to describe the precise manner in which each murder had been carried out. The importance of the similarity of the injuries and the needless attempts at strangulation despite the fact that, in each case, the victim was already dead.

'This man knows something about each woman, and plans his murders extremely carefully. No-one else is around, not even on the car park of a crowded pub. I know you're tired and leave has been cancelled but this man has to be caught. Make that your number one priority.'

Being satisfied that the killings could no longer be considered as random, he now gave specific instructions for all relevant statements to be re-checked for any possible link, no matter how remote that might just start to pull the whole thing together.

'I want to see every piece of background information. It doesn't matter how small you think it is, let me be the judge. I need to know more about the lives these people led before their murder: who they associated with, where they went for fun, hobbies, holidays, anything which might give a clue about what it was that these people had in common. It's in there somewhere and you've got to search till you find it.'

He looked around the room. A bunch of weary faces gazed back at him. But this was the way the murder squad worked. It was the only way it could work. Either a feast or a famine, tired or euphoric. Normal shift patterns went out of the window whenever a murder happened and this team had never failed to rise to the occasion. He had good reason to be proud of the them. 'Thank you. I know you won't let me down.' Deakin turned on his heel and walked out of the room.

A few minutes later Jones walked into Deakin's office.

'I hope to God we're not searching for another Albert de Salvo.' Deakin. said.

'What do you mean?' Jones wanted to know.

'Cast your mind back. Remember Boston, America, and all those killings a few years ago?'

Of course he remembered. Albert De Salvo was believed to be the Boston Strangler, even though he'd never stood trial. But from the time of his arrest the killings stopped. 'Sorry, but I don't get the connection.'

Deakin patiently explained. 'Thirteen women, all murdered in and around Boston in less than eighteen months, between June 1962 and January 1964. The killings were totally random, and the ages of the victims ranged from as young as nineteen to as old as eighty five. For a long time the police weren't able to stop the indiscriminate killing.' Deakin watched Jones's face carefully. 'What do you think they all had in common?'

The sergeant looked lost.

'I'll tell you. Without exception, each one of them either knew the killer or had no reason to fear him.'

'Yes, of course,' Harry Jones still looked mystified. 'But how far ahead is that taking us?'

'Don't you see, there has to be a common denominator? Find that and he's ours.'

'You keep on saying him. Is there a reason?'

Deakin had long since given up the idea of searching for a female killer, mainly because of the amount of sheer brute force used. He knew that at least two of the women had been lifted maybe a foot into the air by someone using only one hand. The stretched strangulation marks were a clear indication that single hand leverage had been used.

In Boston, the simple fact was that thirteen women had been chosen to die only because they were in the wrong place at the wrong time. They were in their own homes, the very place where they would expect to be safe, and which and turned out to be the most dangerous.

'What do we do now? Start making a list of every plumber, electrician and handyman in the area?' Jones suggested.

'No, I think we've just eliminated them. Cathy Wilson, and Janet Stone never went out to some isolated spot to meet any tradesman. Katie Hopkins couldn't afford one and Mary Donovan wouldn't have wasted her booze money.'

Jones thought about it for a moment. 'I feel sure they met the killer for a reason. I'm still dubious but beginning to understand the point being made. The links between the killer and his victims might show up in the background histories now being prepared by the rest of the squad.' He was struggling to think what four women aged between nineteen and fifty six, from different walks of life, could possibly have in common. Only two of them had cars, and as far as he knew, only one of them was a drunk. The process of elimination was tedious to say the least, and the possibilities almost endless. He wondered whether the killer really would show himself somewhere in the ever growing mountain of paperwork.

Deakin now closed the Hopkins file for the moment and put it to next to the other three files which dominated his desk for the time being.

'Do me a favour.'

The sergeant looked surprised. 'Certainly.' He waited.

'Go home, and take a day off. Come back tomorrow refreshed. You're exhausted.'

Jones didn't argue the point.

Deakin went back to his In-Tray and started again, his mind trying to switch off from the four cases with which he was totally obsessed. It was early evening before he finally caught up with the backlog of admin correspondence. He walked out of his office tired but satisfied with the day's work, not failing to notice the WPC still sitting at her desk.

'Working late, Alison?'

She looked up at him, still able to manage a cheerful smile.

'Finishing shortly, sir.'

Deakin nodded his approval. 'Get yourself home young woman. And don't be late in the morning.'

'No sir. G' night.'

Stopping at the enquiries desk for a moment, Deakin looked around for Lloyd, but he was nowhere to be seen. Instead, there was a young constable in his place. Fresh faced, hands clasped behind his back he stood upright as the chief inspector addressed him. Deakin looked at the young constable. Twenty odd years ago he had stood in exactly the same spot, a rookie. Discipline had certainly been a lot stricter then but he'd enjoyed every minute and had no regrets. In those days when a senior officer came through you stood to attention and never dared to smile or speak, unless of course you were spoken to.

'Tell Sergeant Lloyd I've gone home. He knows where to find me if anything crops up.' Deakin walked out to the car park, standing for a moment to take a breath of fresh air. Overhead he could make out the flashing wingtip and body lights of an aircraft. Sometimes they took on the appearance of shooting stars. It was low enough to suggest it was heading for Manchester airport. 'Wonder where you're coming from?

Some exotic location I expect.' He climbed into his car and made for home. Laura would be waiting with dinner in the oven. Whenever serious crimes happened Laura was always kept waiting.

'How you put up with me I'll never know.' He didn't care whether anyone could hear or not.

CHAPTER 19

Pam Lloyd kept an eye on the grill. 'Hope these damned sausages are done enough for old fussy britches.' Tom could eat a sausage sandwich anytime of the day or night, especially the thick pork ones, with plenty of brown sauce. A couple of those with a mug of tea and three sugars was a regular order in the kitchen when he came off a late shift. He never could face a full dinner late in the evening, even when he was younger. She poked her head round the door of the lounge. 'Dad'll be home shortly and if he wants to watch World In Action you'll have to switch over. Just warning you two. And no bickering.' Pam often acted as peacemaker between him and their two feisty youngsters. Mostly it was harmless banter but on the add occasion it could get out of hand.

'Don't worry mum. It's Lulu with The Young Generation. You know he's got a crush on her.'

She knew what that meant. Dad had a bit of a thing for Lulu. World in Action stood no chance against her. Pam wiggled her hips. 'Used to be able to do it properly before I had you pair.' She glanced towards the two girls sitting in the lounge. 'You forget we were your age once.' No-one was listening. She poked her head round the door again.' What time does it finish?'

Neither girl looked up. 'Half past ten.'

She heard his key in the door and turned to greet him.

'Hello Flower.' He glanced downwards at the settee. 'Who's the two strangers?'

'Hi dad.' Two hands raised in a tired wave was all the response he could expect when they were glued to the television. The voice echoing from the television drew him to the arm of the settee. 'Boom-a-Bang-a- Bang' kept him transfixed. 'Has she sung I'm a Tiger yet? He stayed on the arm of the settee, waiting almost reverently while Lulu finished her song, then moved across to his own chair. Making himself comfortable he sat back and watched the end of the show with his other favourite girls. Lulu waved goodnight to them all before disappearing down the tube. 'Why did she have to marry Maurice Gibb? It'll never last.' He shook his head in disbelief. Must be the money bug.' He glanced towards Pam. 'When you think how much kids can earn today. I bet Lulu earns a hundred times more than my boss, and look at the age of her. Makes you wonder what the world's coming to.'

'Want to see World In Action, dad?' A quick glance, one sister to the other, was enough to start them both giggling. Pam went back into the kitchen breathing a sigh of relief. The girls disappeared upstairs, shaking their hips and laughing at each other, thoroughly enjoying the idea of dad 'fancying' Lulu. He watched them go. They were behaving like normal teenagers, he supposed. That's what they were all like nowadays.

Supper was served and eaten with a minimum of fuss. He handed the tray back. 'That was nice, love. Good old bangers. Can't beat them.'

Ten minutes later Pam finally got to sit down. 'Must get my hair washed. It's very greasy. I've got a hairdressing appointment tomorrow.' She pulled gently at the ends. 'Guess what Tom?' she said, changing the subject abruptly.

'Nearly eleven o'clock at night and you want me to start playing guessing games. Found another man have you? I don't know. You'll just have to tell me.'

Pam knew she had his attention until he decided whether it was gossip or real news. 'I heard today about a woman, further down the road, number sixty three, I think, and she was nearly attacked by one of those peeping toms you keep talking about.'

He pricked his ears up. 'What do you mean, nearly?'

Now she had his attention. Anything to do with work was sure to catch him. 'Well, she said she caught him looking through her window and ran out to him.' Pam paused, as if for effect. 'He said something about knocking but not getting an answer, and was just looking through the window in case she was deaf or not well.'

Lloyd continued to give her his attention. 'You still haven't said how she was nearly attacked?'

Pam was not so easily put off. 'Well she could have been, perhaps if she'd opened the door to him in the first place.'

He still wasn't satisfied. 'What did he want? Adults don't normally knock on each other's doors unless they want something, do they?' It was beginning to sound as if she was being questioned personally.

'For goodness sake. How on earth would I know what the man wanted? Anyway she chased him off, so I don't suppose he had a chance to tell her why he was there.'

Lloyd shook his head in despair. 'Why did she think he was a peeper then?'

Pam brought the conversation to an abrupt end. 'It's not that important! I just thought you might want to know about it. That's all.'

'I think there's a vacancy now.' He grabbed the discarded newspaper and made his escape to the bathroom.

'Coward.' She settled down to watch the late night news.

The Daily Mail wasn't his first choice. He was more a Mirror fan but had to take whatever was on offer, according to his shift. Going straight to the sports section he noticed Jackie Stewart had just won his fifth championship race in six starts so far this season, driving the Matra Ford Ms 80. *Love to have a go in that one.* He tried to picture himself on the course at Silverstone, or Brands Hatch. Lloyd's attention was drawn to the Stop Press column.

An article headlined, *Killer to Appeal*, caught his eye. John Stretton, a man from the Gloucester area, convicted of murdering his wife a couple of years ago, was still proclaiming his innocence and taking his case to the Court of Appeal. It went on to say how Ella Stretton was found brutally murdered, her skull fractured and with strangulation marks around her throat. The article however was more concerned with the long delays in getting cases before the Appeal Courts than miscarriages of justice. Most of the evidence, it was being claimed, was circumstantial, and therefore the conviction ought to be declared unsafe. Stretton had now served two years for a crime to which he had always strenuously pleaded his innocence. Nevertheless a jury found him guilty. But it now seemed that they might have got the verdict wrong.

A few minutes later he was downstairs again and rooting through the drawers. 'What are you looking for.' Pam knew where everything in the house was kept. He only had to ask.

'Scissors flower. I need to cut an article out of the paper.'

'Well there's no need to wreck the place. Just ask and I'll tell you where they are.'

Lloyd took it in good part. 'Come on flower. Cough up.'

'Try my sewing box, and don't forget to put them back.'

Somewhere in the back of his mind, he seemed to remember something about the case when it first hit the press but couldn't recall what it was. Walking back into the lounge, he looked around. 'No tea brewing? The service round here's hopeless.'

Pam looked at him. 'Can't find the kettle either eh? What did your last servant die from, exhaustion?' She got up and walked into the kitchen, returning a few minutes later with two cups of tea.

'Found another peeper, have we?' she enquired sarcastically.

Lloyd was too preoccupied trying to remember something else to rise to her bait. He sat, wondering what it was about the Gloucester case that had attracted his attention.

Pam interrupted his thoughts. 'Aren't you speaking to me then?'

He glanced at her. 'For goodness sake woman I'm trying to remember something. If you'll give me half a chance.' He hesitated. 'Don't suppose you remember that Gloucester murder a couple of years back?' Pam read every newspaper from front to back relentlessly and rarely missed a news bulletin.

'You mean that man who crushed his wife's skull with a lead pipe or something? Got life didn't he?' Pamela suddenly started to smirk.

Lloyd looked surprised. 'What's so funny?'

She couldn't help the edge in her voice. 'Not thinking of doing me in are you? If you did, Lulu wouldn't put up with you for long.'

He shook his head.

'You can stay as long as you keep making the banger sarnies and the tea.'

'Deakin.' He waited to see who was calling.

'Lloyd here, sir. Can I have a word?'

'Over the phone or do you want to see me here?'

'I'll pop over. Only take a minute.' Lloyd left the reception desk in the hands of the trainee constable with strict instructions not to make any decisions about stray cats or dogs until he got back. Heading along the corridor towards Deakin's office he almost bumped into a young lady coming out of the tea room. 'Careful Madame.' She nipped smartly out of his way. 'If only my daughters moved as quick as you.' Arriving at Deakin's door he knocked and entered.

'Hello sergeant. To what do I owe the pleasure?'

'Well sir, In yesterday's Mail, there's an Appeal Case that's waiting to be heard in London. Wondered if you saw it?'

Deakin looked at him with a puzzled expression. 'No. Should I have seen it?' The truth was he'd fallen asleep in the armchair after dinner and didn't even see a paper.

Lloyd produced the article from the breast pocket of his uniform.

'Remember a case called Stretton, in Gloucester a couple of years ago?'

Deakin wasn't sure. He waited for the detail.

'He was done for murdering his wife, or ex-wife. Swore blind he had nothing to do with it.'

'Oh yes, I remember now you mention it.' Deakin's powers of recall were exceptional sometimes. 'Man's wife found battered to death. The couple were separated and he'd moved out of the house and took a flat somewhere nearby. She'd been visiting him and that they were argued over money. He lost control.' Deakin failed to see the significance. It was all pretty cut and dried at the time but the accused had refused to acknowledge his crime, insisting throughout the proceedings that he was innocent, and some person or persons unknown were trying to frame him. Trouble was, he couldn't think of a reason why.

'The article says that the wife received a fractured skull. That part didn't worry me too much. But there was an attempt at strangulation as well and that struck me as important.' He waited for some reaction.

'Thanks Sarge very much. Let's have a word with the Gloucester CID and see if they've got anything that might interest us.' He picked up the phone.' Can you get me Gloucester CID.' He added, 'Don't know who I want to speak to but it will be the person who handled the Stretton murder enquiry about two years ago.' He beckoned to Lloyd to take a seat.

'Might as well see it through. It's your enquiry anyway.'

'G'day to you. Chief DI. Deakin here from Ormskirk CID. One of my sergeants has handed me an article from yesterday's Mail. it's about the Stretton Appeal. I'm wondering if perhaps you might be able to help me with a problem we're having up north.'

'Hello chief inspector. Don't know what I can do but I'm willing to give it a go if I can. We had Stretton bang to rights on this one. He was the only person who stood to gain from his wife's death.'

Deakin persevered. 'Did you have any forensics or was the case based on circumstantial evidence?'

The voice came back instantly. 'No forensics but the circumstantial was enough, though the jury took five days to return a majority verdict. Stretton was arrested seven hours after the body was discovered and had plenty of time to clean up any signs of a struggle.'

'Is there any chance I could see a copy of your file.' Deakin pressed him.

'I'll ask the super but we'll have to get it back from the Crown Prosecution Service first.'

'It's just that we have something similar going on up here and it seems odd.' He hesitated. 'Unless of course it's someone copy-catting.'

'Well. It can't be Stretton. He's been well tucked away for the past year or two.'

Deakin kept on. 'Supposing he was framed.'

'Well chief, all I can say is that his wife was no oil painting and never had a lover or boy friend. There was nobody else with whom she was remotely connected and all roads lead back to Stretton himself.'

Deakin gave one last push. 'If I can just have a peep at the file I really would be obliged.' He waited.

'Leave it with me and I'll see what I can do for you.'

It had been hard going but somehow felt like it was worthwhile. Deakin replaced the receiver.

'They are going to let us see the file Sarge. Now let's hope your intuition comes to fruition.'

'It's that old gut feeling Chief. I'm sure there's something there for us. It's the strangling bit that draws me into it. I remember thinking that as I followed the case when it was at trial. It's almost like a trademark.'

Deakin preferred to err on the side of caution. 'They still seem to think that they've got the right man, even though he was convicted on circumstantial evidence. But it was the fact that only he stood to gain from the murder that convinced the jury, nothing else.'

Deakin couldn't fail to notice the look of disappointment on Lloyd's face. As if to reassure him, he added; 'The only thing that seemed to bother the Gloucester team was the lack of factual evidence, such as fingerprints, footprints or bloodstains which would have tied Stretton into the murder inextricably. Of course, that's now the basis of his appeal. 'Maybe there is something in it. Let's wait and see, shall we?' Deakin sat back. 'I'll take a look at their file on the case and do some comparison work. Their man did say that a careful search of the area had failed to produce anything useful, and also that the jury argued for five days before coming up with a majority verdict. There's something not right about the whole scene.'

'Chief, don't you think that there are too many similarities between this Stretton case and our own Cathy Wilson investigation?' Lloyd explained that he felt there may well be a link, even though they were nearly two hundred miles apart, in two different Counties, and with two years between.

'We can't afford to rule anything at the moment.' Deakin glanced at some scribbled notes. 'It is worth an enquiry, I suppose.' He wasn't altogether convinced but would study the Stretton papers when they arrived. Looking up again, he addressed his thoughts to Lloyd directly. 'We're searching for a psychopath, someone who kills pretty frequently once he starts and can't stop unless he's caught.' Deakin rubbed his chin. 'Supposing the long arm of coincidence does point in that direction. It poses another question. Where has the killer been for the past two years? Abroad possibly? Maybe in prison for some minor offence? Or even locked away in a mental institution? These are the things we will need to know.'

Lloyd began to realise the true depth of the chief's thinking. But Deakin hadn't quite finished. 'As you well know, domestic homicide is the most common one of all. I don't want this to become any more complicated than it is.'

The sergeant still clung to his gut instinct over this one. The chief was right. There was no doubt about that. But he hadn't ruled out the possibility of a connection which meant that he too was prepared to explore every nook and cranny of this case, leaving, as he so often said, no stone unturned. Lloyd walked back to the front desk feeling that he might just be playing some small part in this investigation. Maybe his instincts would just prove him right.

Lloyd made his way back to reception, entering through the rear door. Pulling up abruptly, he stared in amazement. It was like walking into another world. A mongrel dog, viciously scratching itself with a hind leg and looking as if it was alive with fleas, was tethered to the end of the long wall bench.

'Where the hell did that come from?'

The young officer stood smartly upright before the towering sergeant.

'You told me not to admit anyone Sarge, so I left him there till you came back.'

Lloyd looked at him astonished. 'If one of my daughters ever brings you home for tea, I'll kick her out with you.'

'Sorry 'Sarge. Did I do something wrong?' He tried to look innocent, but out of the corner of his eye Lloyd had already seen faces peering through corners of the office window. Every team had its practical joker and his was no exception. Generally speaking it was good for morale and building team spirit. He played his part, glaring at the young man.

'Right, clever boy. Now you take that beast to the yard get a bucket of soapy water, give it a damned good bath, dry it off, and feed it. Tie it to the kennel and be back here in ten minutes.'

Deakin thought long and hard before he called Jones to his office. His face must have registered his concern. 'Come on in. Got something special I want you to do as soon as you can manage it.' He pointed to a seat.

'Remember the Stretton case down in Gloucester? About two years ago, I think.'

'Yes Chief. But I had no real interest, only through the papers. There was no connection with anything on our patch.' He listened carefully as the instructions were given.

'I want you to find out which solicitors represented Stretton and ask if they have any objection to our having a chat with him. Make sure they understand we are not interested in his appeal case. See if there's anything in his background that might just help our enquiries.'

'Like what. for instance?'

'Well, he says he was framed and someone wanted his wife dead, or maybe just him out of the way. Is that suspicious enough? After all, Bill Wilson more or less said the same thing and so did Donovan.

Jones didn't look as if he was picking up on the logic of it all. 'It's hard to imagine a husband or ex-husband saying much different really, especially if no-one else has a motive.' He understood the point made but was still confused about the line of questioning to be followed.

Once back in his office, Jones made a phone call before leaving the station. Walking along the High Street until he reached the Central Reference Library he went through the revolving doors and into the wide circular entrance hall, with its busts of famous people staring mournfully back at him. Jones never ceased to wonder at the sudden loss of sound each time he stepped from the hustle and bustle of the High Street and its noisy traffic into the still world of librarians. On the first floor, he went directly to the reception desk and stood, patiently waiting his turn in the silent queue.

The librarian, wisps of hair struggling to escape from the auburn bun perched on the top of her head, looked older without make-up. Maybe thirty five or a little more, he guessed. There was a harassed look about her as she pitted her wits against members of the public who seemed to take it for granted that she was a talking encyclopaedia. She regarded Jones quizzically, inviting him to speak first. He smiled politely. 'Good morning,' almost inaudibly. 'I called earlier about newspaper reports.'

Her face lit up, the voice rising a fraction above normal, an indication that she was excited. 'Oh yes, South Western Editions of the Mail and Express, wasn't it?'

Time was precious. But without her help he was going nowhere.' Had any luck?' he spoke in the same quiet tone.

The bun, waved from side to side each time she moved her head. She really was quite pretty when she smiled. With her hair at shoulder length, after work, she'd be a lot more attractive. But further imaginings were interrupted.

'Yes, I've put them to one side for you. If you just take a seat at one of the tables, I'll bring them over.' Ignoring the rest of the queue, the young woman disappeared out of sight while he looked for an empty table. She returned with an armful of newspapers. 'I think this is what you want but if you need anything else just pop over to the counter.'

'Thanks, I will.'

For an hour Jones pored over reports ranging from the discovery of Ella Stretton's body to the final days of her husband's trial. There was plenty of rhetoric, very little fact and no shortage of circumstantial evidence. He found himself being drawn to the view that the jury found Stretton guilty simply because the police didn't look any further than him. With a friendly wave to the librarian, he left and walked back to the station armed with information from half a dozen press reports, including full details of the solicitors and barrister who represented John Stretton at his trial. He made a mental note to visit the library again when things quietened down.

Back at the office, Jones spent two hours on the phone involved in lengthy explanations, accompanied by promises of confidentiality, before agreement could be reached over the actual nature of the interview. He went home to pack an overnight bag.

The route South would have been more pleasurable if it had not been for the circumstances. The deaths of four women were beginning to weigh heavily on his shoulders. The A449 to Worcester continued south through the Malverns, with the beautiful Vale of Evesham to his left. Miles of green meadows as far as the eye could see, passed with just the occasional glance. Ledbury, a beautiful small market town on the edge of the Wye valley, came and went as he joined the A417 taking him directly to Gloucester.

The final approaches to the city followed a long bend on the banks of the River Severn. A once busy shipping lane now seemed to be silting up faster than it could be dredged. With the tide out there were long stretches of mud banks where not long ago, ships would have been moored. Fishing smacks leaned crazily on their sides, dragging anchors, until the next tide.

Entering the city through Westgate Street he continued towards the city centre, stopping at traffic lights by St Michaels Gate. Ahead he passed a series of car showrooms with their brightly coloured red and green neon signs that looked as if they had been stolen from an American movie. Traffic lights at the end of the row were accompanied by a small sign pointing to the railway station.

The hotel bore the hallmarks of yesteryear. It was as if it had been standing in a time warp since the end of the war. Jones could visualise the steam trains blowing loud whistles, and clouds of white smoke billowing past the bedroom windows. The reception smothered in rosewood panelling, boasted ornate ceilings with bunches of painted grapes hanging from each corner. Lurking behind the desk as if she was lying in wait stood the receptionist.

She smiled a professional greeting. 'Evening sir, do you have a reservation?'

'Mr. Jones. You're expecting me.'

'Oh, yes sir. Need a hand with your luggage?' she enquired, without bothering to look whether he had any.

Jones smiled. 'A brief case, and an overnight bag? I think I can manage.'

'Sign the register if you please, sir.' She turned the book round to face him, at the same time reaching for the room key.

He looked at her only fleetingly. Her boredom was catching.

'Fourth Floor, sir. Lift is on your left next to the lounge entrance.' She continued to look at him, neither friendly nor discourteous, but strangely unemotional. Perhaps it was the repetition of her work, constantly accosting strangers with the same questions. Maybe she just couldn't help it.

'What time do you serve dinner?' he enquired.

'Six thirty to eight thirty, sir. Menu is on the door of the restaurant if you want to order in advance or prefer to eat in your room.'

The phone rang and she reached out. 'Good evening, Station Hotel, Can I help you?' Jones was dismissed.

Selecting an evening paper from the news rack in reception, he made his way to the lift. The long drive had left him tired. Jones needed a hot bath, With relief he noted the room was clean and spacious, with the recent addition of an en-suite bathroom, which though small was adequate. He thought about other places he had visited where bathrooms were located at the end of long corridors and everyone had to queue. He wasted no time taking advantage of the facilities.

It was seven fifteen when Jones finally walked into the hotel restaurant.

'Good evening sir. May I have your room number please?'

The waiter, at least, seemed pleased to see him. Maybe it was because he was the only diner so far that evening. He followed the white jacketed man towards a table set for two people.

'Four-o-six.'

'Can I get sir a drink while he's looking through this evening's menu?'

Jones wasn't used to this sort of cosseting. 'A pint of bitter please.'

The waiter held on to his wine list. 'Of course sir,'

A plain eater, he decided to have the soup, followed by roast beef and Yorkshire pudding. That done, he opened the evening paper. The headline on page three hit him like a hammer.

WIFE KILLER TO BE RE-INTERVIEWED BY POLICE.

Gloucester killer to be interviewed over murders in North West.

The article described how Jones was coming down specially to see John Stretton in connection with other murders committed in the North West, giving a clear but totally wrong impression he was a suspect.

Jones was furious, not so much because the newspapers had got it wrong. God knows they did that often enough. But there was every chance that Stretton might find out about the article and then refuse to speak to him. Anyone could have leaked the story but more than likely one of the prison officers had a contact with the local Press. They would have known in advance about the visit because it had to be logged in the prison visitor's diary. For the next hour he gave up worrying about it and concentrated on his dinner. The Brown Windsor soup with a crusty cob and some butter was served piping hot, just the way he liked it.

'Thanks, I enjoyed that,' he said, leaning back to allow the waiter to collect the empty soup plate. Five minutes later he was back with a large silver tray, from which he carefully selected four layers of roast beef, placing them in sequence around the edge of the dinner plate.

'Roast and boiled, sir?' he enquired courteously.

Jones smiled at him. 'Everything please.' Two Yorkshire puddings quickly joined the potatoes, followed by generous helpings of cabbage and mixed carrot and turnip. A small gravy boat was left on a side plate.

'Any sauces, sir? 'Perhaps a little horse radish or mustard?'

Jones glanced at him. 'Coleman's mustard mixed straight from the powder?'

'I'm sure we can manage that, sir.' He disappeared and within seconds produced a small silver bowl filled with fresh mustard and housing a tiny mustard spoon.

Jones tucked into the meal, thoroughly enjoying every mouthful. It was eight fifteen when he walked out of the restaurant, leaving only a handful of visitors behind. He nodded to the receptionist as he passed the desk on his way to the lounge bar.

'Good evening sir,' she said, in the same monotone voice.

Wonder what it takes to excite you? Quite a good looking woman really. Wouldn't mind finding out. Jones hesitated, 'Don't suppose I could tempt you to a glass of something?'

'Who, sir? Me sir? Not while I'm on duty. Impossible'

'Oh well then, perhaps some other time.'

'Thank you sir.'

Two more pints of bitter and an hour later he was settled down for the night. Through the open window he could hear music being played somewhere nearby. Somebody was playing a piano accordion. Jones easily recognised the excerpts from the shows. Joseph And The Amazing Technicolor Dreamcoat, The Sound of Music, and the West End's latest production, Jesus Christ Superstar. The receptionist was forgotten for the moment.

CHAPTER 20

One last look around the room and Jones picked up his brief case and holdall, satisfied that nothing had been forgotten. The memory of a suitcase left on the platform at Crewe station a few years earlier still haunted him. He would never forget staring, horrified, through the carriage window as the train pulled away and the embarrassment of having to go home empty handed. He crossed the foyer into the direct view of the receptionist. The fixed smile told him nothing about her real mood.

'Good morning sir.' The greeting rang out like someone's favourite record being played over again. 'Everything alright for you?' She managed to squeeze it in before he had a chance to speak.

'Do I get my money back if I say no?'

The enigmatic smile told him she'd heard it all before. One of her ancestors probably posed for the Mona Lisa. He reached for his wallet pulling out two crisp five pound notes.

'Thank you sir.' She reached out for the money, frowning slightly. 'That will be five pounds for dinner bed and breakfast and two pounds for drinks.' She handed him his change. Jones left a pound tip on the small white plate, at the same time picking up the receipt.

'Thank you sir. I'll see it goes to the staff.' She spoke as if she wasn't one of them, and gratuities were beneath her. At last she managed to get it out.' Off to prison now are we?' accompanied by the same enigmatic smile.

'Yes, but not for life, I hope.' Jones turned on his heel.

A grey overcast morning waited to greet him as he walked down the hotel steps and out on to the car park. In the distance he could make out the spires of Gloucester Cathedral, standing like an enormous centrepiece cast in sandstone, its spires clearly visible despite the dullness of the day. 'Must come here again sometime,' he said to himself. 'A city full of history and no time to explore.'

The prison finally loomed into sight. Huge walls, over twenty feet high, made it clear that escape for anyone would never be easy. The entrance to the car park was manned by an officer in a sentry hut. There was no greeting. 'Have you got a visiting order?' The man bent downwards as if to look inside the vehicle.

Jones handed him the order. The man went back inside the sentry hut and wound the handle on his field telephone. 'Detective Sergeant Jones to see 877018 Stretton, A Block.' A minute later he was back at the car. 'Park against the wall by the sign that says Staff Only, sergeant. It'll be safe enough there.' He pointed towards the huge gates. 'Then go to the side gate and they'll let you in.'

Jones thanked him, and God, that there had been no last minute cock-ups. The slightest error on a visiting order would cause a refusal to admit the holder into the prison. The prisoner would be returned to his cell and the whole process started again on a month's notice. He approached the small side door and rang a bell. Slightly above his head a window opened. Jones handed up his visiting order. A few seconds later the steel lined door opened and he was admitted. There was already a queue of visitors waiting to be escorted to their final destinations. It was usually a cafeteria where they could sit opposite the prisoners at tables with hard wooden chairs. There could be no physical contact between guest and prisoner. Jones had two packs of cigarettes each containing nineteen smokes. That way he couldn't be accused of smuggling because they were already open. Cigarettes were just about the most negotiable currency in any prison.

A summons rang out. 'Jones for A wing.' The prison officer looked around, noticing Jones acknowledging his call. 'Just waiting for Stretton's solicitor Mr Jones, and then we'll be on our way.' He had barely uttered the words when another voice spoke out: 'DS Jones, is it? My name's Bradley, I'm Stretton's solicitor.'

A tall, grey haired, well groomed man in his middle years, he looked out of place in such glum surroundings. He held out a hand,' Shall we proceed to the waiting area for A block?'

'Nice to meet you.' Jones felt his firm handshake. He indicated a gate close to the prison officer. 'Over there, I think.' The officer closed a steel gate behind the two men and moments later another gate ahead was opened. It was the prison system, every prison system, without variation.

How prison officers were able to spend so much of their lives in such forbidding surroundings had remained a mystery to Jones for years. It was a way of life which seemed to lend itself to ex-military personnel, used to strict discipline. Finally they reached the waiting area.

Category 'C', trustee prisoners, hovered around the room, swishing damp mops, and polishing cloths over surfaces which were in danger of wearing out. Every once in a while, a cigarette would be dropped on the floor by a well intentioned visitor, and swooped on by one of the trustees, snatching the gift and instantly transporting it to a place of safety for later pleasure or trading. It was like watching a world within a world.

Jones liked the look of Bradley. There was an air of quiet confidence about the solicitor. He looked to be in his middle fifties.

'Shouldn't be too long now. Have a good trip down?' Bradley's voice carried the positive air of a middle class education.

'Not too bad at all. Stayed at the Station Hotel last night. Food was good.'

Bob Bradley looked at him, eyes mocking. 'Hope you didn't get into the fleshpots of our fair city.'

Jones laughed. 'Hardly, I'm only on police pay. Just a couple of pints and a serenade by a piano accordionist.'

The conversation was interrupted. 'You two gentlemen to see John Stretton?'

The prison officer, standing stiffly upright, peaked hat tight over his eyes, shoes gleaming, tunic buttons sparkling, bore all the hallmarks of an ex-military police guardsman.

Jones doubted whether he would have been called a gentleman if it hadn't been for the presence of the solicitor. The small party moved off in the direction of A Block located on the opposite side of the exercise yard. Prisoners, trustees, scurried backwards and forwards from the kitchens carrying trays of food into the building for distribution to those prisoners confined to their cells.

As well as lifers, A Block also housed prisoners detained under rule 43. These were men, mainly rapists and paedophiles, who volunteered to spend their entire sentences in isolation, being entitled to sanctuary within the prison under that rule. It was the only way they could be protected from the other inmates who followed their own code of honour.

Jones glanced towards the solicitor. 'Bit of a route march, isn't it?'

Bradley smiled back. 'Never seem to house the inmates near the gate, do they?'

The officer pretended not to hear them. Once inside the building, the party moved through a further series of locked doors until they finally reached a room which doubled as a canteen. Half a dozen bare tubular steel tables, each with four matching chairs were spread in such a way as to afford only minimal privacy.

'Solicitor and police officer to see 877018 Stretton,' the officer barked, as they walked into the room. A door painted in camouflage green opened, bringing Jones and Stretton face to face for the first time.

'No physical contact. Stretton, stand still.' The prisoner stood motionless. The solicitor and policeman seated themselves at one of the tables.

'Hello John,' said Bradley as Stretton took the seat allocated to him.' Let me introduce Detective Sergeant Jones. He's come all the way from Lancashire to see you.'

Jones took out a packet of Senior Service cigarettes, offering one to each of his companions before leaving the open packet on the table. 'Help yourself,' he added, nodding at Stretton. The invitation was gladly accepted. After drawing on the cigarette a couple of times it was it was extinguished, saving a large stump for later. During the course of the interview he succeeded in emptying the packet into his breast pocket. His brown stained fingers seemed slightly clenched. Jones guessed he had been sewing mailbags. The man looked otherwise in good health and a lot leaner than Jones had expected.

The short cropped hair helped to maintain the impression that he was a man who could take care of himself in a tight corner.

Bradley now addressed his remarks to both men, turning his attention firstly to his client. 'John, you know what this is about and if you find yourself in any difficulty please do not answer without asking my advice.' Turning towards Jones, he said; 'Just two things Sergeant; nothing about our appeal case, and a firm undertaking in my clients' presence that this conversation is strictly between us and not to be used in evidence, or released to the press, without our prior knowledge and consent.'

'You have my word.' It seemed to satisfy both parties.

Jones now looked straight at Stretton. 'John, if you don't mind me calling you by your first name, let me reassure you that my interest might just be a help to you in the long term but at the moment I can't be certain of anything.'

'Don't know what I can do to help,' said Stretton, 'But I will if I can.'

Jones found himself listening intently to the Gloucester accent. The speech was slower than he was used to and words rolled off the tongue rather than being spoken in the harsher northern lingo.

'Tell me a bit about your background John.'

'Like what?'

'I need to know if there is any possible connection between your case and some other murders which I am presently investigating.'

Stretton's eyes opened wide. 'I'll tell you whatever you want to know if it will help my case. You got a line on someone?'

Jones shook his head. 'It's not that easy, but we believe that if we can gather enough information from each source, we may come across some sort of common factor.'

'Mr Jones, what could I possibly have in common with people I never heard of and who are now dead?'

The Solicitor looked intrigued by the conversation between the two men. 'Did any of the victims have children?' he enquired.

'Two did and two didn't,' Jones replied.

'Married?' It was like a cross examination.

'Two were, and two weren't.'

Bradley smiled at him. 'Gets us off to a flying start doesn't it?' Changing his approach he carried on, presumably hoping he might start some bells ringing in his client's head. 'What exactly have your people got in common with my client that brings you all this way?'

Jones was torn between giving the man false hopes and getting something useful from him. 'I don't want to build your expectations, but it does seem possible that since they all met their deaths in similar fashion there could be a connection between our investigations and your client.'

Bradley spoke what must have been John Stretton's thoughts, as well as his own. 'Severe skull fractures, and strangulation marks?'

'That's right. And that's why I'm here.'

A trustee walked into the room unannounced, carrying a large metal teapot on a tray with three mugs, sugar milk and biscuits. Addressing no-one in particular, 'Tea's free, but we have a collection box if you want to make a donation.' It was an invitation not to be refused.

Jones sipped at the steaming mug, as if oiling his throat muscles, before carrying on. 'John, it's not what you had in common with those people that really matters, but what you all had in common, if anything, with their killer.'

Stretton looked surprised. 'You mean your people now accept that I never killed my wife, or ex-wife, if you prefer that?'

The solicitor stepped in quickly. 'Gentlemen, we're getting into an area which is not for discussion.'

Jones looked back at him. 'I understand but I have to say that I haven't seen any evidence for or against your client, except for a few press clippings.' He carried on without waiting for a reply.

The solicitor glanced sharply. 'You mean you haven't had a peep at the Gloucester CID records?'

'No I haven't. But if anything does come of this, then it can only help your client, though at present I don't know who killed any of them.' He turned his attention back to Stretton. 'Was your wife having an affair of any sort that you knew about?'

A haunted look came into Stretton's eyes. 'She wasn't a bad woman. Definitely not the type to have an affair.' There was something positive about the way he spoke. He seemed to be in thought for a moment and then laughed. It broke the tension of having to speak about someone no longer able to speak for themselves. 'No, Ella didn't have another man, or even one in mind. I'm sure I'd have known about that.'

Jones accepted what he was saying without hesitation. 'What kind of life were you leading just before she was killed?'

Stretton's face darkened. 'Pretty miserable really. It was no fun trying to keep two homes going. I couldn't afford to drink. Had to cut my cigarettes to ten a day. Made-do with old clothes.' He looked towards the solicitor for reassurance. 'Missed a few payments. She thought I was spending it on other women, had me followed and I got chased all around the courts.' He shrugged.

'Now look at me; three meals a day, a roof over my head, no maintenance to worry about, and I'm still not happy.'

There was something about John Stretton. Jones already had a feeling that a grave miscarriage of justice would one day come to light. He cast his mind back to the vast amount of evidence which had so recently accumulated against Martin Richards in the Katie Hopkins murder and which might easily have led to a wrongful conviction. It was no use blaming either police or the jury system. No-one had lied or cheated, it was simply their interpretation of the evidence.

The hour allotted for the interview had flown past before anyone realised it. The officer reminded the little group that the prisoner had to be returned to his cell in time for lunch, which was served between eleven thirty and eleven forty five. There were fifteen hundred mouths to feed within the space of an hour and the rota had to be strictly enforced to make sure everything ran smoothly.

'Mind if we just have one more before we go?' Jones pulled out the second packet of 'Senior Service' cigarettes, lighting one and leaving the rest on the table. The three men stood up. No-one seemed to notice what happened to the cigarettes. Jones didn't know whether the meeting had been successful or not but he could at least put his points of view to his own boss tomorrow.

Time for a spot of lunch? There's a nice pub along the 417, more or less on your route home.'

Fifteen minutes later they arrived in convoy at The Carter's Arms. Two farm carts stood either side of the front entrance, each loaded with bedding plants in a wide variety of colours. Hanging baskets in full bloom added to the attraction. Jones had a great affection for country pubs and their home cooking. Finding a quiet corner table, the two men were able to relax away from the prison confines and exchange confidences without worrying about being overheard.

Bradley opened the conversation. 'Trip worthwhile, was it?'

Jones looked despondently at him, and shook his head. 'I can't see anything at the moment which could ever link all these people together but my boss seems to think it was worth a try.'

'If he feels so strongly about it then why didn't he come down himself?'

It seemed a reasonable question. The sergeant might not be privy to everything his boss knew about the cases under investigation. 'He's a damned good detective,' he said defensively. 'Only problem is he takes far too much on his shoulders.'

Running his fingers round the edge of his hair, Bradley was clearly thinking about something. 'You've got four murders of your own and five if you take on board my client, and what does that amount to?' The detective was mystified.

Bradley continued; 'You said earlier that you are involved in cases which embrace a spinster, an unmarried mother, an alcoholic, and a divorcee, and now my client who is legally a widower, simply because his wife died before the Decree Absolute was granted.' He smiled broadly. 'I'll tell you what they all had in common.' He continued without hesitation: 'Courts.'

Jones' eyes opened wide. 'What do you mean?' But he ran the list through his mind. 'Janet Stone was never in court, at least as far as we know.'

'Maybe she was in debt of some sort,' Bradley suggested.

'No. We've already been down that road, and in any case, those involved in court cases all had different solicitors, and appeared in totally different courts.'

He laughed. 'Can't pin this lot on to a judge, can we?'

Bradley laughed with him. 'I'm not so sure. Agatha Christie did, and there's one or two I wouldn't trust not too far from here.'

Changing the subject, Jones posed a question. 'Going to get your man off this time?'

Bradley shrugged his shoulders. 'What I think doesn't matter, but you know our jobs are not really so far removed from each other. My job is not to get people off, or convicted for that matter, but to make certain that they get the fairest possible trial.'

It seemed the proper time to draw the meeting to an end. The soup, followed by Cumberland Sausage and mashed potato with onion gravy, had been a rare treat at lunchtime. Jones was more used to eating on the move, often starving himself in a good cause, or at least in the course of justice.

'Thanks for co-operating and your advice. I'll make sure my boss gets a full report on his desk in the morning.' Jones held out his hand.

Bradley shook it firmly. 'Been a pleasure sergeant. Be nice to think we're in a common cause for once. Goodbye for now.'

Jones drove away from the Carter's Arms taking the road back to Ledbury. The A449 would take him back to the North West and home. He had plenty to think about and yet nothing positive to report to the Chief. He wondered what Deakin was going to make of it, especially the theory about the courts. Maybe he already had it in mind.

John Stretton sat in his cell wondering whether or not he had done the right thing talking to the police but his instincts told him that Jones was trustworthy and he had to let it go at that. Jones had told him nothing really, except that there were a number of similar murders being carried out up north. It seemed for the minute though as if he was still one of only two people who knew that he hadn't murdered his wife.

'Step outside Stretton.' The cell door swung open, Two prison officers walked into the tiny room. 'Random cell search. Got anything you shouldn't have?'

'No sir,'

'Just remember Stretton. You might think you're as good as free but as far as we're concerned you're a killer till someone proves otherwise.' The cell was turned upside down and only roughly reassembled. 'Get this lot tidied up and keep your nose clean.' Having re-established their authority the two men walked out slamming the steel door behind them.

Stretton sat on the edge of his bunk. Now what the hell was that all about? Not being fitted up again am I?

It was almost eight o'clock when Jones pulled on to the police station car park, and walked inside to the enquiries desk. 'Chief gone yet?' he asked the young Constable.

'Yes, Sarge. But he left a message to say if you want to speak to him, he'll be at home for the rest of the night.'

'Thanks. If he happens to call in, tell him I'm back and I'll be here early in the morning.'

'Yes, Sarge.'

Jones climbed back into his car, remembering to read the mileometer before setting off again. Claims for expenses were scrutinised very carefully for errors or guesses. He found himself driving past the Ormskirk parish church and glanced up at the tower and spire. *Maybe not as big as Gloucester cathedral, but it's home to me and give me a good old Lancashire Hotpot anytime.* It was always good to be back.

Chapter 21

Deakin was engrossed in the Hopkins file when Jones walked into his office.

'Morning chief. Still working on my report. Did you want to see me before it's finished?'

Deakin nodded towards a chair. 'What did you make of Stretton then?'

'Wouldn't be surprised if he wins his appeal. Doesn't come across as any sort of hardened criminal. I'm inclined to believe him.'

Deakin wasn't surprised. 'I thought you might, somehow.'

'Well, he wasn't being smart or ducking answers. His solicitor wasn't the type to suffer fools gladly either. Strictly no-nonsense sort.'

'Why were the Gloucester force so keen to put him away?'

Jones never hesitated or attempted to evade the issue. 'Simple, Chief. He was the only one with reason to kill; the only one who stood to gain. They never looked for anyone else.' He stopped for a moment. 'But, the solicitor said something interesting.'

Deakin raised his eyebrows in anticipation.

'He said that all he could see was a lot of people involved in court cases of one sort or another.' I told him we were talking about different courts in different areas, and of course, Janet Stone had never been near one as far as we know. And Katie Hopkins hadn't actually been to court but was due to go.'

'What was his response to that?'

'He said Janet Stone might have been in debt or a witness of some sort, or a defendant. She might even have been a jury member. I told him we'd already run checks on those possibilities.'

Deakin spoke across him. 'Yes, we have done those checks and drawn a blank every time.'

The interview was coming to a close. It was never intended to be a conference. 'By the way. Don't forget to let me have your expenses claim as soon as soon as you can.' It was the signal for Jones to leave.

'Funny you should mention that.' Jones reached into his inside pocket and produced a small sheaf of papers.' Thanks Chief.

Deakin shook his head. 'Should have known better.'

God knows how many times the phone had rung and it was barely nine o'clock. Deakin glanced at the standard issue Timex clock on the wall. It was electric and supposed to keep good time. But whenever there was a power cut or surge, it would either stop altogether or race ahead. He always seemed to be away from the office when these things happened and consequently was never able to rely on the damned thing. However it was police property and stayed on the wall, no matter how useless it might be.

'Deakin.' He spoke hurriedly. It was Alison.

'Your press conference in ten minutes, sir. You asked me to remind you.'

Deakin wondered how long it would be before one of the young bobbies started to make serious advances in her direction. She wasn't just eye catching, but efficient as well. A good combination for any aspiring bobby but a sad loss to the force ultimately.

'Thanks, I'll be along shortly. Tell Sergeant Jones and DC Gray to get their skates on, as well.'

The three men took their seats at the long table and faced their expectant audience. Deakin looked around. 'Good morning everyone. I think we all know each other by now. Who wants to start?'

'Henrietta Furlong, Northern Express.'

'Yes Henrietta, what can I do for you?' She was a good looking intelligent woman

In a man's world. They'd met before. Deakin waited. He couldn't help noticing the broad smile which had appeared on Gray's face. *Must have a word with you, young man.*

'I believe Mr Jones interviewed John Stretton at Gloucester prison yesterday.'

The smile on Gray's face never faltered, though he didn't know what the hell she was on about.

'Can you tell us,' she waved a hand, almost pointing directly at Gray, who would have told her anything she wanted to know, gladly. 'What was the point in interviewing somebody who obviously has no connection with any of our local matters?' She hesitated for a second. 'Unless of course he's due out on licence pending his own appeal hearing.'

Deakin took the question. 'No madam. I can't tell you why we wanted to interview John Stretton. I can however reassure you that he is not under suspicion for any of the murders which we are presently investigating. Neither is he due out on licence to the best of my knowledge.'

'Don Reading, The Mail.' A more familiar voice. Well known to Deakin and admired for his accuracy in reporting. His questions were usually not without purpose. 'Mr Deakin, we've a duty to keep the public informed about matters of importance to the community, which includes crime, as well as gossip.'

'Mr Reading, you know as well as I do that all the murders under investigation in this area took place during the time Stretton has been incarcerated. He couldn't possibly have had anything to do with them.'

Reading came back at him. 'Perhaps you can tell us whether you are following a positive lead or whether this is just another speculative line of enquiry?'

Deakin thought about it for a moment. 'I've said before that we will leave no stone unturned in our efforts to bring this matter to a conclusion. As a matter of course we maintain contact with other forces who may have encountered similar problems to those which we are facing at this time.' Not allowing Reading to develop his theme, Deakin moved straight on.

'Johnson, Telegraph. It seems to me Mr Deakin that you're really not telling us anything at all, are you?'

Deakin recalled the man from previous meetings. He was not impressed by his caustic approach. 'Being offensive helps neither your cause or mine, Mr Johnson. Let me remind you that we have a team of dedicated detectives working day and night on these murders and they deserve better than your criticism.'

Johnson was unmoved. 'So, by telling us nothing, you give us carte blanche to write our thoughts rather than your facts?'

Deakin didn't intend to pull any punches with this man. 'We've spent hundreds of hours interviewing people and searching for witnesses. This is not about pleasing the press but searching for a killer. If anyone offers us a lead we must look into it.'

'So Stretton gave you a lead then, did he?'

'I never said that. Now who's grasping at straws?'

Johnson refused to back down. 'Grasping at straws, or fishing in canals. Not catching anything, are you?' He sat back, smirking.

'Marjorie Halliwell, The Express,' Gray hardly gave her a second glance. 'We know that those arrested previously have all been released without charge. Does that mean you have no-one in your sights at the moment? If so, what guarantees do we have that this man, or men, may not strike again today?'

Deakin relaxed slightly. 'It's true. We don't have anyone in custody at the moment. But that doesn't mean we are without evidence which ultimately should lead us to the person we need to interview.' He held her gaze a little longer. 'With regard to your fear of some-one else being murdered today or tomorrow, or any other day, I can only advise everyone here to inform your readers that they need to exercise great care when dealing with strangers, and take nothing they say for granted.'

Marjorie appeared satisfied for the moment at least.

'One final question and then we must finish, ladies and gentlemen.'

'Max Stenner, Evening Standard.'

Deakin was pleased to see him in the audience. *Thank God. At least I'll get out of here without being roasted alive.* The question was simple enough.

'Does the apparent lack of information at this confer-ence mean that you have something up your sleeve which you can't disclose to us today? Can we at least promise our readership an early conclusion?'

'Well, Mr Stenner,' he started. 'There's nothing in this world I'd like better than to be able to walk into a meeting like this and announce that someone has been charged. Sadly, I can't do that today. Maybe, and it is only maybe, we'll be able to call another meeting soon and make the statement everyone wants to hear.' *Always end on a note of optimism, Dad used to say.* The three men rose and trooped out of the room, leaving the reporters chattering noisily amongst themselves.

'Enjoy that session lad?' Deakin spoke to Gray. A bright red face looked back at him.

'Bit like fencing really. Plenty of cut and thrust.'

'Absolutely right. Cut, thrust and parry. That's what it's all about. Just make sure you don't let the buggers stab you in the back.' Deakin walked away leaving the two men to get on with their work.

Alison noticed him passing her door. 'Coffee sir?'

Deakin was dry as a bone. 'Thanks.' He sat quietly sipping the drink while taking stock of the situation. Four murders already, possibly five, and unless they got a break soon, more might follow. Whoever was responsible was out there somewhere, not far away, challenging him personally. The afternoon was spent checking list of enquiries marked Done and Not Done. Prison records for escapees. Mental hospitals for anyone out on licence. All the local grasses had been seen and no-one had a clue. Usually they could come up with suggestions but this time, nothing.

The Not Done list, which was pretty sparse, included things like trying to trace a white car, possibly a Vauxhall and eliminating prints left by genuine visitors to all of the deceased. Statements from local traders and neighbours also had to be reviewed. It was all part of the unending search for the one lead which might just set him on the path to success.

Deakin called the pathologist, in case he had come up with something new. Hayes had gone home early. Jones didn't seem to be around and it wasn't worth leaving messages at this time of day. He glanced at the clock on the wall. It said six fifty five. He double checked with his watch. it was six fifty five.

'On my God. Late again. She'll be the next one looking for a divorce solicitor.'

Hastily crossing the room, Deakin took his coat from its hanger, threw it over his arm, and walked out, closing the door behind him. He stopped in reception for a brief word with Lloyd.

'Haven't buried your theory yet. Still bearing it in mind. See you in the morning.'

'Thanks chief. Goodnight.' *At least you don't have to go home and fight for the Tele.* He kept the thought to himself.

Deakin's attention was distracted for a moment by the sight of two figures hunched together in the far corner of the car park. *Surely not on police property?* They half turned, glancing furtively in his direction. 'Goodnight Alison.' Without waiting for a reply he climbed into his car. He recalled not so many years ago when the car park was just a field. Laura used to walk down to meet him sometimes when they were newly wed. *Not the most romantic place, a car park, but it's what you make it, I suppose.* The memories flooded back. Deakin stopped on the way home for a minute. There was something he needed to do.

It required a great deal of skill to keep her husband's dinner warm and fresh looking, but Laura Deakin was up to the challenge. Years of practice had made her an expert in that area of the kitchen. Nowadays it was more about patience, which sometimes wore thin when the pleasure of a carefully planned meal was spoiled by a late arrival. He had promised to be home early tonight and it was almost eight o'clock. She heard his key in the door and automatically turned the oven to a higher setting before going to meet him.

Deakin threw his coat over the chair in the hall and came into the kitchen, looking tired and a bit sheepish. Somehow Laura always managed to look good, no matter what the hour. She never just dressed for dinner. It was to please him. The sea turquoise dress in satinised cotton had a slightly oriental look about it. It was well suited to her dark hair. 'Sorry I'm late sweetheart. It's tough going at the moment.'

Accepting his peace offering of a box of Cadburys Roses, Laura pecked gently him on the cheek.

'If I didn't love you, I wouldn't be here. But, if you're trying to buy me, I've seen a dress ring in Boodles window today. Like my new dress?' She posed, hand on hip for effect.

'If you want to keep wearing that, you'd better give me those chocolates back. You look gorgeous. How much?'

Laura knew she could have anything she wanted without asking. 'Ten and sixpence in Woolworth's. Don't know how you put up with me sometimes. What with all the expense I put you to.'

'You mean a thousand quid for a little ring and that's still not enough. You have to have the dress as well. I don't know how I put up with you either.'

Laura's eyes lit up. 'I only put up with you because you're rich, and handsome and generous, and before you fall asleep there's two light bulbs to be changed, and my vacuum cleaner needs fixing.'

'For goodness sake woman. Do you mind if I have my dinner first?'

CHAPTER 22

'Been up half the night trying to fix a bloody vacuum cleaner.'

Jones quite liked the idea of the chief being baffled by something as simple as a vacuum cleaner.

'Managed it in the end though. I think Laura must have been cleaning the streets with it. Brushes were jammed solid.' Deakin yawned as if to emphasise the loss of sleep.

Jones handed him a neatly typed file of papers. 'My report on the Gloucester job.'

'Don't go.' There was a note of urgency in Deakin's voice. 'There's something else rattling around inside my brain and I'm not sure what it is.'

Jones was being nodded towards a chair. 'Like what? A lead we've missed.? Something in one of the statements?' He recognised the signs. When Deakin got into this frame of mind it meant he was on to something.

'Well maybe we're looking at this from the wrong angle.' He still wasn't making any sense but Deakin continued revealing his thoughts in the hope they might lead to better theories. 'We know there was no robbery motive, and that cuts out most of the local villains. We know that there was no sexual motive and that lets the warped minority group off the hook. We know that none of the four obvious suspects could have possibly committed all four murders. That's not to exclude the possibility that any one of them may have tried a copy-cat killing.' 'With you so far chief, but I still don't see it taking us any further.'

Deakin persisted. 'Each one of the men involved suggested that, for reasons unknown, they felt that they were being framed. Yet I'm satisfied as I can be that they definitely were not framed.' Deakin was in no hurry to finish his analysis of the problem. He knew the sergeant would find the loopholes if there were any, but this was a mental fishing expedition. Something that he enjoyed. Something at which he was quite good. 'We've all acknowledged that there's no evidence of framing, but everyone seems to be missing the point.'

'The point of what, Chief? If they weren't framed then what was their role in the whole thing?'

Deakin looked almost relieved. 'They were being used Harry.' He emphasised the word used. 'They were never set up, but someone took advantage of them, or maybe even their situations. Now do you follow?'

'You might well be right Chief but is it getting us any nearer?'

Deakin smiled at him. 'Sergeant, I think we might be getting on to the right track at long last. Supposing someone was able to sit in the public gallery or even the well of the court, maybe like a press reporter, and able to take down details of certain cases?'

'You mean, just sit there and take down names and addresses? The solicitor said the courts had something to do with it. But that wouldn't account for Janet Stone, would it? After all, and I've said it before, she wasn't in court.'

Deakin was thinking aloud, hardly paying attention. 'Either that or checking the court lists and keeping track of cases which are listed but not yet due.'

Jones scratched his head. It was a terrifying thought. 'Could have been in Gloucester on holiday. And checking their lists?'

Deakin looked at his watch. 'Let's get the team meeting out of the way.' The two men got up together and walked quickly down the corridor towards the CID room. Alison was coming out of the tea room alone.

'Good morning sir.' She struggled to avoid direct eye contact.

Deakin wondered if he could detect a faint blush in her cheeks. 'Morning Alison, I'll be back shortly if anyone wants me.' Her secret, it seemed, was safe with him.

The team rose as one man when the two men entered. Deakin's eyes searched the room ensuring there was no-one missing from the team. 'Morning lads. Find somewhere to sit if you can, and ask questions later.'

Before anyone could even begin to speak, he turned a chair the wrong way round and sat down with his elbows leaning on the backrest, facing his audience. He liked the team to feel his presence as a fellow detective and the informal approach made everyone more comfortable. 'Sergeant Jones and I are deeply concerned,' he began, 'at the way some members of the press are now going out of their way give us a bit of an ear bashing. In short, they're looking for a scapegoat. Someone they can point the finger at and shout *Failure*, but we're not going to let that happen.' Deakin was always amazed at the way people sat up and took notice whenever the word press was mentioned. The rallying speech to the troops carried on for a few more minutes before he came to the important part.

'I believe we're closer to catching this person, than you might think.' He raised his voice in case of doubt. 'But I also believe that he is likely to strike again at any time and I want him locked up before that happens. Whatever part you have, play it well, and let's get the rest of this jigsaw put together.' Deakin hesitated, pushed the chair aside, and walked out. There were no questions. There was no doubt about the spring in his step. He left Jones to allocate the day's enquiries.

It was late afternoon before Jones came back into the office, looking pleased with himself. 'Split the lads into four teams today, Chief.' He started to explain. 'Each group making the same enquiries about possible court cases.' Without waiting for the usual invitation, he sat down.

Deakin always knew when he was excited about something. Jones had a habit of rubbing his hands together in a sort of dry washing motion. 'How did you get on?'

'Well, chief, Janet Stone wasn't in court, but she was in the press.'

Deakin was now very interested. 'What was that about?'

'She was the executrix of her parents estate and advertised for creditors.'

It was Deakin's turn to look puzzled. 'What about the others?'

'Cathy Wilson and Mary Donovan were both in court arguing over settlement of property concerned with their divorce proceedings.'

'Surely they weren't reported in the press.'

'I don't think so. Only the rich and famous get themselves reported in divorce proceedings. But I'll have it double checked.'

The more he thought about it the worse it seemed. The idea that some lunatic was picking names out of a newspaper at random was inconceivable, and in any case it didn't fit in with the whole picture. There had to be a connection of some sort. He had an overwhelming feeling about it.

'We know about Katie Hopkins and her problems. But there was no reason for there to be anything about her in the press before she died, was there?'

Jones had to agree that prior to her death, Katie had not attracted the attention of anyone, except the police. She knew what the likely consequences might be.

'What about Stretton's wife?'

Jones livened up again. 'Spoke to the solicitor at lunchtime. Really good man. He says that proceedings were going ahead for a legal agreement to be approved by the court but they ran into a couple of snags and decided to let the judge make the final decision, but she died before that happened, as you know, leaving Stretton a widower.'

Deakin sighed. 'Yes and a wealthy man too, I should think.'

Thursday dawned, giving Deakin the chance of a break. He welcomed the rest after six days of non stop reviewing, examining statements, argument, and counter argument. He was tired and needed to clear his mind. The press were not interested in his lines of enquiry. They just wanted to nail down the lid on his coffin and then go looking for another victim. It was more fun than catching a killer and then having to write about coffee mornings and garden fetes until the next one came along. People in his situation were always sitting ducks. It was after ten when he finally made it down to breakfast, unable to resist the smell of grilled bacon and eggs. Giving Laura a peck on the cheek he sat down at the table. 'Morning sweetheart. What's on the menu?'

Laura picked up the grill pan. 'Bacon eggs, sausage and toast, Sir.' The remark earned her a friendly pat on the backside, as she passed by him. 'Saucy devil. Still think you're Jack the lad, do you?'

Deakin tucked into the meal feeling a bit more relaxed but still unable to get things straight in his head. There was something he was missing. He could sense it, feel it, almost touch it. It was all so damned frustrating.

'More tea dear?'

'Thank you Alison,' he said, absent mindedly.

'Deakin, what have you been up to.' Laura rounded on him in astonishment.

'What's up now?' He looked at her, puzzled.

'Who's Alison may I ask? But you don't have to tell me, after all I'm only your wife.'

He looked sheepish. 'If I tell you, promise you won't divorce me.'

Laura looked at him, pretending concern. 'If you don't tell me, I'll murder you with my bare hands.'

'She's a trainee officer and my personal tea lady.'

'Good God. Don't tell me you've got more slaves tucked away.'

He continued grinning. 'She's got a boyfriend. I saw them in the car park last night.'

'Thank God for that. Can't have you running off with some young floozy at your age.'

'What are you doing today?' Deakin wanted to know, partly in case he was needed to do some driving and shopping, but mainly to find out whether he was going to be free to do some fishing for a few hours.

'Supposed to see Mum for an hour this afternoon. She may come here instead.' Laura poured herself a cup of tea and sat down at the table to enjoy a few minutes with him. She didn't seem to mind what he got up to today.

'Why's that?' He wanted to know.

'Sam, look around. The place needs a damned good spit and polish session. It's getting into a bit of a mess.'

'Can I do anything to help?' The offer was sincere but it made Laura smile anyway.

'Yes. Go fishing for a while and leave me to get on with it.'

As he was ready to leave, Laura handed over a flask of coffee. 'Keep you warm. And make sure you're wrapped up well. Weather's a bit deceptive, so take care.'

'See you later.'

Laura watched as the car eased its way into the road, turning in the direction of the canal.

It was almost twelve noon before Deakin got himself settled in his favourite spot. A gentle flick of the wrist, and he watched as the line sped towards the opposite bank. The bait dropped perfectly, a couple of feet from the waters edge. The small canvas covered stool groaned under his weight as he shifted into a more comfortable position. There wasn't likely to be any boating traffic today so he would be able to leave the line in the same spot for as long as he wished. It was a tactic intended to lull the fish into a sense of false security.

The weather remained overcast but at least it was dry. Looking towards the bridge, he was able to see

271

Jack Donovan's boat still moored, smoke rising straight into the air from the narrow funnel at the front, but no sign of the boatman himself. His thoughts turned automatically to the murder of Jack's ex-wife. She had admitted someone to her home and yet he said she wouldn't let anyone in drunk or sober unless she felt confident about them.

Mary Donovan had been a nervous sort of person even when she had Jack around to look after her but since his departure she must have become more sensitive than ever before. *Who did you let in, Mary? Who did you trust?* Deakin stared across the water, at the same time turning the question over in his mind. He looked up, surprised to see Jack Donovan standing almost on top of him.

'Having any luck?'

Deakin wasn't quite sure what he meant. 'Trying hard Jack. Sure I'll get something in the end.' *Or maybe someone.*

'Fancy a brew?'

Jack Donovan laughed. 'Delighted. Never been known to refuse anything except insults and blows.'

Deakin threw a rug over his basket. 'Sit on that, it's strong enough.'

The two men now faced each other.

'No news on the investigation, I suppose?'

Deakin looked at him. The weather beaten features still showing dark rings around his eyes told their own story. The man probably hadn't had a wink of sleep since the day Mary was killed.

'Feel a bit stupid sometimes, just sitting around and waiting but what else can I do? I've given a lot of thought to your question about whoever Mary might have let into the house, and I honestly can't think of a single person.'

'I think we might be starting to head in the right direction at last.' Deakin looked at him. 'And you might be able to help me.'

Donovan looked at him in surprise. 'What can I do?' He waited for the reply. Deakin's question must have made him even more curious.

'Was your divorce acrimonious?'

Donovan considered. 'Tearful, argumentative, but never any real bust-ups.'

Deakin nodded. 'How many times did you go to court?'

'That's a tough one.' He thought again. 'Three times, I'm pretty sure.'

'How were you served with the documents from the court?'

'That's an easy one. They came through the post. I have an arrangement with the post office.' Donovan sensed somehow that he had said something Deakin didn't want to hear.

'Every time?'

'Yes. I use a post office box number and mail collection is pretty routine for me.'

'Why were you in court on the day she died?' Deakin seemed to be labouring the divorce issue.

'Do you think the murder has something to do with our divorce?'

'I don't know, but I've a feeling there's a connection somewhere, remote or otherwise.'

'Well, we were in dispute over the property and I wanted to be sure that despite her illness, or drunkenness if you prefer, she'd always have a roof over her head.

One she could never sell to support her habit or anyone else's for that matter.'

'Was that all?' Deakin didn't mean it to sound so offensive.

Donovan wasn't offended. 'Well, apart from the boat. She kept asking for half of that as well, not understanding I was actually giving her the house. I was worried in case someone took advantage and she ended up on the street.'

Deakin looked at him thoughtfully. 'What happened over the boat?'

Donovan smiled. 'Nothing really, except I've become a bit of a water gypsy. Moving about the country, making sure I could keep in touch with her but she couldn't do the same with me.' He laughed at the idea. 'Bit old to be playing hide and seek, aren't we?'

Deakin had one last question. 'When you were in court, did you notice anyone in the public area, like a press reporter or just a nosey parker?'

Donovan looked surprised. 'What do you mean?'

Deakin held his gaze. 'I mean strangers. People who had no business or connection with the proceedings.' He watched and waited while Donovan pondered the question.

'No-one really, though there was someone there on the last occasion who might have been a reporter or something to do with the court. Sorry I can't be more helpful.'

Deakin rose to his feet and began to wind the line back to his bank. 'Not much being caught today, is there?' He pointed at Donovan. 'But tomorrow will be a much better day.'

The two men shook hands and went their separate ways, Deakin to his wife and Jack Donovan to the solitude of his boat.

Deakin drove straight into the garage, parked the car and then stopped to remove his Wellington boots and heavy clothing before entering the house through the rear door. Laura heard the garage door swing up and over on its steel rollers and was already in the kitchen with the kettle in her hand.

'Had a good day?' she enquired.

Deakin kissed her on the cheek. 'Great, caught nothing except pneumonia, well almost.'

Laura laughed, pretending to be startled as he threw out an arm, pulling her close to him.

'Fresh air does things to a man.'

She pushed him away, gently but firmly. 'Behave yourself, Mum's in the lounge.'

He grinned. 'One day my girl, you'll run out of excuses.' Walking into the lounge he was about to say 'hello' when he realised the old lady was asleep, snoring gently, at peace with the world.

'Two women.' He smiled to himself. 'The untouchable and the unwakeable.'

Deakin was coming back to life and beginning to feel good about it.

Chapter 23

The desk sergeant checked his day book to ensure no jobs were being missed before the patrolmen left the station. So far, the changeover had gone smoothly but quite often something would crop up, throwing his plans into disarray. 'That peeper's gone very quiet since the Mary Donovan episode.' His eyes settled on the young officer waiting for his partner. 'Was you that found her, wasn't it?'

The man stiffened slightly. 'Yes Sarge. And I don't ever want to find another. I've hardly slept a wink since that night. Blood everywhere. I keep dreaming about it.'

The sergeant pulled him up sharply. 'Alright lad, spare us the gory details. We all know what happened.' He couldn't leave it at that. 'No-one ever said that being a policeman was a soft job. You got the rough end of it that night but you have to move on, not dwell on it. Now get your mate and get out from under my feet or else I'll be after your blood.'

The officers pulled into a lay-by near to the junction of Aughton Street and Park Road. The light was beginning to fade quickly. It was nearly time for the town centre to come to life again, after the end of the day's business. The radio crackled as the call went through to the operations room at headquarters.

They had to report every hour, on the hour, no matter what. Rule number one they called it.

'Tango five to base.' The response was instant.

'Good evening Tango five. All quiet on the western front?'

'So far, so good. Let's hope it stays that way.'

'Don't be wishing.' The operator stopped in mid sentence. 'There's a call coming in now. Keep the line open. You may be needed.' Silence followed for a few moments. The crackling of the radio was interrupted. 'Tango five proceed to Edge Hill Teacher training college, St Helens Road. There's something mysterious going on at the back of the Eleanor Rathbone hall of residence. Might be your peeper. Keep us posted.'

The driver started to spin the wheel to the right. Sparkling blue lights flashed from the roof of the car as it headed into Park Road, preparing to fork left on to St Helens Road. His partner suddenly reached forward, switching off the roof lights.

'What the hell are you doing. This is an emergency, of sorts. isn't it?'

'Don't let's go up St Helens Road and through the front entrance. If he's there, he's bound to see us and scarper. There's a back entrance off Ruff Lane. We can park there and walk in behind him or them or whoever it is.'

The driver turned left into Ruff Lane. Within a minute they were adjacent to the rear entrance. A white Vauxhall cavalier was parked nearby.

'Tango five to base. We are at the rear of the premises and proceeding through a wooded area towards the rear of the Eleanor Rathbone Hall.' He gave details of the car for HQ to run a check.

The two men left the patrol car and headed into the woods.

'Don't forget, we have to catch a peeper in the act, by law. Otherwise we won't be able to charge him with anything except trespass. Let's keep it quiet.'

Keeping to the rough path they walked silently towards flickering lights which filtered through the trees. A hand suddenly raised, fingers on lips, then pointing forwards. Ahead on the edge of the woods they could just make out a hump in the long grass. It moved. The officers closed in.

'What have we here then?' The officer's voice gave Pascoe a fright. he jumped to his feet.

'Bit o' rabbiting lads. Nowt else.'

'What's your name.'

'Er, Pascoe. John Pascoe.'

'How many rabbits have you caught John?' The officer was looking at Pascoe's holdall.

'Er none tonight yet. Can I go now?' Pascoe made as if to walk away.

'Don't go without your camera John.' The policeman lifted a camera out of the grass. 'Minolta XG eh? Bit pricey for photographing rabbits, isn't it? Wouldn't want to leave this lying around would we?' He looked around. 'Binoculars John. All the better to see those rabbits with, eh? Wonder what I can see through these?' He lifted them to his eyes and then towards the Eleanor Rathbone hall. 'Goodness me. All those young ladies. And you're looking for rabbits John? I think not.'

Pascoe maintained a sullen silence.

'John Pascoe, I'm arresting you on suspicion of contravention of the Peeping Tom Act. Anything you say will be taken down and may be used later in evidence.' He pulled out a pair of handcuffs. 'Let's go.'

The three men walked back to the police car. 'Tango five to base. We have a prisoner. bringing him in now.'

'Thank you Tango five. Message acknowledged.'

Pascoe interrupted. 'What about me car?'

The officer pointed towards the white car ahead of them. 'You mean that old banger? Is it yours?'

'Yes it fucking is.' Pascoe began to show his true colours.

'Good. Give me the keys and I'll lock it up. Anything personal in it that we need to know about?' The officer walked over to the white car. The passenger door opened easily. The glove box was unlocked. Inside he found three rolls of used film. He locked the car and walked back to the police vehicle. 'These yours? He held up the films close to Pascoe's face. 'Holiday snaps are they?' Should be interesting Mr Pascoe. We'll pay for the developing and printing.'

'What you going to do with me?'

'We're taking you back to the station where you'll be interviewed, charged and possibly bailed, but that's not up to us.' He hesitated, deciding to leave things as they were for the moment. Five minutes later they were back at the station.

'All yours Sarge.'

Pascoe rubbed his wrists vigorously as the handcuffs were removed.

'Cell two, if you don't mind.' The custody sergeant needed Pascoe in a separate cell. CID wanted a few words with him. Nothing to do with rabbits or unwary ladies. He turned to Pascoe. I have the authority to detain you for a short period and after that it's up to someone else. If necessary you will be permitted one telephone call to a solicitor or your next of kin.'

Pascoe glared at him. 'You can all fuck off as far as I'm concerned.'

'Are you threatening me? The sergeant said. 'There's half a dozen things I can charge you with right now. Shall we start with resisting arrest, assault on a police officer, and threatening behaviour?'

'Do what the fuck you like.' Pascoe remained defiant.

'Mark your notebooks lads. We will be charging him very shortly.'

Jones walked into the interview room. The prisoner looked away from Gray towards the newcomer. 'I'm Detective Sergeant Jones. You, I presume, are John Pascoe. Is that correct?'

Pascoe grunted something unintelligible.

'Well, are you John Pascoe or not?'

'Course I am. What the fuck's all this about?'

Jones weighed him up. He was a big cumbersome man, well able to lift anyone off their feet. But what on earth could he do to attract women. There was nothing attractive about the man. Certainly no charisma. 'I'm making enquiries into a number of murders that have taken place in this area. Did you know or ever meet a woman called Mary Donovan?'

Pascoe knew about her murder. 'Read about her in the paper. What the fuck's that gorra do wi' anything?'

'I'll ask you one more time. Did you ever know or meet a woman called Mary Donovan?'

'And I've told yer.'

Jones changed the line of questioning. 'Do you own a white Vauxhall cavalier car?' He recited the registration umber.

'Course I do. You already know that. What's it to you?'

'Your car was seen in the vicinity of Mary Donovan's bungalow shortly before her death. What were you doing there?'

Pascoe looked mystified. 'How the fuck should I know where I was or why I was anywhere? Free country isn't it? Park where I fucking like can't I?'

'Got a nasty temper Pascoe, haven't you? Lose it with women a lot do you? Enjoy giving them a good whacking now and again? Jones wondered how far he could push this line. It might be interesting. 'Big man with women are you Pascoe.'

Gradually it seemed to be dawning on Pascoe that there was more to his situation than he thought. It was nothing to do with peeping. These people were talking murder. 'You accusing me of murder? I never killed no-one an' you can't prove I did.'

'Have you murdered anyone?' Jones held his ground. 'My men are at your house with a search warrant as we speak. I can link you to a murder. Your films are being developed by our forensic team. Now is there anything you want to tell me before your position gets any worse. It might just help you in the end.'

'I've already told ye'. Don't know what you're talking about.'

A knock on the door interrupted them. Jones went outside.

'A message from the search team Sarge. They've found a load of photos hidden in the house. Mostly local women in various stages of undress, including Mary Donovan. He's the peeper alright. No doubt about it. Wife's terrified in case you let him out and he goes home. Chances are he'll beat her to death.'

'Tell them to keep searching for any personal effects that his wife can't identify. He might just have slipped up and taken a souvenir. Also tell his wife he won't be going anywhere tonight. Might ease things a bit for her.'

Once back inside the room Jones faced Pascoe again. 'Are you still denying any connection with Mary Donovan? This is the last time I'm going to ask you.'

Pascoe remained defiant. 'Told you. I know nowt about her or any murder. Don't even know where she lived.'

'John Pascoe I'm now going hold you on suspicion of murder. If you wish to instruct a solicitor you can have access to one of your choice or we'll call one for you. Do you understand? I take it you would like us to inform your wife. She'll need to know anyway.'

'Tell that fucking lazy bitch nothin'. I'll sort her mesel'.

'You're just a natural born bully Pascoe, aren't you?' Jones hardly expected him to agree. 'I know you're lying. I've got the proof on the way right now and I'm going to make sure every last ounce of it goes before a trial judge.'

'Well fuck you too, mister. You're not havin' me for something I haven't done. so I took some pictures. So what? Doesn't make me a killer.'

'Supposing you had an accomplice.' Jones kept trying.

'An accomplice for what?'

'Maybe casing the place for a burglary that went wrong, badly wrong.'

Jones stood up. 'No Pascoe. We're not finished with you by a long way. Take him back to the cell.'

'I want bail. I need to go home.' Pascoe's voice dropped for the first time. He was almost civil.

'No bail Pascoe. And if I have my way you won't be going home for a bloody long time.' Jones turned his back and walked out. Once in the corridor he spoke to the custody sergeant. 'Let him stew for a while. I'll see him later, after I've had a word with the super about a detaining extension.' He carried on towards the CID room.

Joy Pascoe answered the front door.

'Hello. Mrs Pascoe is it? I'm Detective Sergeant Jones and this is Detective Constable Gray. May we come in and have a word with you?'

Joy was still in a state of shock from the visit by the search team. They'd had her identifying photographs that Pascoe had kept hidden. Joy knew Mary Donovan and the lady from the boutique.

'Yes, of course. Please come in.' She was glad to have them off the doorstep. God knows what the neighbours might be thinking.

'I have to inform you that we are holding your husband for a series of offences but most importantly on suspicion of murder.' Jones waited for a reaction.

'Oh my God. He's killed someone. I was always afraid his temper would get the better of him one day. When did this happen? Today?'

'No Mrs Pascoe. We're talking about Mary Donovan, the Irish lady whose pictures you have seen today and which your husband took immediately before she was murdered. His car was seen at the scene of the crime.' Jones was looking for a link. 'Does your husband have a particular friend who might go with him on some of these undesirable ventures?'

'As far as I know he has no particular friends. He's not a very sociable person, as you've probably already guessed.' She thought for a moment. 'I suppose you could ask at The Lion. He's there almost every night.

The barman might be able to tell you something. Pascoe never tells me where he's going or what he's up to and I'm not allowed to ask.'

Jones noted the absence of a Christian name. 'Is your husband prone to violence Mrs Pascoe?' It was a risky question. She could reach for a phone and call someone. But she didn't.

'Yes Mr Jones, especially in drink. No point in denying that. I've put up with it for years. But I never dreamed he would deliberately kill anyone, except perhaps me. You see, we don't get on very well.' Tears welled up into her eyes.

Jones looked at the woman. *Quite pretty really. Some decent clothes and a bit of make-up, and a hair-do would work miracles. Pascoe must enjoy bullying you. Seeing that downtrodden look and the spark gone from your eyes. The bastard.* The thought stayed in his head. 'Off the record, this is your chance to save yourself. Maybe you should see a solicitor while your husband is locked up and get some wheels in motion in case he gets out sooner rather than later.' It wasn't his place to give advice but he guessed that if they had to let Pascoe go then he would likely take his spite out on Joy after a drunken spree.

'Thank you sergeant. I think I might do that. Will he be kept in jail for very long?'

'It's hard to say at the moment. Our enquiries are still ongoing. He could be bailed within seventy two hours if we're not finished with him. He might also be brought before a magistrate and bailed on the porno charges. Conditions could be attached to bail with regard to yourself because you would be a material witness. It's all a bit complicated in the early stages. Sorry I can't help any further.' Jones left her with something to think about.

CHAPTER 24

The wiper blades slashed relentlessly across the rain soaked glass. The struggle to get through early morning traffic seemed to be getting worse every day. The town centre showed signs of being gridlocked. It was frustrating, not being able to exercise the power deep inside the engine of his Wolseley fifteen hundred twin carburettor. Second hand maybe, but Jones had it tuned to perfection and it never let him down. He stared unblinking through the windscreen.

Turning into the Police Station car park shortly before eight o'clock, he drove directly into one of the spaces allocated to CID personnel. Deakin's car was already languishing in its own reserved place, looking as it had been there for some time. When he was worried about something, Deakin would often come in early to work undisturbed on the problem. The sergeant knew the signs only too well. Without either a mackintosh or an umbrella, Jones hurried through the rain and up the steps leading to the rear entrance.

'Morning Sarge.' The duty constable unlocked the steel door.

He barely glanced at the young man as he hurried towards to the CID office. He could hear the phone ringing before he reached the door. 'Sergeant Jones,' he said, trying to pull his wet jacket off at the same time.

'Morning. I spotted you through the window. Pop down as soon as you've got a minute.'

'On my way Chief.' Jones went straight to Deakin's office.

'I understand you've got a fellow called Pascoe in cells. Is it just for peeping or do you have something else in mind?'

'He denied all knowledge of Mary Donovan. But, our search revealed otherwise. There were photographs of her semi-naked. His car was close to her house around the time of the murder.' Jones waited to see whether Deakin wanted to comment but there was no response.

'Anyway, the patrol lads got him bang to rights on the peeping job. He's bound to cop a plea on that but we needed to hold on to him a bit longer.'

'Why not just bail him and keep tabs on his movements? Deakin had his own way of doing things.

'I'm not satisfied that he doesn't have an accomplice tucked away somewhere and they might have been casing Mary Donovan's place. Or he might have seen something and daren't cough it to us without incriminating himself in other ways.'

'Do you really think he killed Mary?' Deakin clearly was not impressed.

'I'm not saying that. I believe it's possible he knows more than he's telling us. We've got him on peeping and also on other minor charges so why not let him sweat for a while? Never know what he might come up with.'

'The chances are he couldn't have killed all our victims. Don't you think that we are wasting valuable time and resources?'

Jones felt embarrassed. The Chief knew he was up to something and was sure to figure it out eventually.

'I interviewed Pascoe's wife yesterday evening. She's living in fear and dread of him going home and beating her to death. The woman's on the verge of a complete breakdown. She needs protection while things are being sorted legally.'

'I didn't hear what you said and I don't want you to repeat it. You can hold him on suspicion of the Donovan job while you check alibis for it and any others. You're only going to draw a blank anyway.' Deakin instantly switched the conversation. 'I met Jack Donovan yesterday on the canal.'

Jones pricked his ears up. 'Thought you were supposed to be on a rest day.' For a moment he sounded as if he were the boss.

'Nowhere to run, nowhere to hide, not even on the canal bank.'

The sergeant knew only too well that the Chief wouldn't turn anyone away whether it was Jack Donovan or a tramp at his front door, particularly if it had anything to do with a case. His treatment of Joy Pascoe was really no different. He waited to see whether this was the reason for the early start.

'It was interesting that the only stranger he noticed at any of his hearings was someone he took to be a press reporter. Now what the hell would a newshound be doing reporting on a case which was of no interest to anyone?' He paused for a second.

'Christ, Chief, you don't think it's one of them, do you?'

Deakin remained thoughtful, choosing his words carefully. 'Leaving no stone unturned, nor even a pebble. that's what we said, or at least I said.'

Jones remained mystified. 'I don't get it.'

The phone interrupted their conversation. It was Howard Phillips, the solicitor.

'Good Morning Chief Inspector. You left a message on my answer service. There was a slight pause. 'Not thinking of getting divorced, I hope?'

Deakin laughed. 'No thanks. You'll have to look elsewhere for your big fee today. I'm just making a few enquiries in connection with Katie Hopkins, and I wondered when it might be convenient to have chat with you?'

'I'm at court from ten o'clock. Should be clear by twelve, if that's OK. Your place or mine?' It was his turn to laugh.

Deakin didn't hesitate. 'I'll come to your office if that's alright.' He turned back to face his sergeant.

'As a matter of some urgency I want you to get in touch with Keith Taylor. Not by phone. I want you to see him and push him as hard as you can about any connections Janet Stone had with the courts. Anything at all, no matter how remote.'

Jones stood up, ready to move off, but found himself detained.

'Do that this morning, and take DC Gray with you. We need to do the same with Cathy Wilson's ex-husband.' He thought for a moment. Tell the custody sergeant to get the patrolmen to take statements from Pascoe on the peeping job and anything else they can think of. When they've finished he can call a solicitor. We might as well try and make it look authentic.'

Jones left the office with a sense of urgency he hadn't felt for some time. Deakin's enthusiasm was rubbing off on to him.

Deakin turned his attention back to other matters. Eventually he glanced at his watch wondering where the last two and a half hours had gone. It was already after ten. He left the office in good time for the meeting. There was no point in taking the car. It was only a brisk walk and the early morning rain seemed to have stopped for the time being at least. He reached for his top coat and then made his way out of the station, stopping briefly to tell Tom Lloyd where he was going. 'Back in an hour Tom, if anyone needs me.'

Walking along the High Street towards Imperial Chambers, his attention was constantly distracted by the endless offers of bargain upon bargain. Suits, shirts, socks and ties piled high in the windows beneath the gaudy new style flashing neon lights. There was an undeniable vibrancy about the place. He recalled when sales were only held in January and July. When people shopped in a more leisurely manner. The transformation was remarkable.

The Odeon cinema at the end of the High Street was now advertising a change of programme. Barbara Streisand in Funny Girl had taken the place of The Boston Strangler, now withdrawn to avoid offending public taste. He made a mental note to mention it when he got home and carried on walking towards his destination. Laura, he was certain, would love to see it.

Being familiar with Imperial Chambers, Deakin didn't need to read the polished brass plates, already knowing most of them off by heart. Through the glass fronted entrance, he walked directly to the lift, and groaned to himself out loud, 'Oh, bloody hell.' Some fool had left the gate open at one of the floors above and it wouldn't operate until it was closed properly.

Frustrated, he set off down the passage and through the fire-doors towards the main staircase, reluctantly beginning the long climb. The old treads seemed to twist and turn every ten steps in a spiral, making the journey seem twice as long. His legs began to ache with the constant knee bending as he climbed to the third floor. He finally arrived at the offices of Howard Phillips and Co and walked into the reception area, face now reddened with the physical effort.

'Not as young as I thought I was.' He said to the grey haired, bespectacled secretary as she ushered him through to meet the solicitor.

'None of us are, sir.'

Howard Phillips had arrived back from court early and was waiting for him. The two men shook hands in a genuine show of friendship and mutual respect. He was ushered into a padded armchair.

Deakin sat back in the chair, facing the lawyer across the broad desk, recalling how, only recently, Katie Hopkins must have sat in the same chair. She must have hoped like him that he could somehow solve her problem. Deakin could almost sense her presence in the room, one eye smothered in makeup, a swollen cheek, and a dried blood spot on her split lip. Phillips seemed to be reading his thoughts.

'Not long ago Katie was sitting just where you are now.'

'I was just thinking the same myself.'

'Well whatever I can do, will be a pleasure. How is it going with Martin Richards?'

'It's not him. I'm sure of that as I can be.'

Phillips looked surprised at such frankness. 'Good God. Don't tell me she had two men abusing her. She certainly only mentioned one to me.'

Deakin could see that the lawyer was also worried in case he too was missing something. 'Not really, if you accept that she was approached only once by the killer.'

Phillips was puzzled. 'Got anyone else in mind?'

'That depends on developments which I can't explain at the moment, but if things turn out as I hope, the answer could well be yes'

'What can I do?'

Deakin kept it as brief and confidential as possible. 'Do you see many press reporters in the civil courts?'

Phillips looked intrigued. 'Yes we do. Usually it's in connection with commercial matters and large compensation claims but not so much in the family courts.' He thought for a moment. 'Or in exceptional cases, like battered children, but not battered wives. They don't seem to attract much sympathy.' He kept on looking straight at Deakin. 'That much I could have told you over the phone, and our coffee's not that good.'

'Sorry, I didn't mean to sound secretive but I need to get one or two things straight in my mind. So you wouldn't have noticed anyone hanging around the court waiting for the Katie Hopkins case to come on?'

Phillips was certain that no-one was anywhere near the court that morning. 'There were only three of us there, otherwise the place was empty. I was waiting to go before the judge, without a client, and another solicitor was coming out of court with a client.'

Deakin tried to appear satisfied with his answer and carried on. 'Do you know for certain whether or not

Martin Richards was served with a summons to appear on that case as the official defendant? He says he wasn't.'

'Just a minute.' Howard picked up his file of papers on the Hopkins case. It was thin by his standards, legal aid forms taking up most of the folder. He fingered through the pages, pulling out the original summons with an invoice still pinned to it. 'Must get that paid.' He looked at the document. 'This is the actual summons, so it couldn't have been served.' He looked at Deakin. 'Looks like he told you the truth.' He handed the document over for checking.

'Can I see the invoice as well, please?'

Phillips curiosity was building rapidly but he knew better than to try and question the questioner. He handed over the account.

'Can I borrow this?' Deakin was no longer smiling.

'Of course you can, but let me take a photocopy first, so I can get it paid.' He pressed the intercom button. 'I need some photocopying done right away please.' There was a tap on the door and a young clerk appeared.

'Anything else or just the invoice?'

'Can I have the summons as well?'

Phillips handed the document to his clerk.

'Don't mind my keeping the originals for a while, I hope?'

Phillips shook his head. 'Of course not. I won't need them anymore.'

Deakin looked at the invoice, slightly puzzled. 'I thought these were served by the court bailiff.'

Phillips laughed. 'Depends on whether you can afford to wait till they get round to it. If it's an emergency or the hearing is likely to call for some sort of evidence then we often go private, so to speak, and use enquiry agents, or process servers as some like to be called.'

Deakin was curious to know what sort of evidence.

'Well,' said Phillips, 'Perhaps we need to know something about the background of the individual, so we serve him, talk to him at the same time, and then the enquiry agent can give evidence about the conversation.' He smiled. 'Fancy teaching you the tricks of our trade! On the other hand, if there's an urgent hearing, the enquiry agent, or process server, will attend court and prove the identity of the person he served with the summons but that's only necessary if the defendant fails to arrive. The court bailiffs don't often do that type of work because it's too time consuming and there's no profit in it.' Phillips sat back in his chair looking as if he had just delivered a lecture.

Deakin had a look of intense concentration, not wanting to miss a word. He had never given much thought before to the work of process servers and enquiry agents, and found it interesting.

'Going to let me in on your little secret then?' Phillips smiled, obviously hoping for some morsel.

'Well, at the moment I'm still on my fishing expedition but getting nearer all the time. We were wondering whether Richards had been served with a summons, and if not, then why not?'

Phillips still didn't follow the reason for concern.

'Well, if he was served then it might seem logical he went round to Katie Hopkins home to try and persuade her to withdraw the summons before it got to court.'

Phillips interrupted his flow. 'And if she refused?'

'Precisely, we have motive, including time, opportunity and inclination, which sets him up nicely. Pity that theory has been kicked out. I'd love to see that man behind bars for a while. He needs to be taught a lesson.'

Phillips leaned back and shrugged his shoulders. 'Can't help you there.'

'The problem is,' Deakin continued, 'We know he couldn't really be tied into any of the others. Yet they're all connected somehow. There was always the chance of a copycat killing but I'm inclined to disregard that possibility.' He rose heavily to his feet. 'Anyway I'm grateful for your help. Hopefully I might be able to bring you some good news shortly.'

Phillips walked around the desk, hand outstretched. 'If there's anything else I can do, don't hesitate.'

Walking back through the shopping centre, Deakin hesitated by the florist's before going inside, and ordering a dozen yellow roses to be delivered to Laura.

'Card sir?' the assistant enquired.

'Thank you.' He leaned on the counter to write the message.

'Love You' was all it said.

The florist raised her eyebrows, wondering what sort of misdemeanour was causing him to make the sentimental apology. Usually it was a forgotten birthday or anniversary but he didn't look apologetic enough for that. *If she's kicking him out, I wouldn't mind giving it a try.*

Deakin sat down and opened the file of papers, trying to sort things out in his mind Everything seemed to depend on something else. Nothing was going quite as he had planned. The phone disturbed his train of thought.

'Not caught you at a bad time, I hope?' It was Laura. 'Don't worry if you're a bit late tonight: you can get me some more flowers tomorrow. These are gorgeous.'

'I still hope to be with you by seven thirty.'

'Don't be late. Mum's not here tonight,' she said. There was a touch of mischief in the voice which he recognised.

'Can't wait. Bye for now.' Laura's infectious laugh was still ringing in his ears when the phone went down.

CHAPTER 25

'Call from Gloucester, Mr Bradley, the solicitor is on the line.'

'Oh good, put him through.' Deakin felt a twinge of excitement as the Solicitor's voice came down the line. It was as if things were finally beginning to come together. 'Good afternoon. Thanks for returning my call.'

'That's alright Chief Inspector. What can I do for you?'

Deakin hesitated for a second to get things right in his mind. 'With reference to the Stretton case, would you know for certain whether or not any court bailiffs, enquiry agents, or process servers ever attended personally upon your client for the purpose of serving a summons?' The speed of the response left no room for doubt.

'I represented Stretton throughout his matrimonial problems and all documentation intended for him was delivered directly to me at all times. There was no need for him to see anyone.' He seemed positive.

'Can you recall seeing any strangers or newspaper reporters in court at any time?' The question seemed to surprise the solicitor.

'The court was full every day during the trial.'

Deakin corrected himself. 'Sorry, I meant during the matrimonial proceedings.'

The solicitor needed no time to consider the question. 'Heavens, no. Reporters and their like don't bother themselves with domestic wrangling, and the only other people likely to grace the court would be university law students studying a thing called Practice and Procedure.' He explained briefly how students study cases actually proceeding in court in order to develop an understanding of real life legal pleadings.

Deakin thanked him for his time and drew the conversation to an end. Something; some small detail, locked away in the back of his mind still evaded him. Jones knocked and entered, looking worried, grunting a sort of greeting.

'We've seen Keith Taylor, and Wilson but they don't seem to be able to tell us anything we don't already know, except,' he paused as if for effect, 'Janet Stone engaged a firm of solicitors to sort out her parents' estate, so she had no need for either enquiry agents or process servers.'

'Who were the solicitors?'

'Carter and Manning. I've spoken to them and they say they used some guy down south to trace a couple of beneficiaries but that's all.'

'What about Bill Wilson?'

'Well Chief, like I said, nothing much there either. Wilson received most of the papers through the post or through his own solicitor, and as far as he was concerned his wife was treated the same.'

Deakin rubbed his chin. 'We're missing something and I don't know what it is.'

'Are you sure we're not becoming too obsessed with the idea of a court agent of one sort or another?' Jones waited for a response. He tried again. 'Why not a policeman?'

Deakin looked at him. 'Because police officers could- n't give us the link we need. These people were involved in civil and domestic issues, not crimes. Policemen would hardly be aware of their existence.'

'OK. Why not a random killer.'

'Well, the way I see it, there's a loose connection between all the victims, including the Stretton murder. They were all involved in some form of legal proceedings.' Deakin smiled at him. 'Why not a solicitor. Phillips, or your friend Bradley, perhaps?'

Jones scratched his head. 'Thank God we don't even have to consider that possibility. Imagine having to investigate a couple of seasoned professionals like those two. Anyway, four or five firms have been involved so that should let them out.'

Deakin leaned towards him. 'Go through the five main statements one more time and let's see what comes out. The answer has to be there somewhere and it's staring us in the face. I can feel it.'

Jones walked down the corridor to the CID room thoroughly dejected.

Alison knocked and entered to collect the empty cups. She smiled politely. 'I'm finishing early today sir. Can I get you another drink before I go?'

Deakin looked up from his desk. 'Young lady. You'll have to stop fussing around me, else you'll have my missus after you.'

Alison's face showed her surprise. 'Don't understand what you mean, sir. It's only coffee.'

He smiled. 'Called my wife Alison the other night. She threatened to divorce me.'

'Can't have that sir. Fancy having private detectives hanging around the police station watching us all day.' She giggled at the idea. 'I'd end up making coffee for them as well. Did you say you wanted another one sir?'

Deakin stared at her. 'What did you say?' His voice suddenly took on a sense of urgency, almost snapping at her.

Alison felt herself going bright red. She was shocked and embarrassed at the change in him. It was out of character.

'Sorry, sir. I just asked if you wanted another drink?' She stood still not quite knowing what to do next.

Deakin leaned towards her. 'Before that.'

She was becoming embarrassed, not knowing what he meant.

'I just said fancy us having private detectives on our tail. That's all.'

'Not by any means, it's not. Private detectives on our tail, doing what?'

She stared back as if he'd gone mad. 'I was only joking sir.'

'Doing what?' Deakin insisted.

'Well, trying to get evidence for a divorce, I suppose.'

Deakin ignored her obvious discomfort. The whole situation seemed to be getting out of hand. He cut across her thoughts. 'Never mind the coffee. Get Sergeant Jones back in here. Tell him it's urgent.' He thought for a moment. 'Then ask the switchboard to try and get Mr Bradley back on the line. She's got the number.' Without stopping for breath he continued. 'And when I've finished with him, I need to get hold of Mr Phillips as a matter of urgency.' Deakin's face relaxed for a moment. 'And you'll need to get a move on if you still want to meet your young man on time.'

Alison almost ran back to the sanctuary of her own office.

Deakin's conversation with both solicitors was brief but a faint look of contentment appeared on his face as he replaced the receiver after the second call.

Jones knocked and entered. 'You wanted to see me Chief?'

'Did you say a summons was issued against Bill Wilson but returned on the morning after the murder, unserved?'

'Yes Chief. That's right, I did.'

Deakin face showed his relief. 'That's what I thought.' He pulled the invoice from his file of papers, reading the name and address out aloud. 'Get round there right away. I need to be having a few words with this man.' Jones started to say something. Deakin brushed him aside. 'And don't come back without him.'

Jones and Gray left the police station, the portable blue light on the roof of their car already flashing its warning to anyone not to get in their way. The address on the invoice lay down one of the side alleys which ran between market Street and County Road. The two detectives hurried up the steps into the now decaying Victorian building, their feet echoing on the uncovered floor-boards. At the rear of the second floor they found what they were looking for. The sign read Ralph J Bergman Private Investigator.

The inscription, printed in black and white on a piece of white cardboard and stuck to the glass panel, seemed to have a lack of permanence about it. The door opened to expose a room poorly lit by a single unshaded light bulb. It looked as if it hadn't been decorated in years. The remains of chocolate coloured paint no longer able to contain the damp was swelling into bubbles and peeling away from the walls. Furnished in a style more in keeping with a scene created by Dickens, it was apparently sufficient for the needs of its tenant.

'Mr Bergman?' Jones stepped inside holding out his warrant card and addressed the occupier.

The man sitting behind the desk looked surprised.

'Detective Sergeant Jones CID and my colleague DC Gray. It is Mr Bergman, isn't it?' Jones held his gaze without wavering. *Not as big as I thought you'd be.* Sharp unsmiling eyes peered back at him. Wisps of dark hair flattened across a balding head. Pale features gave him a slightly sickly appearance. Nothing like the private eyes depicted in books and on television.

'Yes, that's right. What can I do for you?' He stood up. The unpressed suit had seen better days and a bigger man.

'We're looking into the death of a young lady, name of Katie Hopkins, and others, and you may be able to assist our enquiries.' Without waiting for any comment, he continued. 'Because of the serious nature of our business I think it best that I should formally caution you and explain that you are not bound to say anything at this time, but anything you do say may be taken down in writing and later used in evidence against you.' He waited for the reaction.

A look of astonishment came over the man's face. 'I don't know any Katie Hopkins. Never heard of her. Why are you asking me?' He leaned towards the phone. 'I think I should call my solicitor.' Gray moved it out of his reach. Bergman's face twitched in sudden anger.

'I've just bloody told you I don't know what you're talking about. What the hell are you two after? I know my bloody rights and I want to speak to my solicitor right now.' He made an exaggerated move towards the phone. Gray lifted it from the desk and pulled hard on the cable, watching the connection box rip away from the wall. 'Oh, dear. I think it's broken.' The young detective seemed almost to be enjoying himself. 'Never mind Mr Bergman, you can use ours down at the station. It's working fine.'

Jones interrupted again. 'You can come down voluntarily and assist our enquiries or I can arrest you on suspicion of murder and take you in handcuffs. Which is it to be?'

Bergman took a step backwards as if to distance himself from the two men. 'Why the hell are you picking on me? Think I've been following you for your wives? That's your game is it? Trying to put the frighteners on me. Well it won't work. I want my solicitor and now.' His voice rose to a high pitch. Jones produced a set of handcuffs as if by magic. 'Ralph Bergman, I'm arresting you on suspicion of the murder of Katie Hopkins. You're already under caution, now put your hands on the desk and keep them where I can see them. He walked around the end of the desk.

Bergman chose the moment to go berserk, gripping the edge of the desk and tipping it upside down, forcing Jones to jump clear. Gray moved in to make the arrest. Bergman started to throw a punch. A hand seemed to come from nowhere and hold his wrist in a vice like grip. Jones spun him round with his left hand. Bergman ran into a right hand punch that would have floored an ox. He fell to the floor screaming, blood steaming from his nose and above the left eye.

'Resisting arrest. Assaulting two police officers. One more peep out of you mate and you'll never live to see the station.' Jones snapped the cuffs tightly around his wrists, while pinning the man's arms behind him. He dragged Bergman to his feet. 'You alright Gray?'

'Yes Sarge, I'm fine.'

Taking an elbow each, the two men pushed Bergman outside into the corridor. Pausing to lock the office door, Gray put the key in his pocket. A group of tenants had left their offices to look for the cause of the disturbance.

'What's going on?' Someone enquired.

'Mr Bergman's had a bit of an accident.' Jones kept him moving quickly towards the staircase and down into the street. The blue flashing lights had already attracted the curiosity of passers-bye. The sight of Bergman's face acted as a warning that the two men holding him in handcuffs had to be taken seriously. Murmurs rippled through the group as Jones dragged him to the car. Opening the rear door he pressed the prisoner's head down to avoid further damage, at the same time pushing him inwards and on to the seat. Gray climbed in next to him. Jones jumped into the driving seat, switched on the siren to shift the crowd now gathering, and moved off towards the station.

'Tango two to base. Message for chief inspector Deakin. Suspect under arrest. We're bringing him in now. ETA ten minutes.' The car swept on to the car park at the rear of the station right on cue.

'Duck your head as you get out, otherwise you might hurt yourself.'

Bergman bent forwards, leaning out of the car. His face, shirt and jacket were all blood soaked. Jones looked for a moment as if he was pitying the man. Standing behind the cover of the open door he reached down, grabbing him by both ears.

'There now, Let me help you to your feet.'

He pulled him out of the car suspending him by the ears, at the same time thrusting his own face close up. The fight had gone out of Bergman. Jones could see the fear in his eyes. 'Welcome to our house tough guy.'

Sergeant Lloyd had the documentation ready. A charge sheet already made out with specimen charges was sufficient to take Bergman to a cell and strip search him, sometimes a painful process in itself. He took a long look at the prisoner. Natural instincts and years of experience told him that the entry in his day book might well become a milestone in the murder hunt.

Deakin rang Laura. 'Hello sweetheart. Can't afford more flowers so I'm ringing to say that I'll be late tonight. Got a lot on at the moment.'

Laura knew better than to question him about his work. Don't worry. These'll last a while longer. Bye for now.'

Word had already spread through the station that they had an important prisoner in cells. A curious silence fell over the building as Deakin, carrying his file of papers, walked down the corridors towards the cell area. Faces peered out behind him, voices whispering, 'Good luck Chief. Nail the bastard.'

'Chief Inspector Deakin, sir. This is Ralph J. Bergman and I have cautioned him. He is under arrest for assaulting two police officers in the course of their duty, resisting arrest, and of course we are also holding him on suspicion of the murder of Katie Hopkins.'

Deakin placed his file of papers on a corner of the table leaving room for Jones to sit next to him with his own notebook, while Gray stood close to the door, acting as an observer and guard. Bergman sat facing the two men.

'I want my solicitor here right now and I'm not talking to anyone till he gets here. And I'll tell you something else while I'm at it. You can see these two heavies gave me a going over at my office. I'll be making an official complaint.'

Deakin couldn't fail to notice the south western accent. It had a ring of Bristol about it. 'Bergman,' he began quietly. 'You will have access to the solicitor of your choice in due course but not until you and I have had a few words.'

Bergman glared at him. 'I've got nothing to say to you or anyone else until my solicitor gets here. You can stick your interview.'

Deakin, ignoring the remark, opened his file of papers, ensuring that the unserved summons and invoice were clearly to be seen.

Bergman stared down at the documents in astonishment. 'What are you doing with my paperwork?' Despite having had his face washed and a change of shirt, he was still a mess. A large swelling with discolouration was beginning to stand out.

'You do recognise this invoice and summons?' Deakin put the question to him.

Bergman glared at him again. 'Of course I recognise my own invoice. The summons has got nothing to do with me.'

Deakin held up the documents for his examination.

'Oh yes. Martin Richards. Couldn't serve him, he was out somewhere.'

Deakin looked at him. 'So what did you do with the summons?'

Bergman sneered at him. 'Took it back to the solicitor of course. If I can't serve anyone, I just take the summons back with an invoice and charge them for the visit. They can do what they like with it after that.' He sat back on his chair, levering the two front legs into the air in a rocking movement. 'Makes me a fucking murderer does it?'

Jones nodded at him. 'Now mind your manners. You know what I said.'

The fear came momentarily back into his eyes.

Pointing to the date on the invoice, Deakin continued; 'Is that the day before the hearing date on this summons?' He offered the two documents side by side.

'So bloody what?' The sneer was now turning to grudging interest.

'How long have you been in the business?'

The curiosity deepened. 'About five years. Why?' His question was ignored.

'But only in this area for less than twelve months?' Deakin looked at his notes. 'In fact nine months might be more accurate.'

Bergman looked confused. 'What's that got to do with anything?'

Deakin continued; 'Where did you live previously?'

'Place called Minching, near Avening, down south. Not wanted there as well, am I?'

Deakin's expression never faltered. 'Really. That's the west country, Gloucester area, if I've got my geography right?'

Bergman stared at him. 'So what?'

'Did you ever meet a lady by the name of Ella Stretton down Gloucester way?'

'Never heard of her.' He coughed. 'Could do with a drink of water. Who is she anyway?' His eyes had narrowed to slits. Nervous fingers felt their way along the edge of the table.

Deakin ignored the request and continued to study him at close range. 'Bergman, as we speak, my officers, with search warrants, are visiting your offices and your home, and are taking possession of your car, which we found parked at the back of the building where you work.'

He watched as the pale features turned a greyish hue. 'We'll be looking at your paid invoices over the past couple of years or more, your reports and lists of clients, and we may also just come across some forensic evidence. Now I'll ask you the question once more.' He almost spat the words out. 'Did you ever meet a lady called Ella Stretton and wasn't she the reason you left the Gloucester area?'

Bergman looked relieved. 'Can't fucking touch me. They've already nailed someone for that.'

'For what?'

'Her murder of course. Got the husband didn't they?'

'The question, Bergman was whether or not you knew Ella Stretton.'

'Well, if I did, it was confidential and I don't have to tell you about it.'

'Yes or no. Just answer the question.'

'Well yes, I suppose so.'

'Thank God for that. What about Cathy Wilson?

'Who's she?' Bergman growled.

'Another of your confidential clients, no doubt.'

Jones joined in the conversation. 'You'd be far better off telling us the whole story. It might just help you at trial.'

'Story about what? Trial, what fucking trial? You can sod off, the lot of you.' He was flushed but still defiant.

Jones looked at Deakin before continuing, hoping he wasn't overstepping his authority. 'The story about why you killed Ella Stretton, Cathy Wilson, Mary Donovan, Janet Stone and Katie Hopkins.' He sat back watching and waiting.

But Deakin interrupted the questioning before Bergman had a chance to answer. 'I am now terminating this interview while the prisoner has his mandatory break and a hot meal.' Collecting his papers together he stood, ready to leave the room. 'Think about things carefully for the next two hours Bergman. I'll be back.' He turned on his heel and walked out, leaving the prisoner in the care of the two detectives.

Back in his office, Deakin rang the CID office. 'Any news for me yet?'

'Lads are on their way back now Chief. Got some very interesting stuff. Be here in about ten minutes.'

'Good, tell them to bring it straight through here.' He sat back, fingers now tapping together.

It was a curious mixture that landed on his desk. Amongst the bric-a-brac taken from the boot of the car was a shiny new jack handle. 'What the hell is this about?' He was mystified. The search officer explained that he had delivered the actual jack base to forensics for checking. Deakin looked pleased with the collection. 'Good man. Now I think I'm ready for another chat with our Mr Bergman.'

Bergman was already in position when Deakin took his seat.

'You've had time to consider your position. Is there anything you want to tell me now?'

Bergman sneered. 'I want to see my solicitor. You lot can't prove nothing.'

Bending slightly, Deakin picked up his weighty brief-case from the floor. One at a time he laid five files across the desk, counting them individually. 'Ella Stretton, Catherine Wilson, Mary Donovan, Janet Stone, and Katie Hopkins. You knew them all. didn't you Bergman?' He reached inside the case to produce a second bundle. 'Fee notes, paid invoices, summonses, reports. They're all here. All in your name. What's your answer to that?'

Bergman tried to hold his ground. 'If they were all dead there was nothing for me to do except send in my accounts. Now I want to see my solicitor. There's nothing I want to say to you.'

A knock at the door stopped him in his tracks. A note was passed to Deakin. He read it carefully.

'Have you had a flat tyre recently?'

Bergman looked surprised. 'So what?'

'I take it that's a yes?'

'Of course.'

'Did you call out the AA or RAC?'

Bergman shuffled uncomfortably and scowled at Deakin. 'Did it myself. Why?'

'So the hydraulic jack in the boot of your car is yours. Not stolen or borrowed?'

'Of course it's bloody mine.' He was sneering again. Or was it nerves?

Deakin reached into his briefcase once more.

'This yours as well is it?' He pulled out the shiny new jack handle,

'I left the old one at the roadside by accident. Had to buy another.'

He sneered once more. 'No bloodstains on that are there?'

Deakin sat back in his chair. The old fox could sense victory was in sight. 'Pity you didn't buy a new jack base as well. When you came out of Katie Hopkins' house that night you changed the wheel before throwing the handle away. Some blood and hair are still stuck to the base where you jammed the handle into it. According to our forensics team they are a certain match to Katie's blood and hair.' Deakin still wasn't finished. 'The fee notes you sent out were dated before the bodies were discovered. You couldn't possibly have known that they were dead. Not unless you were there, that is.' He put his finger tips together. 'Now I really do think you need a solicitor. A damned good one.' His voice was suddenly drowned out by the screeching noises now coming from Bergman.

'Scum, whores, all of them. Got what they bloody well deserved.'

Deakin turned to Jones. 'Get him back to his cell. He needs a doctor and a solicitor. Then we'll see about charging him. I doubt whether he'll be fit to plead.'

Bergman had stopped screaming and now sat quietly staring into space, waiting for God knows what. He was neither hearing nor listening.

'For some reason he developed a hatred of women who were in control of their own lives and capable of maintaining some form of independence. They were all giving him orders albeit indirectly. We may never know what started it but no doubt some psychiatrist will cure him in due course and let him loose to start again. That's the way the world seems to be heading nowadays.' The two men walked out of the interview room leaving the prisoner to be taken back to his cell.

Jones was still puzzled. 'Where does Janet Stone fit into the frame?

Deakin explained. 'In amongst the fee notes was one which charged for several visits to a client. On the night in question, Bergman went out to kill that client but for whatever reason, she never showed. Janet Stone had just engaged him to trace her brother who had moved house and so he went after her instead. It could have been anyone that night and might have thrown us off the scent altogether.'

It was only minutes before midnight when Deakin put his key in the door and walked quietly into the house. Laura was asleep on the settee. He sat down to pull off his shoes, as she opened her eyes, staring sleepily at him.

'How did you get on?' She almost whispered the question.

'We've got him.' He leaned back in his chair. 'And that bloody peeper.'

Epilogue

A nest of squawking sparrows in the eaves, roused John from a deep sleep. Half closed eyes stared, unbelieving, at the bright beams of light pouring in through the open window, while his mind struggled to recall the last time he'd faced the early morning sun, an open window, an unlocked room. Closing his eyes again, he tried to recapture the dream. Something he wrote years ago, a poem for Ella, drifted in and out of his brain.

'If only dreams could be reality,' it began.

'Hi! Breakfast in bed. Not bad eh !' His sister smiled down at him, holding out a tray laden with bacon, eggs, toast, marmalade and a mug of steaming tea. John's first taste of freedom.

'You broke my dream,' he said.

Pulling the morning paper from the crook of her arm, she handed it to him. 'Thought you might like to read this.'

Unfolding it, he exposed the headline.

FIVE TIMES KILLER JAILED FOR LIFE
Don Reading. Mail Crime Reporter

John Stretton remembered the last lines of his poem.

'And So I dream and dream anew,

'And in each dream, reality is you.'

About the Author

Cyrus Ferguson lives on the Wirral Peninsula just a few miles from his birthplace in the city of Liverpool. He has enjoyed a wide and varied career which began with regular service in the Fleet Air Arm followed by 25 years as a national and international investigator. Besides being a member of the Association of British Detectives, and the World Association of Detectives, Cyrus also found time to study law at the John Moores University in Liverpool, specialising in divorce and crime. More recently he was awarded an MA in Writing Studies by Lancaster University. Cyrus also writes short stories and poetry, some of which has been broadcast on BBC local radio.